THUNDERPAWS
AND THE
TOWER OF LONDON

BY
BEN HOUSDEN

illustrations by
MonoKubo

layout and chapter ornamentations with
Robyn Lawrence

First published in Great Britain in 2021 by
High Gate Press, an imprint of HGP IS Limited.

Illustrations by MonoKubo
Interior design with Robyn Lawrence
Art direction Ben Housden
Cover by Chameleonstudio74

A CIP record for this book is available from the British Library.

Colour softback ISBN: 978 1 914956 01 0
Colour hardback ISBN: 978 1 914956 00 3
Ebook (standard ebook text formatting) ISBN: 978 1 914956 03 4
Audiobook download ISBN: 978 1 914956 05 8
Audiobook CD ISBN: 978 1 914956 06 5

HGP IS Limited
www.hgp.is

www.thunderpaws.com
www.benhousden.com

This book is printed on paper from wood grown in sustainable forests
and uses vegetable-based inks.

'I so much enjoyed Thunderpaws
– it (and he) were very entertaining, and I was gripped!'
– Emily Thomas, Carnegie Medal long-listed author of Mud

'A fun romp through history....with a twist...Thunderpaws moves into the Tower of London and wow, what a bunch of characters he meets there! As a big fan of cats, history and books this was a no brainer. Done in a light hearted way, with excellent humour, this was enjoyable and I look forward to any sequels.'
– Rachel S, Waterstones Manager, UK

'There is so much to love about this tale, it's hard to know where to start... I cannot recommend it enough, achieves something really special... crafted so perfectly, I almost want to stand up and applaud.'
– Becks, Wiltshire

'Kept me reading all day and I read it in a day.
Perfect for any magical Harry Potter fans. Definitely recommend.'
– Katie H, UK

'Smart, funny and incredibly cat-like... horrible histories vibes... really did make me laugh out loud... anyone over the age of 9 will enjoy this...'
– Erin, Devon

'Ambitious, original and hugely entertaining.'
– Sarah House, runner-up, Bath Children's Novel Award

'Thunderpaws was a delightful book to read, full of history, magic, and humor. I would recommend this light-hearted mystery to anyone who enjoyed the Harry Potter series as well as all cat lovers out there.'
– Monica B (Librarian), Texas

'I was really lost for words to describe it. It was so different from anything else I have read... Loved the way it rattled along and I did find it difficult to put down for long. I enjoyed it immensely because it was unpredictable –
I couldn't guess where you were going to take me next.'
– Sharon, Rutland

'Loved this book sooooo much!'
– Lucrecia, Florida

'At last a book told from the cat's perspective that is actually believable.'
– Paul S, UK

'A ruddy good read – it's playing havoc with my sleep routine – just got to read a couple of pages more.'
– David, South Yorkshire

'This is a rollicking tale from within the Tower of London, madcap with plenty of mayhem and will keep readers from 9-99 entertained… It has a unique print layout where the words follow the action… it's a fantastic way to read and will really add to the reading experience especially for younger readers.'
– Jen, Somerset

"This is a truly delightful read. If you love cats, or history, or both, this is the book for you. It's fun, experimental and glorious… The story navigates itself so brilliantly to keep you engaged along the way. Packed with action, dramatic tension, and one not-so scaredy cat, this has it all.'
– Emma, Neath

'Cute, funny, and entertaining. Read it if you like all-ages books with talking cats, rats, a mouse, spirit felines and royal ghosts.'
– Graisi O, Ontario

'A delightful adventure involving cheeky cats, well-known ghosts, ravens and legends of London… a ghostly story of intrigue, suspense, double-dealing and danger… It was exciting and thrilling whilst at the same time being charming and heart-warming. I loved it and cannot wait for the next instalment!'
– Maddy, Merseyside

'A terrific light-hearted read… The colourful illustrations are so beautiful and unique that they speak volumes in themselves… can be enjoyed by older children (teens) and adults alike. I thought it was tremendously unusual, eccentric, weird and wonderful.'
– John D, UK

With lots of paws and thanks:

Rev Paul Abram MVO and Jo Abram (Chap & Mrs C)
Jane & Sheg

Teufel
(also known as Thunderpaws)

Legal disclaimer

Teufel's lawyers have asked him to point out that although based on real events and being true stories and everything, some characters and scenes are fictional for storytelling purposes. Teufel is not sure he agrees with this, but when pushed will admit that he occasionally bigs things up if readers need a bit of oomph – "it's a story!"

He acknowledges under duress that the Governor and Ravenmaster are actually lovely (eventually!) Do not mention birds, rodents or responsibilities.

Also, he says, 'wait for book 2 – you lawyers will have a proper fit at that. True story!'

WORDS

TEUFEL* AND THE ENGLISH LANGUAGE...

Memo from:
HGP's department of Dictionaries and International Relations & Translations

The department requested multiple grammatical and spelling changes. Teufel's response was, 'bog off**, it's words, innit.***' He accepted a list of hints. Some words he claims come from Shakespeare – the department remains unconvinced. The department does admit English can be weird, with the same word meaning different things, the same sound being spelled in different ways, and all the regional variations of dialect because of hills, history and stubborn locals. Hence, a dictionary of terms for discerning worldwide readers, with explanations of more uncommon words for those where English is an additional language. For friends across the Atlantic who are used to z for s, no u by o, a general efficiency in spelling and kibble for cat biscuits, we do hope you'll forgive our old ways. It is hoped in due time translations will follow. You may well note Teufel has many, many words for the word stupid. He's got plenty more where they came from, too...

* *Teufel as in toy full*
** *no chance*
*** *goes at the end of answering a question*

AN A TO Z OF TEUFELISMS

armabrillo – armadillo
assing – messing about
attichoo – sneeze sound
atwitch – to be making small movements
baba – father
barmy – wrong-thinking
beaky – with a beak
beardo – someone with a beard
bhuna/kahuna – type of curry/wise man
bluss-fussering – acting loud and confused
booyaka – crack-like sound
boshed – bash something
bosher – one who bashes
brisks – move quickly
cabbies – taxi drivers
catisfaction – happy
cattin' – swear word used by dogs, birds and rodents
cattitude – see the world perfectly
cattus non gratis – cat not welcome in Latin
chet/chets – Devon word for kitten/kittens
chillified – covered in chilli powder
chings – sound of metal hitting metal
Chiron – asteroid in the outer solar system
chop-chop – be quick
chuggle-chunk – small and chunky
chunky-lunks – chunky cheeks
corvids – crow family of birds including ravens
crims – criminal
cuppa – cup of tea
deffo – short for definitely
Devon – county in south west England
Dickers – alternative for Richard
Dickie – alternative for Richard
Dicko – short for Richard
diddly-squat – nothing
dingbats – stupid
discombobulated – confused
doggin' – swear word in cat and rat land
doofus – stupid
doolally – stupid
dred – means many things, including friend
duked – receiving the title of duke
dukeship – title of duke bestowed on someone
Dukey – duke-like behaviour
erm – hesitating
ew – sound of disgust
fanging – putting fangs into something
fangled – something invented
fella – a male
flappy – flaps
flump – something heavy
foetid – unpleasant
freakin' – short for freaking, as in weird
freakoids – strange

gawps – look
geeze – term used when addressing a man
ghosty – like a ghost
ghouling – doing ghoul-like things
ginge – being ginger in colour
gloaty – gloats
gloop – slime
go-wah – surprise
gobsmacked – surprised
gonna – going to
gorm-dork – looks stupid
gotcha – got you
Govvie-boy – alternative for Governor
gran – grandmother
grockles – Devon word for tourists
gruffs – like a grunt
higgle-piggle – messy
holler – call out to someone loudly
innit – said at the end of answering a question
interweb – the internet
Janey – alternative for Jane
justa – one word for 'just a'
kaboof – disappear
kingy – king-like
kittenhood – childhood but for cats
knifer – someone who uses a knife
knobbled – nobbly, has lumps
looning – foolish behaviour
loonville – a place with lots of fools
lovedog – the strange place of dog lovers
Maccy D's – McDonald's
malarkiness – nonsense
mangey – in poor condition
manky – dirty and unpleasant
Mau – Egyptian breed of cats
mices – more than one mouse
moggy – common name for a cat
moochy – chilled and casual
mooding – threatening
moreish – want more of
mouseball – batting a mouse head across a floor
muppet sack – a sack of stupid
muppets – stupid
my lordy – expression of surprise
nah – no
navigatory – used in navigating
nighted – something viewed at night
nutbunk – stupid
oathed – get under oath
oomph – bigger scale
overalled – wearing overalls (workwear)
padder – those who pad (walk with paws)
pah – take that
perma-tan – permanent sun-tan
plonk/s – put down
prawny – very prawn
primo – of superior quality
pukey – feeling sickly
ratty-watty – dismissive term for a rat
ravey – like a rave
redded up – made the colour red
Rotti-Doberman – Rottweiler/Doberman style dog
Salcombe – Devon town where Teufel was born
salvos – a succession of things
SAS – UK special forces: the Special Air Services
sashays – move with swinging hips
scarpers – gets away quickly
scowly – bad tempered or suspicious expression
scraggle – small and scruffy
scuse – shortening of excuse
sextanted – using a sextant, a device for navigating
shagster – something excessively hairy
sharpish – fast
shingly – containing small pebbles
shippies – ships and boats
shouty – shouts
sith – mythical Celt beast
Sixy – shortening of Henry VI
slabby – an apparent flat surface
slime-fest – lots of slime
sneaker – trainer/running shoe
sparko – flat out
spick and span – clean
stooled – been made Groom of the Stool
swiggle – a small wiggle
tad – a bit small
terra-firma – solid ground/earth
Teuf – short for Teufel and genius, brilliant, etc
thickos – stupid
thingies – variation on things
thingy – used when you forget the name
toodle pip – goodbye
tosspot – idiot
twizzles – twists
verms – vermin (pests)
Waltie – pet name for Walter
Walts – shorter pet name for Walter
wanna – want to
whiffy – smelling badly
whinging – complaining
whiskering – exploring something
whizz – move quickly
wittering – talking
woh – hang on
wonking – wonky, not straight
wot-sits – when you don't know the name
wuss-pants – scared person
wussface – scared person
Yorkist – of the House of York royal family
yuk – disgusting
yup – yes
zoom-zoom – move quickly

MAP

THE TOWER OF LONDON

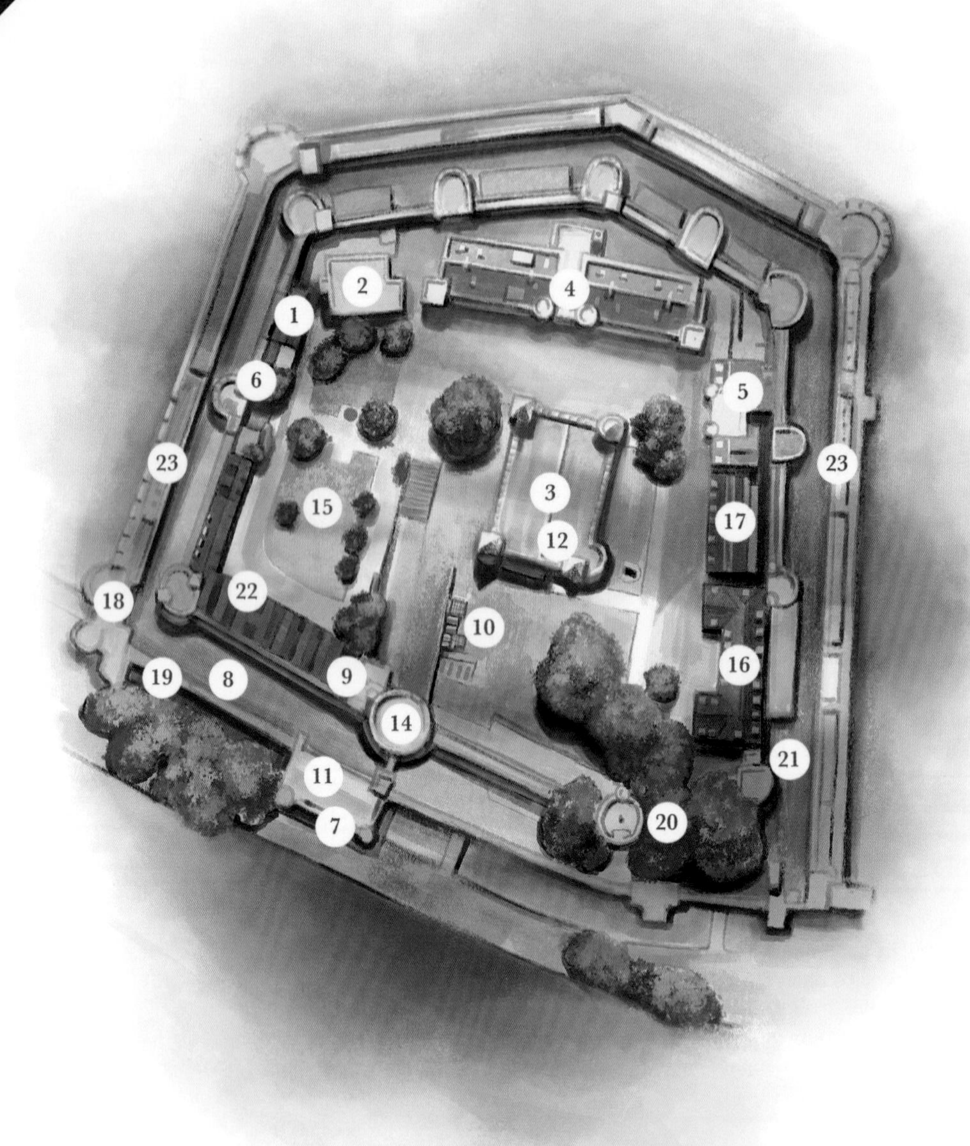

1) Chaplain's house
2) Chapel of St Peter in Chains
3) White Tower
4) Waterloo Barracks
5) Fusiliers' Museum
6) Beauchamp Tower
7) Traitor's Gate
8) Water Lane
9) Bloody Tower
10) Raven cages
11) St Thomas' Tower
12) Little Ease
13) Secret Garden
14) Wakefield Tower
15) Tower Greens
16) New Armouries Cafe
17) Old Hospital Block
18) Byward Tower (exit)
19) Outer wall
20) Salt Tower
21) Outer Ward
22) Governor's House
23) Casemates

Free character biographies and digital map

For a free pdf specially formatted for phones and tablets including short character biographies, portraits of the Tower's ghost community and map, please register at the address below (if you are under thirteen please seek the permission of a parent or guardian).

www.thunderpaws.com/treats

By registering you will receive the PDF by email and register to receive first info on the next instalment in the Nature's Claw series, currently titled The Cat and the King, and be added to the Thunderpaws clawletter… only ham, never spam.

Find Teufel online through:

Thunderpaws London

ONE

'You gonna sleep forever, Thunderpaws?'

My left paw flexes.
Head rotate, I shift and turn.
Yawn. Rub ear, back to sleep.
'Go away.'

'That's the plan, actually.'

Eyelids haul up. Full paw flex. Claws out.
'Dog off.'

'I can't.'

From across the blackness, a mouse stares from the top of an old, wonky dresser.
Thinking it's safe.

Great. I'm still who-knows-where in a locked, cold cellar, and now
there's a bonkers-chatting mouse who somehow knows that name.
I must have been muttering in my sleep.

'The thing is, Thunderpaws. To save your future, your country, the whole world,
very soon you're going to need to defeat ghosts, ghouls, and all manner of monsters.
So, I think you need to wake up.
The good news? It's gonna be a blast.
Ready for a trip?'

'You what?'
I stretch up. Full-body crank.
'Listen, whisker-twitch,
I'm a cat, I've got a headache, and wherever this is,
I can assure you that trip won't be our journey.'

I jump from my blue cushion and land on the cellar floor.

The w e i r d, b u g – e y e d rodent keeps staring.

'I just arrived too. You're truly a gift from the gods!'

The floor is a cold clammy slime-fest.
'Excuse me?'

'A gift. From the gods! The nub of our adventure
is to save everything. It's going to be tough.'

'I bet...
Come on, come down…'

A snack always helps. One less mouse–

'There are biscuits there. That bowl by your cage. The table. Behind you.'

'I don't do biscuits.
Fresh or human food only.'

'Oh…
you're one of those,
okay… I don't judge.
This is a bit of a secret, but,
I think I love cats.'

Oh, do you, now? I think.
This I love you. This saving the world stuff is gutsy.
If porky-pie mousey-lie kinda gutsy. Admirable but stupid.
Croakers and their tales trying to escape being fanged...

'What's a croaker?'

I.
No.
That didn't happen.
I did not say it aloud.

Flick my head. Shake the nonsense away. Off with you.

It.
Did.
Not.
Happen.

She leans over the dresser's edge.
'It did, you know.'

Nothing strange here, Teuf. Just another soon-to-be-dead mouse.
She's not in your head. At all.
Those staring eyes of hers should be bullets – little black bullets.
Why are they cat-like, cat-shaped?

'You're a mouse. A weird one, granted, but a mouse.
Have some guts, come down and I'll be quick, I'm a gent. Accept your destiny.'

'You accept yours.'

'Excuse me?'

She scratches her ear.
'I know you're a church cat.'

What?
'I am not a church cat. I live with a vicar. It's a very different thing.'

'You're a church cat. You have to come on my trip.'

'No one tells a cat what to do.'

She scuttles over the dresser's edge and
drops
in
on the highest shelf by a line of jars.

Her fur is flat and greasy. Puddle mud grey.
You'd think rat, but she's got big mouse ears.
And a tail that's a disco of coloured rings.
Who is this mouse? What is this mouse? No matter.
A final few steps and I'm beneath her.
Striking distance.
These distractions are smart, but smart doesn't stop dead.

The old
dresser
is propped
against
the wall.

I can jump the drawers,
kick off the counter, past the tools –

✓ claw,
✓ neck bite,
and done.

All over.
I can then return to my focus.
The vicar.
What is he up to and why?

So, tail-still, torso-primed,
I'm ready.

The plan is tight.

If you're *fuzzy*-headed, if mice play you, dis tr act you, lie their tail off
no matter, you con cen trate.

This battle is beyond time and circumstance.

Hunter – prey.
Cat – mouse.
Power – less.

There's only one winner.

'That won't work,' she says.
'Let's introduce ourselves.'

'Of course, little one.'

She scratches her ear again.

Fleas, I bet.

'The name is Teufel.
Toy, and full.
What you *are*, and I shall be!'
I spring up the dresser.

She scrambles at jars, crashing over lids.

But it's too late. I'm there.

Mid-air, I swipe.

A blast of light.

My vision blacks, I slap the shelf and tumble down. The dark fills with flashing stars.
Air rushes my whiskers, glass clunks clattering my ears.

The dresser must be fa
ll
ing too.

With a twist, I double-kick against the wannabe cat-crusher, leap for the floor and scoot under the table.

The crashing and bashing stills, my vision stumbles back.
A broken jar rolls past my paws. Stupid fat paws. Clumsy big things.
Was that flash the mouse?
The gloom is silent and still.

'Are you there, mouse?'

Nothing.

Something else is missing too. I lean forward and sniff. No melon smell.
What mouse doesn't whiff of overripe melon?

From somewhere high above, another noise begins.

Thud,
thud,
thud.
The skeleton of the house crunches and shakes. That'll be the traitor.

The cellar door yanks open. At the top of the steps, the vicar's huge silhouette stands black in the middle. He hits the light switch, tugs the door to and lumbers down in heavy pyjama-flapped feet.

The cellar blinks into light.

His face is a fire of frustration.
'Teufel, what have you done?'

I leap past his feet and shoot up the steps. A paw at the door and I'm gone.

His huge feet flipper-flap up the stairs behind me while I scan a small cosy kitchen.

My nose drifts over the room and finds the lovely scent of cardboard boxes. But they are flattened and stacked. Useless. Days of closed ones. Now this. Perfect pleasure palaces broken and bust.

'Three days, Teufel.'
He joins me.
'Derek said three days. Get you acclimatised.
Do you ever do what we want?'

Oh, whatever.
I tu
rn
and give him the general "you stupid" cat stare.
If you want good, be good, Vicar. Sleeping tablets from Derek, your *I'm a vet, don't you know* cousin, because I like singing in cars is out of order.
I return to surveying the kitchen.

He doesn't answer.
There are never any answers.

Mum said humans lost the skill generations ago. Chucked the universal language for progress-zoom-zoom. She was full of stuff like that at kitten school.
The bits I remember.

The vicar moves across the room
and switches on a radio –
a brown one like the one from home.

Big Ben tolls the midnight news.
Vicar fills the silver kettle (from home),
gets two plain white mugs (from home),
opens the red tea caddy (from home)
and drops a teabag in each cup, which
Mrs V would never do – she's a teapot person, always.
Teas brewing, he stands by the table (from home)
and flicks at a newspaper (not from home – wrong shape.)

Where are we?
Because
this is not home.

After milk from the fridge,
he kills the radio, the lights and my hope for answers,
by leaving through a glass-panelled door.

'Night, Teufel,' he calls.

The door rattles.
The house creaks.

His feet fade upstairs to silence.

Through a window above the table, bundles of cloud shift beneath the sliced moon.
At least I'm out of the slime-fest cellar. The table is best for sleep, so I jump up and settle on the paper.

Height is safety, and safe in the light, always.
Tail stilled, I tuck my paws,
shutter my eyes
and close out the world.

'Oh, Teufel,' calls the mouse from behind the cellar door.

I'm down and land eye-level with the gap under the door.

Her shape is there in the murky murk.

She scurries forward, whiskers twitching excitement.
'As I was explaining. You and me to save the world.
Every man, woman and child.
From Matsumoto to Mumbai, Preston to Peru,
Adelaide to Zhangzhou. Moscow too.
But first you must survive here.
I have lessons, amazing adventures, but there's a number one rule,
you gotta be nice!'
She flicks an ear.

My tail beats the kitchen floor. With laughter.
I mean, she's funny. This is funny.
'Survival? Mum-a-zoo-what and where?'

She comes close. Cat-eye close.
'My first advice. Don't touch the birds, no matter the temptation. Not here.
Second. Rather important. Don't annoy the lions, or monsters.
Bit harder. Survive all that and the adventure begins.
Do you like sports?'

I ram my head against the wood, snarling fangs,
'What? Like mouse-head ball?'

She scurries closer.
So close her nose could tickle mine except for this stupid dead tree between us.
'Seriously, Teufel. You're going into a beam of light on 5th November to save the world.
That's Bonfire Night in two short weeks!
We'll set the skies afire.'

I reverse back, settle my fur and turn away, accepting the physics of solid doors
and the annoyance of maddening mice on proper spaced-out wind-up missions.

'Yeah, right.'
The lies they try!

'I can make you.'

The soft click of a door handle breaks my sleep.

'Morning, Mr Crash Bang Wallop,' says the Vicar.

Very funny. I s t r e t c h up, arching my spine.

His face is a happy fresh pink,
all summer-blue eyes
behind the half-moon
glasses
perched
on his nose,

and resplendent in a new red cassock
– the ankle-length coats he wears for church service. He drops letters on the table, *scruffs* my head, then pulls the newspaper from under me and
d
u
m
p
s it in the recycling. Charming.

I resettle on the envelopes and watch as he scans through high cupboards on the far wall. Why's he in red? Vicars wear black. It's what they do. Every, single, day.

The door clicks.

Mrs Vic enters
all a-smile.
Takes a seat and
nuzzles my neck,
lazing out a yawn.
'Handsome fella.'

This is all strange. Furniture from home. Acting like home. What's going on? As I push into her hand, Vic pulls down a small tin and pops the lid. Fishy salt smells sparkle across the room, Tuna à la Teuf. Bingo.

I ju
mp down. Above, two small plates are prepared. One for now, one for later.

The saucer lands.
'Welcome to the Tower,' he says, whatever that means.

There are other rattles and clicks. I'm not the world's greatest listener, least of all with a gob full of fish, but I miss little with these eyes. However, when I next peek up, Mrs V has my blue cushion from the cellar.

'What spooked him?' she says,
placing it down by an old brown cooker sat squat across the hearth.

'No idea,' replies Vicar. 'Not a spot on him though. I'll clean up later.'

The cushion is an excellent result, but I need to investigate last night.
That gibberish-talking flash-disappearing mouse.
It was weird. Too weird.
But there's a more important job first.
The task of payback.

With whiskers wiped and more than enough tuna to satisfy me until elevenses at nine, I p a d to my cushion, take a long investigative s n i f f, dismiss its familiarity, head to the centre of the flagstone, arch my back and THROW UP.

THAT'S for the tablet.

I stroll to a table leg by the wall and puke again.

THAT'S for putting me in the vet box.

And THIS – I saunter to the fridge and wrench up a last hacking dollop by a small rubber foot – is for shoving me in the cellar.

A leisurely high-tailed return visions Vic and Mrs Vic's grizzle-faces.
I take a seat and set about a clean, occasionally admiring the view.

The results are a delight.
Puddles of sick.
Nice slow-popping bubbles.
Solid stink.

Dashing humans.
It's a triumph, I only wish I had more to give.

'Teufel!' says the Vicar, from the sink.
'As if downstairs wasn't enough.'

He's right, it wasn't.
Now I'm ready for mouse investigations. To be or not to be, that is the question. The mouse is real, I suspect. Deluded, certainly. Demented, perhaps. I'll settle on deceased. Time to croak the croaker. 'Monster lions' – mice are such liars...

I pad to the cellar door and give it a long, rising cheek rub.
'Miaow. Miaow.'

Vic glances up from the fridge, rag in hand, patience on frazzle.
'You want to go back?'

'Miaow.'

'Oh, cat!'

Somewhere a door knocker raps. Three sharp knocks. The Vicar jumps up, fumbles for his watch, then washes at the sink muttering. A quick brush down, and he's out the glass-panelled door. **Oi**, don't you disappear –

'Can you take over love?' he calls.

Mrs Vic bristles to the sink. Cellar opportunity lost; other duties remain. Like investigating where I am. I follow the Vicar and find him at the end of a narrow hall, facing a sturdy white door. He pulls the thick iron bolt, lifts the latch and tugs.

Crisp autumn air swirls down the hall with a sharp chill.

Stood on the step, tapping his heels, is a tall willowy man in a grey suit. Short silver hair, tanned; there's a large rectangular package under his arm. He steps forward.

'Morning, Governor!' says Vicar.

The man extends a spidery hand in welcome.
'Settling in, Chaplain?'

'Excellent so far.'

'The red looks splendid,' the man says, crossing the threshold.

A shrill caw breaks over the introduction. Another. ***Another***. That's birds. Big birds.
I am so overdue bird.

I get up. Vic sees me and thuds the door shut. Attention forced back to the hall, I retake my seat and wait for the visitor's dutiful head pat. Then it strikes me – *who's Chaplain?*

The visitor brisks straight past. Not even a glance. Charming.

He enters a room on the right. Vic follows, so I follow the Vic. If this fella's a dog lover, he's getting it – I'm over him like a wasp. This room is full of vicarage things too. The low pillowy sofa. Vic's favourite red chair (pure claw heaven). His less favourite brown one (also claw heaven); lamps, books, ornaments, e v e r y t h i n g. Even that darn model clock on the mantelpiece. Vic built it to explain the church-tower renovation campaign. Took him weeks. An ever-turning complication of circles and nudging tick-tocks; that clock cost me a lot of strokes. Infernal thing.

The man hands the package to the Vicar.
'A little gift,' he says.

Vic smiles. 'Most kind.'
He signals for the Governor to sit.

The thing, practically a tombstone turns out to be a large book.

Vic studies the cover.
'Prisoners of the Tower, marvellous.'

The Governor's attention has moved to the mantelpiece. His eyes narrow.
He checks his watch, steps over to the Vicar's model clock
and pulls its minute hand back a fraction.

'So you know which souls to pray for,' he says, perusing the clock's workings.
'Chaplain to Her Majesty the Queen, two royal chapels, soldiers, yeomen, millions of visitors a year, and the most famous birds in the world. This is the national stage.
A show for the world.'

He returns to the sofa, adjusting his cuffs as he sits.

My tail beats with intrigue and delight. Most famous birds in the world?
Now that would be a debut.

I find his eyes have met mine. I'm not sure it's love.

'We're not a place for mishaps or mistakes, Chaplain. As I stated in my welcome
letter, if this cat...'

What is this 'Chaplain' nonsense? His name's Vicar. You're the mistake. And less of the glare-eyes, Lank Plank. Staring is rude. I pad to the sofa and take a seat next to him. I'll keep guard here – eyes front, facing the Vic. A real man, he was a soldier, in the SAS, and everything. You, flake, couldn't lead a basset hound to beef biscuits. I gaze the ceiling for a think.

Hmmm... that croaker mentioned birds. Love bird.

Cooked bird is delicious. There's the slight shame that I haven't caught a live one yet, but I will. That's what destiny's for. Everyone knows it. A famous bird under my claw, and I'd be on my way to being like Dad. I didn't meet him – but Mum told me everything. I've just got to believe.

Hunt those birds, flush the mouse. Get this place owned. Yep, that's the plan.

A spark of light pulls my attention back to the room. On the mantelpiece – from nowhere – is that doggin' disco-tailed mouse, moseying across like she's on the way to a party. She lifts a rodent hand in welcome, turns, takes a seat, then stares at me.

'Hey,' she mouths.

I speed-scramble over this Governor fella.

Halfway, Vic yanks me to the floor.
'Apologies, Governor – you were saying?'

I stare back to the mantel. Tilt my head. Change my angles. Move views. Alter heights. Nothing.

The mouse is gone? Not behind the clock's wheels, levers or cogs.
How can it disappear,
again?

'No mishaps,' the Governor says, '...the ravens. You're the first Chaplain with a cat.'

My ear flicks to a quiet, dull, tingling sound. Cheap metal, keys I expect.
Where is that mouse?

'I should be off', says the Governor, rising. 'A yeoman's debut today.
The boys always give them something special. Local kids this time, I understand.
I'll say hello.' He brushes at his trousers.

'My granddaughter's coming the weekend after next,' says the Vicar.

'I look forward to meeting her.'

My heart flushes. Ella!

'Thank you for the book,' says the Vicar. He peers over his glasses. 'Teufel, stay.'

Yeah, right. Explorations, Vic. There's bird out there. Famous ones, and I got itchy claws. The mouse can wait. I allow them a few seconds to leave, then follow them out.

At the front door, the Governor digs in his pocket.
'I almost forgot. Another small gift.'
He pulls out a thin strip of red leather.

A cat collar!
A red cat collar.
With a bell!

Vic lifts me to his chest, arm squeezing tight.
'Look, Teuf, we'll match.'

The Governor – gleeful and smug – fixes the buckle, tugging tight. Freedom isn't freedom with a bell. The Vicar opens the door and drops me onto the step outside and I shame off, tail low, sounding like a toddler's pull-toy.

'Have fun,' he calls.

Dog you, traitor!

Where am I? There are castles. Castles everywhere.

I am. I'm at the Tower. And.

Oh.

Double dogs.
Triple dogs.

There's a church.

THREE

In the middle of a vast square of lawns stands a tall white castle. A bad mood of bricks and crushed dreams, crowned in battlements and turrets, the other buildings around the square almost bow in awe. Two golden castles – one long and boxy, the other like a posh house, are both guarded by cannons and guns. High trees stand like lollipops by the lawns.

And there to my left is the church. A church I want to ignore, like I did with the one at home after Mum died. That was bigger, not small and shoebox-shaped like this one.

I am not a church cat. I'm just a vicar's cat. I am not responsible for policing ghosts. It's just wild kitten stories. I can't have Mum's job now she's dead, can I?

The new red collar itches like a fleece of fleas.

Me, though, in charge of a set of castles. In London.
I told those Salcombe cats I was special.

'The cat's well behaved?' says the Governor
from behind me.

He's holding a railing by the steps.

'Generally,' replies Vic, touching his ear.

'And the name? Toyfell.'

'It's Teufel. German for the Devil.'

'Peculiar choice.'

Vic nods.
'Peculiar cat.'

The Governor brushes fur from his trouser leg.
'Well, keep him in line, will you?'

With a wave, he turns down a cobbled road towards a castle with battlement hedges. The castle sits in a line of houses. The furthest are black and white, and look like chopped-up Battenberg cakes under higgle-piggle roofs. Outside one, a man stands in a red uniform, a big black toilet-brush hat on his head and a rifle by his side.

Is he a soldier? Is the gun for monster lions? Who has lions in London?
Lions are Africa.

Another mad mouse story. Impressive in a way. But our story, hers and mine, is about the natural order. An order that needs to be restored. We will meet again, mouse. But if it's stories – what are all the guns and soldiers for? You don't need guns and cannons for lions. You might for monsters.

The white castle is scarred. Charred with black marks. Almost like scorches.
Castles mean battles, knights, kings and queens. They also mean dragons.
Dragons are monsters.
Dragons scorch.
Calm down, Teufel.

I shake the nonsense away.
From the far side of the tower, a strangely dressed man barrels forward like he's got a thermometer up his bum. Growly face, sharp white beard with fighting eyes, he's gripping a long spiked pole over his shoulder. He might be annoyed at what he's wearing – a thick navy dress, its front flashed with red rectangles, a large crown motif and the letters ER, with a hat like an upside-down cooking pot – or he could be dogged off at the line of kids following him. Yep, my feeling, it's the kids. Heads down, hands in pockets – kids do stuff to adults at times. Excellent. I pad over.

The man stops. He turns, stamps his staff to the ground and waits for the teens to catch up. A boy in a thin grey jumper arrives first.

'It was in that tower, back there,' the boy says.

The man leans forward, resting his weight against the spiked pole.
'I'm an army warrant officer with more than 22 years of good standing.
We all are here. No one stole your coat. This is the safest place in England!'

'It was a hoodie, not a coat.'

The man shakes his head. 'Can I get on with the show?'
He opens his shoulders, yanks a smile across his face
and steps past the boy to address the other kids.
'Now, delinquents. I mean, lovely young nippers. Welcome to the execution site!'

What?

'Anne Boleyn,' he booms. 'Noble queen. Not stabbed to death like our devout,
peaceful King Henry VI earlier –'

'Err, sir?' calls a girl.

'What is it?' replies the man.

'He was a bit of a chump really wasn't he?'

His knuckles whiten around the staff.
'You do not call Royals chumps!'

'You do in Hackney, mate. He was soft. Now the knifer, that Richard –'

'Young lady...' He puffs his cheeks. 'Anne was beheaded here.'
His arms sweep out.
'And so too Lady Jane Grey, just seventeen, queen for nine days. A crown she didn't
want or know she was getting. One of the finest minds of her century – dead.
Eyes pecked out by you know who?'

Who?

A boy calls from further back.
'What happened to the crims, Maccy D?'

The bearded man scowls.
'What did you just call me?'

'Beefeater, bro. Mr McDonald's innit.'

The others chuckle.

'I am Yeoman Warder. We do not like
the name Beefeater, Maccy Diamond D, bro or innits!'
His eyes flick to the sky.
'Commoners were executed outside on Tower Hill.
It's that way if you want to try,' he says, pointing past the boxy golden castle.

'I only nicked it last week. Who do I talk to about my hoodie?'

The man curls a finger at the boy.
'Come here.'

The boy steps forward.

'Crime does not pay, lad. That's the lesson there. Back then we'd have you
hung,
drawn
and quartered, with your head off –
so you wouldn't be needing or caring about blinkin' hoodies!'

He looks back to the group.
'Now, I'll get back to my speech. If we were being kind, or the traitor was a female,
it was the stake. Roasted, from panic to dead in forty-five minutes,
depending on the weather. We judge hard, fast and cruel.
So next term, be good or else.
No more exclusions!'
He cracks a half smile.

'I bet the rich got off,' someone says.

The Yeoman nods.
'It's a rich man's world. The wealthy
bought gunpowder collars to finish things off quickly.
The traitor's head going all *kaboof*,
as my granddaughter calls it.'

I feel sick. The collar tightens around my neck.

'Whatever the way or weather, Londoners would cheer your misfortune over a few
beers. There, young charges, lay the fate of the guilty, and sometimes the innocent.
So be careful. I'll certainly need a beer after you lot this evening, my lordy.'

The kids laugh.

'Yes. This palace, this prison, began with the White Tower almost a thousand years
ago. Tragedy, torture and terror; deception, deceit and denial – the heart of English
history. A state prison for VIPs, but alas, for others, so much more. And these people
are still here. They walk at night as mists, whatever the weather. For the Tower of
London is the most haunted place in the world.'

'Yes dred... Woooooo.'

'Micky, bet your gran's 'ere.'

Oh.
Quadruple dogs.
There can't be ghosts.

I can't have Mum's job as a church cat, I can't. She said I wouldn't be suitable.
This is just stories. Stories for tourists, surely? No way ghosts are poking through here.

'Now, boys and girls,' the man says, with a tug of his cooking-pot hat. 'Your tour concludes. We've seen Traitor's Gate down in Water Lane, and Bloody Tower's torture tools. We finish with the Chapel of St Peter in Chains, where our most famous prisoners are laid. They'll be under your feet, so please, respect the dead. After, you are free to visit the crown jewels in Waterloo Barracks behind you, which should now be open. Good luck nicking anything in there!'

The warder steps towards the church, and I turn away, trying to shake off thoughts of Mum. As the group moves off, something promising moves in. A wisp of wind with a whiff that blows mouse's overripe melon out of the fruit bowl.
The hot, tropical, fruity sweetness of live bird.

I turn, crouch and scan the square. *Famous, eh?* Most famous in the world.
Is this the home of the last doddering dodo? A pluck! of parading peacocks?
Better not be OUTsized OGling Ostrich.

A flash of black reveals nothing more than a boring old crow, stood by a water fountain. Dullness. Common as dogs, crows are. Cocky and arrogant. Tricksters too. A kid takes a snap like it's one of the famous ones. Idiot. It's a crow. A large one, granted, but a crow's a crow. I'll give you some real action, boy. Watch this.

Right, this time do it right. For once. Follow all the rules.
Low and slow to keep the collar quiet, I stalk behind a
black
railing
post.

A post as black as me and my plans.
I take a moment. Close my eyes and picture success.

Mum said it's what Dad did (when he was very, very hungry).
Dad would never be seen dead in a collar.

All I need is speed, I've just got to believe.
Speed will overcome the bell.
Speed will deliver a squall of feathers,
and the proud noble silence of death.
Speed will lose my stupid Thunderpaws nickname,
for having never caught a bird and being a bit clumsy
when I get excited.

Speed will deliver a new Teufel,
a magnificent Teufel, Teufel the Magnificent.
Now that's a name.
A name to be respected.
Alone in the world, as all cats should be.
I will have my first uncooked bird (if I can get the feathers off).

Thunderpaws will be dead.
The bird will be dead.
My past will be dead.
My future?
That's mine to decide.

I will own this place and destiny. A real CAT, not a loud PAW. And not a church cat, because church cats can't kill, have fun or anything. I am not living a life of duty and service. No way. I am freedom.

I edge towards the crow.

*Closer, ever close*r. Slower than slow. Back low, shoulders low.

Tail still.

Not a single tinkle from the stupid bell. Superb, Teufel. Striking distance and it hasn't got a clue.

What's mousey gonna do about it?
What's that Governor fella gonna do?

The sun lasers through dull grey cloud. It's like a sign. The square dazzles.

Take this.

Glory.

I'm a *bullet* of speed.
Buildings *blur*, people freeze. My focus narrowed to one thing: *the bird.*
The pit-black eyes and dagger-hook bill, the feather shine and knobbled feet.

The bell at my neck tinkles.

The bird turns.
It sees the *rocket* of blackness. A cruise missile cat.

Wings beat and pUMP. The rush for LiFT
Legs scurry and pound, hunting air.
Alarm SQUAWKS BURST.

Close enough to pounce,
I punch my back legs,
open my front paws into a pincer and soar, claws out, fangs a-go-go baby!

Thumped back and side, my vision goes black.
Violence engulfs me.
Buffering slaps, salvos of stabs.
I drop my spine, twist and scramble away.

Silence.
The air still.

I look back. The attackers are gone. Somewhere a clock strikes.
Dizzy, sore, I search for what just happened.

My senses pull
UPWARDS.

From the dark heart of a rain cloud,
two black shapes
hammer down.

Crows!
'Welcome to the Tower!' they scream.

Birds did that to me?

More dive from other buildings. It's a full-scale attack!

I sprint to the cobbles, past the hedged castle towards the houses. Every door and window is shut. The red-uniformed soldier doesn't even look, never mind help. It's useless, the crows will be on me in seconds. The road ends in a high wall. I could jump. But what's on the other side? Height makes their attack easier. I'll be clawed to pieces.

My first day. Murdered.

I scoot beyond the final house. A small courtyard. A house in the corner. The door is open! That will do. Birds don't do doors. I shoot in. Heart chugging and collar ringing like a summer church wedding, but safe, finally safe. Stuff you birds.

Inside, away from the murder of crows, the bell stills, my heart eases and my fur calms. Never seen crows that big or foolish in my life. Outrageous. I take in the surroundings. A wooden wall is covered with ancient graffiti carved deep into its grain. A spiked gate sits across a giant fireplace, next to a rack to stretch humans, judging by a diagram.

Very strange, but humans and their vices are not my business. My business is getting rid of this bell, then getting rid of crows. I need genius for the tricky corvids and a helping hand for the bell. And from the floral scent hanging in the air, someone's just been by.

Cut into the far wall, a spiral of stone steps curls upwards. Stairs are full of promise. I'll take a gander.

A woman gasps somewhere above, 'Hang on.'

I climb to my first target. The space is older than time and coffin-tight, but at the top, I find her. A white-haired little lady in lime-green and pink, holding the hands of two young boys. One reeks of peanut butter and trickery. I wonder if he'll help. Here mate, want a bell?

She addresses the younger boy,
'This is where the feeling came, Robert. Sense anything?'

They stare into a white room.
The windows are barred, but there's a four-poster bed.
I love beds.

'Everywhere, gran,' says the younger boy.
'Black-eyed ghouls and dream monsters.'

'Shut up,' says the older one.

'That's what I feel.'

Monsters. Again.

They leave through a far door.

I stay. Not because the collar can wait, but because, as usual, stairs have come up trumps and led somewhere private and comfortable. My whiskers twitch on something. An energy. As if hope or a similar emotion died in this very room. But, on reflection, I decide it's human nonsense, no matter for a cat.

Peace, quiet and a bed. Perfect.

What more could you want? I push under the four-poster to check for surprises. You don't want surprises hanging about in dark places. Cats don't do surprises.

'No!' shouts a gruff man's voice.

A siren WALLOPS the room.
I JUMP, *smash* into the bed then HIT the floor.
Cowering, ears flat, eyes on dart, my legs jelly, a siren whirls and wails around the walls.
The bedding yanks up.
This yeoman doesn't look happy either.
'Here kitty,' he snarls.

His hand swipes forward and I do the only decent thing. I slam him with eight claws, a deep set of fangs, then shoot off.

He stands. You'd think
I'd ripped a finger off
from the language.

Serves you right. Play with the devil, and you're gonna get scratched.

I leave him and head outside.

The doorway exits
to battlements above the greens.
Wind rips at the trees.
I fluff my fur and scurry
down some steps to ground level.

Rough situation back there, but a most excellent response. Tip-top – well done.
Why alarm a bed?

Now, where to find proper peace?

Back home with the Vic
and Mrs Vic,
that's where.

I pump my tail and stride onto the lawn, pride and paws puffed right up.
Teufel's in town.

Oh, yeah. Sing it, people.
And hooligan over-stuffed crows.

For there they are,
flapping about by my house,
like they own it.
Seven of them.

I swear, the smallest one at the front,
the one I attacked earlier, is laughing.

These can't be special birds. No way can flea-factory crows be famous. I know something though. Catch one and the rest are done for. Their cockiness will crumble to dust. I fancy me some crow pie. This is my place now. They can't do a thing.

Feeling I'm being watched and knowing it, I pad across the grass, swinging my hips and tail...

Sing, Teuf, sing!

'Sing a song of sixpence, a pocket full of rye!
Four and twenty blackbirds, baked in a pie!
When the pie is opened, get ready to be fed!
Wasn't that a dainty dish, and you're all dead!
Four and twenty blackbirds, baked in a pie!
Dead! Dead! Dead!'

The crows are going mental; flaps and squawks galore, and they daren't say a word back.

Hilarious, except there are quite a lot of them and they are quite big. For now, I'll do a little of that *patience* thing Mum said. I pass them with all the high-tailed, high-nosed disdain I can muster, and leap to the kitchen windowsill.

Vicar, Chaplain, or whatever I'm supposed to call him now, smiles and a few moments later opens the front door. He immediately gets all a-flinch at the flapping flappers. Worry not, old man. Not yet. I zip past his feet on other business.

A quick sniff for any melon-mouse, a tuna munch, and then my beloved blue cushion for a sleep, with maybe a bit of planning before dreamy-dream time.

Arrival wobbles set aside, I'm back on track. First day, new place, territory setting done. Strong work. Next time a kill. Bird or mouse first, I don't care. No, I do. Mouse. No rodents in residence – worse than a dog. I'll croak it. Only dead mice allowed. Get tactical, beg some cheese – a mature cheddar with good aroma – lay a trap and wait. That mouse will be history.

After a good nosh on the requested tuna, I'm settling – doing that circle thing: finding the right angle, changing my mind, circling again, selecting another, changing again – when the phone rings. Chaplain answers.

'The Bloody Tower, Governor? I am sorry...
Sir Walter Raleigh's bed... Ah, oh dear...
He has moments...
I'll make sure I control him, yes.

Four hundred years old? An injury?
Deep? A bite?

I apologise... no... he shouldn't...
only trying to help...
quite.

The ravens? Yes, I realise...
the legend and the promise...
a bigger bell?
Well, I could...'

The Chaplain cups the phone to his chest and throws narrow-eyes at me.

I love you, Chap, but don't give me no mood face. And don't be thinking about ideas from idiots on phones, either. A bigger bell and there will be consequences, fella. Riots of sick. Mouse heads on pillows. I'm not above pee in tea.
He gives me a *don't do that* frown.

I give him my *not your business* head-turn and return to fur alignment licks.

Bloody is a strange name for a tower. Yet apt for birds and mice. I will shake off Thunderpaws here, I can feel it. This is Teufel the Magnificent's territory now, and I feel bird is coming my way. How do you spell the words victory and revenge?

You spell them:
C. R. O. W.
Catastrophic Results On Way.

Out on the lawn, I'm the size of a house.
Mammoth flappy ears, fire-hose nose, and upturned bananas as fangs.

Sky is purple, the castles glow blue.

And this mouse.

This disco-tailed mouse who is now neon yellow,
is staring up at me.
'Climb aboard!' she says.

I go to speak, and this gargantuan moo-grunt noise blurts out.
I snort demented elephant calls.
And even more embarrassing,
I obey the mouse.
My massive, cracked leathery foot lands on her back.

And she takes the weight.
'Jump!' she says, 'Jump!'

And I'm on board and she scampers around the Tower like I'm a flea.

'You must learn,' she says. 'Be nice. Start with me and the heavens are ours!'

I've had enough. This is a nightmare,
and what do you do with nightmares?
You get the dog out and wake up. I open my eyes into a thick brain fog.

That yanked-from-sleep feeling.

My claws flex in the cushion's rough fabric. I need air. Fresh air. Any air.

Outside the kitchen window, everything is dark.
Upstairs, the Chaplain and Mrs C are asleep. I jump up and bosh his face.

'Miaow.'

'Teufel.'

I'm dumped to the carpet. He resets for sleep. Charming. I jump back up.
'Miaow.'

Bosh! Bosh!

'Cat!'

Chaplain stomps me downstairs in a flurry of swishing pyjamas.

Bottom step, I leap for the floor, land, turn back to him and stare.
Tail high with my cutest face on – head tilted, big eyes, cat grin –
the negotiations begin.

'Miaow, miaow.' Come on. You know how this is going to end.

And he does. With zero resistance, beyond scowly brows, he tugs the heavy bolt
and releases me to freedom.

Good man, but quicker next time.

The door thuds shut.

Now what?
I sniff at the darkness.

Across the lawns and square, the Tower is new, different. Empty and silent.

Mist falls from every turret, battlement and roof. Tall lamps stand like scarecrow
policemen, arms out, glowing heads fighting into the deep gloom.
Vision's never a problem when you're a cat, and there's not a single crow in sight.
Up in the trees *shivering* I bet, wishing they had a home and staff. SUCKERS.

The White Tower is true to its name, gleaming in a sliver of milky moon.
Under the cake-house roofs, small windows glimmer like the backs of pirate ships.

All is quiet until a roar rips the silence. A long rrrrumbling RoaR.

My ears dart towards a low wall. It came from the other side. Now there's a clacking
sound. Lion big clacking! I've heard it on Chap's telly, watching them bang around fields
praying they'll get lucky.

The mouse has to be lying. Why would lions even be here? But I have to check.
Top rule of catting: own your place. If trouble exists. Know.

I reverse my tracks and sneak around the back of White Tower.

Beyond the tower, a great lawn opens out. In the distance, tucked into the arches of an old wall are sheds. Modern sheds with big cages attached.

Don't like this.

I edge forward, ears on point. A rough drizzle falls. My heart pleads to leave, but I need to know, I must master this place. I get closer. The cages have water bowls. Lion-size bowls.

Don't like this.
Don't like this.

Can't smell cats, though. There's a sharp ammonia pong, but not sweet, cat pee. What lingers in the drizzle is different. I can't get my whiskers or nose around this... From a shed window, a small, beady eye blinks at me. Then another...

Dog off. Can't be.

A crow hotel!

I prowl the cages, eyeing birds in each cheap shed. Pathetic homes. Pathetic human manipulation. Where's your radiators and duvets? You've got a long way to go to catch up with cats.

Two of the crows launch at their windows, smashing beaks and beating wings. Yeah, yeah... Whatever. When daylight comes and you lot are turfed out, terror's calling, birdies, I've just got to find my spot.

The drizzle drenches down. But above the clouds, the light is changing. Darkness heading home. Beaut. By nine I reckon I'll be good and hungry. I hoist my tail, give the crows a view of my bum and push out an extra-stink cat fart. Suck that up your nostrils, flappers!

'See ya, losers!'

I skip over some large rocks half-buried in the grass and head for the house. On the green, I hear laughter from near the cake houses. Through the drizzle, two boys in nightgowns are being chased by an old woman with a white flag.

Are they ghosts? The middle of the night means it's technically not illegal. No one can see them poking through. That's right, isn't it? Why wouldn't Mum tell me the rules?

Still, it's not lions.

The roars shall be fully investigated after crow pie. I wonder if it tastes like cooked chicken, or will Chap have to cook it up first? Time to find out.

I cast around for my breakfast attack plan and see the perfect spot.

A breakfast of crow requires camouflage. Well before tourists arrive, safe from used nappies, sloppy drink-ends or any other nasties, I find my place. The hole, height and position are perfect. Yes, your loveable Teuf is inside a bin, paws on the lip, spying for crow. Genius. A black bin for a black cat; spot me now, freakoids.

Best of all, I silenced the bell. Dunked the end in soil from the lawn's edge – everything has its uses. Victory through brilliance. What's your plan, Governor?

And here's the crow. The cocky youngster from yesterday, hopping by a tree in front of the flat-faced castle. All shiny eyes and glinting feathers – after a worm or whatever they do when they peck grass. There won't be laughter today, mate.

Well, not yours.
Not the Governor's, either.

Teufel's?
Oh, yeah, sing it, people.

A hop and another hop and the crow's behind the trunk. Hauling myself out of the bin, I sit blended into its blackness, eyes narrowed. I give my neck a wiggle. Not a sound. Total ninja.

I'm safe because the bird's safe.

He checked this way minutes ago.
Everywhere a cat-free zone.

Gotcha, pea brain.

I shut my eyes and do the thing Dad does, visioning – picturing my success.

I am the warrior,
the master.

Eyes open and the crow's out from behind the tree. Action time.

Wings spread, tail fanned, it's quite the scene.
He stabs the grass.

That's it! Don't worry, worm, I'll save ya! Faster and faster. I'm a panther. The black bullet of speed shoots again. And again the fool hasn't got a clue. I'm so fast the lawn mud dislodges from the bell. The doggin' thing tinkles. The crow turns, screeches a panicked caw, drops the half-pulled worm and scarpers. Too late. With a jumbo grin and outstretched claws, I leap across the sky. Hello breakfast!

Smacked by an invisible tornado, I slam into the castle's hedge and crash
to the cobbled road. What the fox was that? The crow's gone.
No pain. Shaken, but okay.
Out of here. Run.

I try to move but can't. My legs won't work. But I'm moving.

My body's dragged like prey. Sliding over stone after stone, I try to claw the cobbles, grab the hedge. Nothing works. I'm thumped down a flight of steps, past a thick garden to an arched door at the base of the castle. I stop but still can't move. Then I'm flipped onto my back like an upturned beetle. This is beyond scary.

Above me, set against the grey sky, a ball of mist appears
and forms into a semi-transparent, scowling black-and-white cat.

'Were you born a muppet sack?' she shouts.

Mind paralysed by shock, all I can do is stare.

A ghost. A cat ghost.
Hovering there.
A black-and-white.
White heart on her chest,
White paws and nose.
The rest black, except for
eyes of pure green anger.

Strangely, staring at a shouty, hovering, semi-transparent cat while paralysed upside down isn't the weirdest part of my situation. What's weird is that she's wearing a cat-size navy-blue baseball cap with a red M on the front.

'Speak boy, speak!
Are you an IDIOT?
You're a church cat and you do that,
here of all places?'

I try to shake my head. Why can't I move?

The ghost cat comes close, whisker close.

'I said, what gorm-dork attacks ravens?'

'R...a...vens?' I stumble out.

'The birds!'
She turns away,
shaking her head to the sky,
'Up all night for a clown.'
Her tail flicks, two short stabs.

The hold on me releases. Is she holding me? Has she released me without realising?
I flex my paws. My toes twitch. I can move. I edge my legs down, then stumble up.
My senses are cat-nip city – wobblier than an earthquake factory. Play for time.
Get yourself together, work this out, then boom her.
Just for now, I curl back down.

'Who are you?' I say.

She flushes her long whiskers, tips her tail,
and lifts her head to the side.
'Magnificat, 1601.'

'You have a serial number?'

Her eyes glare.
'Do I look like I have a serial number? 1601 is the year, fool – the greatest century this
country ever had. You've met a ghost before? As a church cat?'

I'm stumped.

'The training?'

Play this stupid.

'You're supposed to be a helper?
Comforter of the dead? Or the not-quite dead, to be precise.'

Is that what Mum did?

Her whiskers drop a fraction.

A sign of confusion. Confusion is opportunity. I test my claws against the stone.
My strength's almost back. Just a few moments. I lift myself to full height and bristle out.
I'll blag it with what I do remember.
'Dog off, Misty. Church cats are ghost police. You know it. I know it.
What are you lot doing poking out? That's what I want to know.'

'Excuse me?'

'The cooking-pot dude said there are more ghosts here than anywhere.
You are not supposed to be in front of living humans. That's the law.'

She laughs.
'You're telling me?' She shoves forward.
'Do you know who we are? Where you are?'

I look about.

'Some glorified Lego set, in a town with attitude problems.'

'And you think we'll take orders from you?'

'You have to.'

'Of course we do.'
She puts her nose to the air.
'Boys, honestly.'

'And speaking of rules – never interrupt another cat's kill?
Remember that one?
I should mouse you for that alone.'

The returned stare is slightly to the left of dumbfounded.

'Kill ravens. How are you going to do that?
They are the gatekeepers to the other world. Lords of the dead.
Heard any of this? Every church cat knows. It's basics.
I mean how could you not know?'

What this is, is lies.
Mouse-size whoppers.
She's gaming me.
Birds are vermin with wings.
This is a size-up for who's boss, and I'm not losing to a misty old windbag.

Her ears drop.
'Ravens always take their revenge.
They are the most feared birds in the world.
Hail the ravens!'

'What planet are you on?
They're fat crows.
What's next?

Obey humans?
Be kind to mice?
Dogs' rights?'

'Attacking ravens is almost treason.'
She stomps off, giving me space.

Giving in. Weakness.

I think about following her, but stand my ground.

'Dog breath, is it treason.
Birds are food.
Food is not illegal.
Food is not treason.
You're talking nonsense.
It's you who is illegal!'

She turns around.
'You ruined my Friday night;
you are not wrecking the weekend.
Guards!'

Four towers of mist
form around me.
In a flash they are armoured men
in helmets, visors up.

Scabbed faces,
patchy beards
and missing teeth.
Each holds a staff
topped with axe-blades and a spike.

They bang the staffs against the ground
then tip the spikes at my head!

The front guard leans forward
and rubs his main blade with a metal-gloved hand.

'These, you furry cockroach,
are halberds.

Double-axe spiky magic.

Time to behave, get polite and stop messing around.
We've got other stuff to do.'

I hiss, flex my haunches and weigh up launching at his scabby face.

A spinning whizz of metal arrives glinting at my nose.
I need another plan fast.
The garden. They've got no chance if I'm in there.

'Ravens!' I scream.

Everyone turns.

I jump for the shrubs but don't even land.

Frozen mid-air,

blades are tight against my neck.

'You think we're fools, do ya?'
blasts a guard with one eye.

He drops to his knee
and strokes my cheek,
mouldy vomit breath washing over my whiskers.

'You need to behave, little fella.'

No. What I need to do is claw that last eye out.

'Enough with the games,' he says, rising to his feet.
'Right, gents.
Excellent work.
I'll hold the first hover.

Keep him up.
If he tries anything,
if anyone loses grip for a second,
take his head off.'

The blades ease but I can't and daren't move.
My body's stuck.

Magnififluff
or whatever she's called,
swans between two guards
and gets right in my face.

'Welcome to the big time,
and the delightful pleasures
of Royal Court guards.
You'll find amateurs don't last long here.'

She looks up at the metal-suited men.
'Boys, shall we?'

Now my brain's proper wobbles.
'You're talking with humans?'

'Yep. This side of death, you can.
You going to be respectful now?'

'Wrong cat, sister.'

'You are here for a king's business.
This is London. Decisions matter. You better cat up!
We are not Devon.'

She takes a seat, her cap lifts and turns backwards on its own.

'Dog off.'

It's all I can muster. How does she know I'm from Devon? A king's business? The guards clank their staffs and we march up the steps with me in the middle hovering like an invisibly trussed barbecue pig. I give Magnificat burn-eyes.

'Is this necessary?' I hiss.

'I do what I dog well please,' she says, not looking back.
'So wise, so young, never live long, remember that.'

What's she on about?
'Yeah,' I say, 'well, you did well.'

She turns.
'What do you mean?'

'You copped it. Couldn't die! Didn't make it to Heaven. You're a failure. A ghost. Spelled L. O. S. E. R! Loser!'

'Whatever.'

At the top of the steps, I pray the Governor's on the green, a yeoman, anyone. The Chap! They spot a floating cat, they've gotta help? The yeomen are ex-army like Chaplain. Bound to assist a mate's moggie, surely? But there's not a soul. Useless. Just trees and rubbish buildings. And me, and I can't do a thing.

The guards scan the square. All clear, we march down a wide sweep of steps beside White Tower. The pace is quick, and if I ignore the situation, floating is quite good. Better than rib-digging fingers or that cradling nonsense humans do before they are invited to realise you're not a baby, you do have self-will, claws, fangs and other places to be.

We head towards a big set of open iron-clad doors beneath the Bloody Tower.
A loud caw breaks the quiet.

Another.
Ravens swoop from the rooftops. In seconds, a swarm of black wings and beaks are coming at us. Magnificat races ahead. The guards panic, ramping up their speed.

Me, I'm bouncing around like a washing machine on spin.

'Will you be careful!' I scream.

Safe under the arch, the guards collapse to the floor, huffing and puffing. Magnificat pants by the wall. No one's let go, though. I can feel the hold. Armoured men and a decrepit moggie scared of birds – what a bunch of pigeon fanciers.
I look to the ceiling in disgust.

There's a spiked gate like the one in Bloody Tower embedded into the stone.

'What do you think that's for?' a guard asks, getting to his feet.

I ignore him.

'Oi!'

I suppose I better meet his enquiry. I turn my head.
'Me?'

He tips an annoyed nod.

'Why would you think I care?'

'It's called a portcullis,' he snarls.
'Snaps down and booyaka! Spiky, spiky.'

I give him Cat Stare 22.
Which is the same, basic, you're-a-gormless-idiot stare as 1 through 21.
'Ooh, petrified,' I say, and reach to clean my face.

He huffs and goes to help one of his mates up. Magnififluff flicks a back leg, pushing out adrenalin. All recovered, we cross a narrow high-walled road to a half-timbered building sat above a berth of river water.

'See that?' barks the one-eyed guard.

A shackled gate lays half-submerged in the dock.

'Better than you. What's this, an architectural tour?'
'That's the route of the condemned.
Traitors' Gate.

Prisoners come here for death.
You're very near, and not too lucky, so far.'

I toss my tail like I don't give a dog's, because I don't.
'You lot are sooo scary.'

'Don't push it!'

His spike pokes my bum. I ignore that too. I've got a plan. The guards make a right turn. In the distance there seems to be an exit. Am I being chucked out? Excellent.

Halberds strike the ground.
Clack!

We shuffle left and face a thick wooden door.

'Silence entering Court.'

We enter a dark, rough-walled room. The next is worse. No ceiling, just exposed beams and broken slats for walls.

From a doorway there's laughter.

One-Eye nods to Magnificat.
'The cap, my Lady.'

She shakes her head.
'It's the weekend, Queen Anne won't be back until Monday.'
Her tail lifts.
'Did you bring the fish?'

'I did, Ma'am.'

'Fish?' I say.
Are things looking up?

Magnificat's tail rises, her ears erect.
'Yes. A small piece of fish in your mouth as a sign of respect
to our mother river, the Thames. You hold it on your tongue, say "thank you, Mother",
then you can eat it. It's tradition entering Court for the first time.'

'Gotcha.'
Free fish is free fish.

'Don't mess about when we're in there. Not a mew. Theses are very important
humans. We are commoners, we wait until we're spoken to.'

I roll my eyes. Whatever.

'And don't interrupt.'

'Where's the fish?'

One-Eye's gauntleted hand reaches down to my face.
'Open wide, little cat.'

'I can't smell it.'

'Fresh fish doesn't smell,' he gruffs.

I shove my tail up.
'Not to humans. You can barely smell a turd. There's a whole world you can't whiff. I say I can't smell fish. There ain't no fish.'

'And this ain't no argument. I said, open wide.'

He stares at me narrowing his beady eye. They're all staring.
And then it happens. My head pulls upwards, my jaw goes down. They're controlling my mouth. His gauntleted hand reveals a small ball, that's not made of fish! He fingers it forward and wedges it across my back teeth.

'That's better,' he says.

They all smile.

'Eeghh, ggmmm...'
I can't speak.

Magnificat's eyes flush wide, whiskers soft with full-on catisfaction.
'Nice and quiet.'
She glances to One-Eye.
'Should have used that from the start.'

I try to spit the ball out. The guards grin, settle their armour and brush at marks. All set and me all a fume, I am hovered into the next room. Everything changes. Elaborately decorated walls, candles and drapes – proper Royal style. Light floods windows across the far wall.

A misty young woman sits in a window bay, the river and London framed behind her. Hoodie up, head down, she watches her trainers swing. A silver-haired man observes her from a table. A ghost too, he's dressed in lavish blue silk dotted with jewels. Beyond him is a grand fireplace, shuttered windows painted with golden lions, and a four-poster bed, its red privacy drapes closed.

'You shouldn't have stolen it,' he says to the girl, 'and you definitely shouldn't wear it here. Any of it. What's wrong with a good brocade? Some silk slippers?'

'I'm not partying dressed like a curtain.' She tugs on the hoodie's strings.

He turns. His face is all perma-tan,
chisel-cheeks and fancy-point beardy whiskers.
There's a strange, white ruff around his neck, like a stack of paper plates.

He sweeps his hair back, says nothing and turns back to the girl.
'London is changing.'

'London is always changing,' she says, still tracking her feet.

'Anne's not going to like it.'

'So? She didn't like the Stones, punk. Now it's hip-hop and rave.
Hip-hop and raves are hoodies and sneakers. Get over it. All of you.
It is possible to like more than one thing,
more than one time. It is possible to grow.'

'She doesn't like you going out. You are seventeen.'

The girl lifts her head, her face a dance of freckles circling an impish smile.
'I was seventeen four centuries ago. I'm not staying stuck. I'm living. Modern
ghosts are fun. Now is fun. London rocks.'

'It's dangerous out there, Jane. We are ghosts. Old-world ghosts.
The modern world and modern ghosts can't be trusted. Inside the Tower is safe.'

'Whatever.' She kicks a sneaker again.

The man picks up a long, feather quill, dips it in an ink pot
then lifts a scroll from a pile on the table.
'These new-fangled things have their pleasures, but we stay in our time.
Their world is... just... it's just... different. The past is certain... known.
But stealing is wrong,
whatever the century.'

'Says Mr Pirate Robber of the high seas. You're a thief. We're all thieves really.'

'I'm not a thief. It was government business.'

'I was government business, too.'

'We were all government business. Everyone gets the chop. It's what happens.'

She finally sees us and jumps down.
'Mags, there you are. Where were you?'

Magnifitude sashays forward.
'Sir Walter had me watching that idiot,' she says, looking at me.
'It attacked the ravens. Can you believe it?
Was the party good?'

It? Idiot? I try to spit the ball out again, but it still won't budge.

'So good,' says the girl. 'Proper mash-up. South London came. Crew got moves.'
She breaks into a little step dance, feet tip-tap shuffling across the oak-beamed floor. 'It was boss.'

Walter gestures to the bed.
'Lady Jane, this is Court. A king sleeps.'

She stops and eyeballs Sir Walter.
'He wakes once a year in May for one day.
Been the same for five-hundred years. Chill, dude. You're such a worrier.'
She leans down and strokes Magnificat.

They all just ignore me.

Sir Walter stands. He fusses buttons on his tunic, then lifts out his chest.
'That was until yesterday, my dear Lady. Our whole future changed. While you were raving at the Wag, or the Four Aces, or whichever hit parade hall it was.'

'They're called nightclubs, Walter. It's not hard. Night. Club.'

'The King woke. Spoke a great prophecy.
About a black cat, no less.
And that very moment,' he turns to me, 'this black cat arrives.
Truly a gift from above. Save us.
His very words.
The time is upon us. I feel it in my mists.'
He checks me up and down.
'Guards, sit him on that stool.
Remove the gag.'

A guard pulls a stool from under the table and dumps me on it.
He yanks the ball from my mouth.
'We're off back there, kitty.
Don't go thinking nothing clever.'

While I spit away the ball taste, Mr Blue Eyes Pirate Face gives me an oversized smile.

'Cat, I'm Sir Walter Raleigh.
You've heard of me?'

I shuffle my fur.
'No.'

He retakes his seat, resting the quill back in the ink pot.
'Explorer? Adventurer? Poet? Sailor of the high seas? Spy? Courtier?
Writer of the best book ever – available in all good bookshops
– we don't mention online – all-round genius?'

'Mr Humble. As I said... No.'

He adjusts the ruffle of white around his neck.
'Well, you should read more. Get about.'

'I'm a cat, Plank. And you know why I'm here.'

He laughs.
'Yes, I do. Looks like Heaven's brought you to serve your country.'

'I don't fall for lies. I'm not stupid.'

'You attacked ravens, so you must be a little bit stupid,
do you not think, given their position?'

'I'm a church cat. Ghost police.'
I think this is what I remember from the Salcombe cat stories anyway.
'And you lot, it seems, are running riot. Showing yourselves to living humans
is forbidden. That yeoman fella said this is the most haunted place on the planet.'

The tips of his moustache twitch as he plays with his beard.
'You don't know what a church cat is, do you?'

'I do.'

His eyes tighten.
'No. You're bluffing.'

Hold it, T, hold it. They challenge you, go large, attack.

'You are here to serve us,' Sir Walter says.
'The ghost world. And in this instance Royal ghosts.
It's new to you. You've seen our powers. There are rules and dangers here.
The world between life and death – the half-life we call it – is very different.
The world of the Tower is different, too.
Believe me when I say, we control both, and we control you.'

'Dog off.'

'Excuse me?' He looks towards the bed. 'Petulant little beast...
Let me introduce the boys...'

There's a clack.
From between the four-poster bed and fireplace
come three doggin' lions!
Male lions!
The size of doggin' LIONS!
They pad forward in a line,
hefting manes, grunting and sniffing.
All musk and power,
the front one pads up to me.

Hot ghost nose-breath to live cat nose-breath. His huge amber-black eyes tighten to a stare. A cat-off stare, right in my face. He can't do that. It's like me doing it to a kitten, totally unfair.

'BEHAVE,' the lion says,
growling through the word.

He turns, wafts his tail, giving me a punch of pee smell, and leads the other lions back towards the bed. They flop around the base, each eyeing me as they settle. I feel sick.

'Walter!' a woman's voice shouts from somewhere I can't work out.

Panic sparks across the room – the lions drop their heads, ears flat. Walter straightens, shoulders back. The young woman grips her hand.

Magnificat bolts to my side, eyes flaring terror.
'You say Your Majesty first time, then Ma'am – like you do jam. Be careful.
Very. Whatever you do, stay still and be polite!'

She jumps to One-Eye's chest, dumps her cap behind his armour, then drops to the floor and hides behind his legs. Everyone stares at a drape to the left of the bed. A woman in a gold dress glides through. Tucked under her arm is a gem-encrusted model animal, the size and shape of a small badger. The woman's eyes are black, her tight hair is black. A jewelled letter B hangs from her neck...

is this, this... Queen Anne Boleyn?

'Walter!' she says. 'Excellent news from a new hotel by the Duke of Wellington's place.'
She chucks the animal at him, and thumps onto the bench where he was sitting.
'Do something with that?'

'Err, what is it, Ma'am?'

'A pango-something. £1.2 million they wanted. Can you believe it?
Buy a country for that.'

'You paid for it?'

'Of course not. Oh, and here,' she pulls at her dress, 'three watches.'

'For?' asks Sir Walter, taking the three gold timepieces from her hand.

'I don't know! They were in the case.'

Walter sets the sparkly animal and the watches on the table.
They sit gleaming by a round, leather bag with a drawstring pull.
He touches the scrolls.
'Of course, Ma'am.'

Her black eyes track the room. She pauses at the girl.
'Nice dress, Jane.'

The younger woman crosses her arms.

The Queen's eyes fall on me. 'What's that?'

Sir Walter picks up a scroll.
'Ma'am. We have our own stupendous news.
I was due to inform you on your return tomorrow.'

Her eyes narrow.
'Is this about the internet, Walter? Have you got an actual plan to get rid of it?'

'Not yet,' he says, pointing the scroll at me. 'Another matter, pertaining to this very cat.
The king woke last night, would you believe? A momentous event.
While you were courting with...'

'Never mind who with,' says the Queen.

'This cat is here to save the world. Those were his very words. I heard them myself.
A sign from above, if ever there was one. For full transparency, there's been a small
teething issue with the ravens. He's a church cat who doesn't seem to know his role.
Quite strange. He's from the country, so perhaps just a little thick.
We'll get him trained up and spick and span for the mission.'

I want to doggin' explode. THICK! THICK! Mission?

'Have you mentioned this to the Bishop?
He needs to know everything, always.' she says.

'He witnessed the dream,' says Sir Walter, 'but I haven't seen him since to mention the actual appearance of the cat. I believe he's on Bond Street. He'll be delighted.'

She straightens her back.
'He's shopping? Well, we can't risk the ravens. They're more important. Kill the cat.'

'Ma'am?'

Enough. If no one's saving me. I'm saving myself. I jump to a stool by the fire, leap for the mantle and scramble over to the top of the four-poster before they can start any of that hovering nonsense. You can always rely on the good old cat rule...
Height is safety.

I look over the privacy curtain. A sleeping King. Crown on his head and everything. Cute. From the other side come snarls. The three lions stare, fanging me. Dog off!

'Right, you lot,' I announce to the room. 'My Mum was a Siamese and my Dad a Mau. Proper cat royalty. Famous, the lot. So, lions and queens, don't go thinking you're better than me because you certainly aren't. I may be a very humble church cat, in addition, but that does not,
I repeat, does not,
remove my natural right to attack birds. A cat's gotta live.
It's nature. Get over it. Birds know the rules. I know the rules. Same with mice. Those flappers are a doggin' liability. Hooligans! You humans, it's none of your business. Don't mess with nature or it will mess with you.'

The Queen's face drops. Walter is aghast. Lady Jane is smiling.
The rest are busting with panic. This might just work.

'Ma'am,' says Sir Walter. 'He doesn't know. No oath. No induction. You have truly caught us out arriving back so early. Allow me a few moments, a morning. Pop back and see your new beau in town. We'll get this yob sorted. Get him oathed up. No more trouble then. Get him on track and in service, Ma'am.'

'Nope!' I say. 'Don't be bothering with that Walter Wannabe Wussface. I ain't saying no oath. Cats are not beholden to others. Ask them lions. The Queen could be Cleopatra and it wouldn't matter. It's just against nature. And nature trumps human, always has, always will. Here way before... It's nothing personal mind... I'm sure–'

'Cleopatra?' the Queen strangles out.

I pad across the top of the bed-frame, to make sure she fully gets it and isn't a little thick or anything...

'Yes. Egypt worshipped cats. We respect her. Very cultured Queen. Very cultured people. Thais too. Ancient histories. Primo blood pumps these veins.'

I give Magnificat a fat smile. Instructions? Behave? Ma'am and jam?
How's that darling? Take that with your backwards baseball cap.

The Queen stands. She turns to Sir Walter,
'I leave you alone for a night and what happens?
Take note with that quill on the following.'

'Yeah,' I say, 'and look what you do to birds. Right there with that quill. A bird died so you can pontificate! You lot should all shush it up.'

Sir Walter fumbles to unfurl a scroll, quill all a-quiver.

'Jane is grounded,' says the Queen, 'for a hundred years! You are on your last warning.
And the cat. The cat is dead.
Kill it.'

What?

Sir Walter scratches the words into the parchment at break-neck speed.
'Ma'am, let me just get him under oath...'

'Get rid, Walter. I don't have time for nonsense. You have one focus – the internet.
Take it down. Rid us of evil and to Little Ease with this venal, foetid, fleapit cat.'

'Little Ease, Ma'am. Right away.'

What's Little Ease? Anyway, good luck getting me from up here. I've already spied my route out, across the mantelpiece to the far door. A sack flies over my head.

'Oh, and get my champagne,' says the Queen.

NINE

Every minute and seventeen seconds, a gloop of slime wreaks through my left whiskers, down my shoulder and drops into a small depression of other slime on the stone floor.

There is no other sound. No light. No bowls for water or food. The place stinks like dead fish. I'd move, but an inch in any direction and the gloop is worse. This is the driest wet spot there is. My paws stand in the gunk. Night's grip owns my bones and day never comes.

It is a darkness akin to the Devil's soul.

Even the air pinches and moans at the stench. And I need a pee and a poo. This space, this box of stone and blackness, made so no human can sit nor stand, as the guard said bringing me, is Little Ease indeed. Abandoned for centuries and reopened for me.

Me and my big mouth. Me and my big everything. Me and my overconfidence. What happens now? Do I die? Alone and thin? Waste away?

The darkness refuses to answer.

Magnifimoan does though. Oh yes, she won't shut up from the other side of the door when she visits. Berates my stupidity. I refuse to answer with even a hiss. Sometimes I see sparks, but that's just madness and tricks of the dark. The Chaplain and Mrs C should launch a rescue! Guns, explosions, the works. Take me back to Salcombe, our seaside home in Devon, never to see this palace of fools and fear again. Away from Queen Anne Boleyn, a woman ignorant of basic facts. Telling a cat is like telling a pebble. Pointless. So is telling a queen it appears.

No food or water, and I've been here, what, two days? Hard to tell when time moves like a depressed snail. Little Ease's door remains as closed as a vet's heart. My claws, blood-raw and sore, gave up yesterday.

Hope's gone, too. Everywhere is stone. But this gloop, this endless drip-drop gloop, is going somewhere, otherwise I'd be ear-deep, drowned in the dark. I wish I could sleep.

BOOM!

A thud smashes the cell; the floor twists and shakes. Walls shudder and groan, rocks hit my pelt. Little Ease will collapse! As fast as the boom hits, the cell settles and silence returns. Cowered in the blackness, I sniff the stagnant air for clues. What the dog was that? The gloop is stronger. I scan for injuries. Something stinky hits my back. My neck. My tail. More and more...

The slime is pouring in. I will drown! There's nowhere to go. I dig at the floor. Paws plunging. A way out. Any way out. Gloop rises up my legs. Pushing at my shins. It has a direction, Teuf! It's flowing behind you. The floor must have shifted. Somewhere there's a gap. I drag myself around. There. The back of the cell. The gloop's sliding under the wall, like the edge of a waterfall. I stab a paw past the stream of cascading gloop. Beyond is air. A void. I stretch and stretch. A ledge. Yes!

I duck my face into the gloop and squeeze under the wall. Pushing my body claw by claw, limb by limb under the heavy stone, then over the void to the black safety of the ledge. The air changes. I'm safe. Gloop-less except for my sodden fur. I clamber further into the space and hit that distinct smell – the stench of death.

My eyes adjust to the dark. Woodlice speed over my paws in panic. Something grunts ahead. A deep muffled grunt. More of the little armoured insects scurry past, faster and faster. My senses are smashed; the death smell overwhelming.

But I can only go on. If trouble exists, know. An object looms in the gloom. A tipped-over cauldron. The smell and grunts are from inside. I peer forward. But I'm a cat. I need data. Whatever's inside begins to move. A giant's head! From leathery cracked skin, two huge grey eyes start to open. I turn away. The head issues a soul-tearing scream. I'm outta here!

Another explosion. A thunderous bang. I smash into the head. It screams. I howl, kick and run – fighting my way back to Little Ease. Over the ledge and under the wall, I'll drown in slime rather than be eaten by that!

Back in the cell. Adrenalin gone, fear shuts me down. I tremble. This place is too much. I can't cope. But the gloop has stopped. Cowering in the debris, the gloop's stench is taken over by something new. Acrid, almost chemical. Towards the door, long splinters of blackened wood litter the slime. I can see them; that means light.
I splutter and cough. Stumble up.

The caustic stink fades. Fresher air touches at my nostrils. In the middle of the blackness where the door was, a match strikes mid-air. The pear drop flame hovers yellow in the dark.

A ginger-black cat's face leans forward past the quivering flame.
'Come, my friend. Let me lead you into the light.'

The gingery-black ghost cat retreats into the gloom of the tunnel, leaving the flaming match hovering mid-air. I stumble through the debris into the smashed doorway. Across the floor lie battered metal sheets, a metal rod and matches. Matches everywhere.

There's a hole in the wall at floor level. Cold wisps through, freshening the musty sulphur, firework air.

'Come, my friend. Come,' he says, from beyond the flame.

Matches spin from the dirt, hit the lit match, flare and trail to a brushwood torch on the far wall. It crackles and pops into light. The now-revealed cat is large, dirty. Kinda burned, with droopy whiskers, torn ears and a red collar. He pads forward, dragging a back leg, and sniffs.

'You don't smell so pretty, church cat.'

'The name is, Teufel. Teufel. And I ain't even telling you what went on in there.'

'I know the name,' he says.

I lean against the wall, not caring about the muck and grime against my sodden fur. Should I push my tail up to show gratitude? I'm not sure; I don't trust this place. Or him.

'You did this?'

He nods, pawing dirt from his front. Comes close.

'Wanted it smashed up. The explosion will confuse Court when they investigate. You're in a mess. Deep in a pickle jar of problems. Big problems. Court has you by your whiskers. We've got to show you've got power. Explosions show power. It's taken days to track you down.'

'Who are you?'

'My name is Citizen. We're going places.
Starting with that hole there. Come.'

He turns to the hole which seems to be the start of a small passage.
I stop and hold. My tail droops.

'I'm sorry but–'

'What's the problem?'

'One minute I'm beaches and lanes. Next it's chop-chop street and bang-you're-dead terrifying doom holes. Now explosive-expert cats. I need a moment.'

'Welcome to the Tower. We feed fear. Keep your secrets to yourself.
Don't worry. I'm here to help. Just so happens you've stumbled into something bigger than you could ever dream.'

I stare down the tunnel. Abandoned torches hang from the walls far into the gloom.
'Where are we?'

'Deep in the base of the White Tower. A ghost land, long forgotten by the living. Come, we don't have time. Follow me.' He dips his tail and pushes into the hole.

We emerge into the deep night, tucked in by a pillar, shadows of something vast above us. He comes whisker-close.
'We're beneath the White Tower's entrance. William the Conqueror put it one floor up to fox his enemies. We must fox ours. From this moment on, consider yourself on a secret mission.'

'Secret mission?' I blurt.

'Yes. Keep quiet. The ravens are there. See?'

The cages and huts are across the lawn.

'Those birds are dangerous. Don't think about anything within ten feet.
They can read your mind – but you know that, you're a church cat.'

'Naturally, of course,' I say. Mum never said anything about doggin' birds, except don't eat them unless you really have to – she could be proper annoying.

'Leave them alone. We'll sort them later.'

Everyone's obsessed with these doofus birds. Kill 'em, situation over. There are cannons galore. Blow 'em up. Simple.

'I'll be in touch,' Citizen says. 'Don't say a word to anyone. I need to tidy up back inside, but over there,' he signals to where the stairs meet the ground, 'you'll find a treat. Fill up, then head home and clean up. You stink.'

'You seen a mirror? You aren't looking so great yourself. I didn't choose to go through that in there you know?'

His eyes are sharp and cold.
'No one chooses here. Don't you get it? Lose the cattitude. You've just been rescued from hell, remember.'

'But why? Why the help?'

His head drops,
whiskers
down,
ragged ears
fallen.
He rises fast.
Swipes my face with a big misty slap.

'Because you, mate, despite looking like a feral and stinking like a skunk
and being doggin' ungrateful, are an exceptionally lucky cat.
Powerful ghosts have your back.'

Stunned, I shake the hit off.

'They do?'

His tail rises.
'They do. More powerful than you can imagine. What Court have planned is going to take every millimetre of fur to survive. Do exactly as we say, and you might live to become the most famous cat in history. When Court ask, say you broke out. That'll put the bricks up 'em. Powers. Hint at magical powers – black cats are lucky, and all that.

Now go.
Say nothing to no one and we'll be in touch.
Oh. And no oath.
DO NOT, on any account, say the oath.'

'Why?'

But it's too late.

He's disappeared in a pocket of exploding mist.

ELEVEN

Confused – and as Citizen, the explosives-expert ghost cat noticed – whiffing like a basket of old mackerel, I gaze across Tower Green.

I can be the most famous cat in history?
Is that why I'm here? I can be like Dad.
And a church cat? Mum said I was special.

I just have to behave. I can't make any sense of it.

But as promised, tucked under
White Tower's giant staircase, is a saucer of fat pink prawns
in a cream sauce.

Now, I'm no fan of cream or milk – that's my Siamese side – but when you've not eaten for days, you don't give a dog's privates. I rip into the flesh and lap up the fishy-prawny yum-yum cream; it's a smack-down meal.

After two very satisfied belches, I waddle for home – stuffed-penguin style.

Over the lawns, I see the lights are on downstairs. Excellent. I jump for the living room windowsill and peer in through the steam-drippy glass. It's toasty warm in there.

Chaplain is reading in his red chair.

'Miaow. Miaow.' Scratch of the glass.

He looks up, clocks me and drops
the
book.
His face is
Christmas morning
and the best present
in the world.

A few seconds later the front door flies open.

'Teufel! Teufel!'
He's almost singing it. He shouts back into the house.
'Teuf's back, Love. He's back!'

I give a bum wiggle to judge the distance and thud down to the step.

At his feet, my funky aroma lifts lifts into his nostrils.
His joy crumbles.
'Love, bring a towel!'

Mrs C arrives with two tea towels.
'Oh, my boy... Oh, my... Ew... What's that?'
She thrusts the towels to Chap.
Using them as gloves, he stoops down and grabs me around the belly.

Oi. Easy fella.

Another belch comes and suddenly I'm not so well; my stomach's a gas factory.
I go to get down.

Chaplain's fingers lock against my ribs.

Not now, Chap.
Not now.

We thrust into the kitchen, straight for the sink.
Mrs C blasts the taps on.
Water smashes against the stone basin. She squeezes in washing-up liquid.

Water and dish-soap is not happening! I'm food ends!

I squirm and twist at the Chap like a Japanese ninja.
He tightens down and the inevitable comes.

I growl a deep, undulating yowl, my stomach explodes and a puke-flume bazookas out of my mouth like a confetti bomb. A Great Dane couldn't chuck up more. I am strangely satisfied, and yet broken.

'Teufel!'

I surrender.

I am washed and cleaned for five doggin' minutes, Chaplain on me, Mrs C on the sick.

A skunk of washing-up liquid and indignity. After a dry down with a real towel, I am released. I stomp to my bowls for a drink. My cushion isn't there.
'Miaow. Miaow.'

The Chap's face goes soft.
'Gone, Teuf. Came down this morning and... the strangest thing.' He shakes his head.

Missing? How do you lose a blue cushion? What nonsense.

Mrs C brings a sofa one and pops it by the cooker. I give it a sniff.

The Governor's yucky cologne slaps my pride. But I don't care.

I climb on board,
plonk down,
curl my paws,
and I'm gone.

TWELVE

In the morning, I barely wake when the Chaplain comes to make tea.

Thirty minutes later, he's dressed and I still don't move. But when a small plate of chopped chicken arrives by my nose, and I receive a top-notch head rub, I stumble to my paws.

A while later, I'm let out without fuss when Mrs C leaves, wrapped in a big coat and a purposeful expression. Bag over shoulder, shopping list in hand, she's got that curry-night expression – Chap likes it spicy!

On the front step, it's a dark autumn morning. All mist and murk. But inside I feel like spring. A bad experience (or sixteen piled on top of each other) – you move on.

I'm free, fresh and clean. Not a drop of Little Ease gloop passed my tongue.
I've got powerful new friends, although I don't know who they are.
And I'll be famous. Proper, world-beating famous.
Take that, idiot Royal Court, Walter Wuss-Pants and Anne Baloney-in.

Simple pleasures get you back on track, too. Like a good poo. It's important when you're a cat to have a private spot. Nothing worse than being tail up and a beady pair of eyes slapping on you. And most important – you gotta be doing the do somewhere else – neighbours' gardens preferably. But the Tower doesn't have those, and there are more windows than a glass factory.

No more trouble with the Governor. Not yet.

Chaplain needs to settle in.

By chance I find a little garden at the bottom of the Tower.

It's private and tended by loving gardeners, who keep the vista pretty and their heads out of my business. And when you're at your business, and things are taking a while – you get to thinking. Kinda helps it come out in some weird way.

Court think they've got me in their dastardly plans, but they're wrapped up in a cat's even better ones. And good luck getting around that.

Humans always think they're better than everyone else.
I can't wait until Citizen shows them his paws.

'Dude!'

I follow the sound through a bush.

Lady Jane is peering at me, smiling. 'Dude. What the– ?'

'Do you mind?'
I cover up my donation with some fresh black compost, lower my spine and slink off in the opposite direction.

She mists in front of me, blocking my way. Hands in the pockets
of a thick grey dress, rather than her punk-ravey-hip-pop stuff.
She looks like she's been dragged from a museum.
'Dude, you're supposed to be in Little Ease.'
Her freckles bounce as she laughs.
'Anne's gonna proper do one at this.'

'What's with the sack?'

She pats at the bulky folds of her dress.
'Anne thinks she's won for now. But I've got a little surprise.
Never mind the dress – how did you get out?'

Power is in presentation and timing.
I take a seat, lick a paw, and stare into her impish eyes.
'I told you, I'm not just any cat. Your Little Ease is smithereens.'

She pulls a hand bell from a pocket and jangles it hard.
'Mags!'

In seconds, Magnififluff mists in.
Idiotic blue baseball cap, all crazy cat shock;
whiskers back, ears back, eyes flared.
'What the fox are you doing here?'

I decline a reply. A cat that comes to humans like a dog has no self-respect.

'Anne's going to blow her gin,'
Magnifishame says to Lady Jane.

Jane stoops down and rubs her back.
'I know. Can't wait. He might be what the King said. Who'd have thought that?'

While Magnififuss gets all high faced, gloaty, I-loves-you purr-purr nonsense,
I pad forward. Time to get front and centre.

'I am the one,' I say. 'And if any of you old misty have-beens try anything like that again, I'll do the lot of you.'

Jane chuckles.
'Anne's gonna so love you. Walter's going to have kittens.'

'This fool needs to be careful, Jane,' says Magnifinonsense.
'He knows nothing of the real world, never mind ours.
He's a chump.'

'Oi,' I say.
We cats can handle any insult, but that's just rude.

Magnificat turns to me full-fluff.
'It's Scorpio up there,' she says, with a nod to the sky.
'Manipulation, treachery and death. The wound that never heals is weeping – the sun in Chiron. Darkness is coming. You know nothing.'

'Excuse me?'

She nods to the heavens again.
'The stars and planets – how they align.
We are in foreboding times. That's what I'm saying.
Up there.'

'You follow *stars*? That's what you're telling me?'

'Of course,' Magnificat says.
'How they align affects everything.'

I'm in a palace of loons.

'Right you are...'

'The Bishop's feeling it. The ladies of the rods, too.'

'The Bishop's rods?'

'Yep. You don't want to mess with them.'

'Okay...'
I spy a tree with excellent scratching bark.

From behind me she calls:
'Science is serious.'

Science – if only. I turn and face her.
'And does this cap of yours shade you from these magical stars and their looning rods?'

'What?'

'The baseball cap.'

'You like it?'
The cap floats off her head and hovers between us.
Like she's showing it to me.
She hasn't even removed the sticker, the tramp.

'Got it off a tourist kid's doll. Some mascot thing...'

'You steal from children?'

'Where else am I going to find my size? Snapbacks are boss.'

A red-plastic lighter hovers out from inside the cap's rim.
It floats past her face, the flame sparks and the lighter sways side to side.

'Hip-hop, rap, rave,' she says, head swinging to the same rhythm.
'Anything with the boom. I'm gonna be a rapper – the Snook Moggy Mog.'

Please.

She cuts the flame, hovers the lighter back into the cap and returns it to her head, this time on backwards.

Double please.

Lady Jane pulls something else from her pocket.
'I got these last month...'

A pair of grey headphones drift up.
A press of her pocket and a fast boom-boom blasts out.
Another press and the music stops.

'What does your bishop say about all this stealing?' I say.

Jane laughs.
'You should see his room. Biggest thief there is.
He could hide a giraffe under a stamp, that man.
He leads the old Court. You'll meet him soon enough.
A fusspot as full as his belly. And he's going to have a proper problem with you.
The oath would have kept him quiet. The Queen too.
But you got all back-chatty and now Walter's in trouble.'

'I was presenting facts.'

I check the potential scratch tree. When you're setting up power relationships, negotiate from a position of strength, always ask for what they can't give.
Keep them off centre.
Annoy them – just never enough so they walk away.
'Get me a Sir-ship like that Walt has, and I'll think about the oath.'

'The honour of a knighthood. For you?'
She puts the headphones away.
'For doing what?'

I put my tail tip up and ears forward to show I'm serious.
'For being a cat. That should be enough. Never mind being your saviour.
A king's mission is status and status requires it thus. Treated properly. Bows and stuff.
From them guards particularly. That One-Eye is proper annoying.'

She crouches down and tickles my chin. Her mist is warm.
'Teufel, my sweet Teufel.'

Humans get cosy when they want things. Transparent as mud.

'You really don't have a clue, do you?'

'Yes I do.'

'Do something for me,' she says.

'What?'

Her hand moves down my back. Fussing attention on a cat when you have an agenda is null, void, and remembered.
'Meet Sir Walter for me. You and him. Smooth things over.'
The back of her hand runs down my flank. Now her fingers dance on my tail.
'A king's mission is an incredible honour in itself.'

'Maybe,' I say.
I nudge for some cheek. Love a bit of cheek.

'He'll be in the king's private chapel before Court.
Wakefield Tower across Water Lane.
You can't miss it – big, round, sticks out like a drum.
He studies there, anything to stop the queen dragging him by his beard
when he's done something wrong.'

She rubs my head.
Now the other side.

I gaze into her eyes.
'What time?'

'8.45.'

'You realise I'm feline? We only do our versions of time. Very rough to non-existent when you want something, very precise when we do.'

She smiles, fingers scraping into the base of my tail.
'You need to be kind with Walter. He's been through a lot.'

'Has he now?'

'Can't cope with clocks. His execution was delayed so many times, hour bells send him crashing to the ground, unless he's being very quiet. Some kind of fit. Terribly upsetting. His death was rather traumatic.'

I nod.
'Noted. I'll think about it.'

She ruffles up my back with light reversed-hand action – proper skills, actually.
'I've got plans for Queen Anne. They'll keep her distracted enough.'

'How are you going to do that?'

'I'm going to bust up her house, next weekend.'

Magnificat rushes forward.
'Jane!'

'What?' she says.

'The Bishop's Halloween prayers.'

'Oh yeah, weekend after, then,' she says, scrunching her freckles.
'I'm going to organise a rave.'

THIRTEEN

Back near home, the clock strikes nine.
Better go.
Old moustachio Sir Walter will be waiting.
I've got to help the Walts, have I? Listen to what he has to say? Very well.

Keep friends within a paw and enemies at claw.

As instructed by Lady J, I find him in the chapel of Wakefield Tower.
Stood at a table in a rainbow-dazzle of light from six stained-glass windows.
He's studying something, his back to me. I take a seat on the tiles and observe.

'Lateness is unbecoming,' he says.

Eh? He hasn't looked back. How does he know I'm here?

He turns, his silver-fox perma-tan face all serious.
'Of a man, mouse, or chets who won't grow up.'

How does he know a Devon word like chet?
I pad up to him.
'Oi. What you doing calling me a kitten?'

'I'm from Devon too.'
He taps the table with his ring.
'Come.
Sit.
You're with a friend. Let's talk mess and, please, don't be late again.
Up.'

I p to the table. A huge book of ornate script covers
a most of the top.
e
l

'You don't speak like you're from Devon,'
I look for a place to sit.

'Nor do you.'

'I was born at the Chaplain's, but grew up in a yacht club for a while.
Full of grockles.'

'That's not a word I'm familiar with.'

'Tourists, incomers. I'm from–'

'Salcombe, we know where you're from.'

'How do you know that?'

'The ravens. Birds provide all kinds of services, and corvids
– the crow family run an intelligence network.'

'An intelligence network?'

He nods.
'Country-wide. We can find out most things.
They are very intelligent.'

Very intelligent birds? Please.
'Fascinating.'

'Now, we haven't got all day. The mess–'

'What mess?'

'Do you know how dangerous escaping Little Ease was?
There are whispers at Court. Of sorcery, witchcraft...'

'Witchcraft? Sorcery? I'm a chaplain's cat, practically angelic.
You lot are from Planet Lovedog.'

'There are old ghosts here, Teufel. Much older than I.
They like the old ways, old thinking. The certainty of their beliefs warms them.
And black cats haven't always been treated so well.'

I want to pace, which is difficult because of the book, so I decide to sit.
Love books. Warm bums are books.

He shoos me off.
'Good heavens Cat, have you no decency?'

'What now?'
Humans have so many issues about where cats sit, we've given up and sit anywhere now.

Walter blows a gentle caressing breeze over the scribed page and closes the book.
The thick leather cover is embossed with a cross.

A Bible. Whoops.

Head lowered, he grips the table.
'What am I supposed to say to Anne?'

'What about? Do you love her?'

'You. You fool.'

I shake my whiskers.
'You get a message from your king about a *special* cat. You *get* a special cat.
Darn lucky I'd say, but then it's all
moan,
moan,
moan.
Think I'd sit in a dark mouldy hovel and be grateful?
I busted it up. It's what I do.
Church cats are more than you know. Police, remember –
with tools and magic and everything.
Your behaviour was outrageous.
Jane said I'm special, treat me like it.'

His eyes are pained.
'I'm under a lot of strain, Teufel. Help me.'

I shake my head.
'Human problems.'

His hand smacks the table. I flinch but don't move.

'You'll talk yourself into your own death, cat.
Independence is dangerous here.'
He leans over me.
'Do you understand?'

I hold his gaze. Human stares are amateur.
I'm certainly not being outdone by a half-dead old geezer.

He blinks.

Told ya.

'You need a cat. You get one. Fortunate, from where I'm sitting.'
I look around the admittedly palatial setting.
'Who'd want to be here?'

'A well-behaved cat. Not one called Thunderpaws.'

I stop dead.
'How do you know that name?'

'The head ravens, Thor and Munin, told me.
As I said, they're an intelligence network.
We don't let just anyone waltz into Court. But that very name might save you.
If I can sell my idea to the queen and you're under oath.
It might stop this internet plan she has.'

That again.
'A Sir-ship and I'll consider the proposal.'

He tuts.
'A knighthood helps nothing. I lost my head.
Anne did as Queen. And Jane. The list is endless. Court is tonight at six thirty.
Humility and deference will serve you well. Proper court behaviours.'

I know the words, of course, but do I regard them? No.

He carries on wittering.
'The Bishop and the rods will be there. You and I can meet before for a briefing.
Everything should go fine. Might I suggest six fifteen?'

My tail-tip swirls. I peruse the ceiling above.
What did Janey say about his things with hour bells? Oh, yes.
I look into his face.

'Let's do six! I'll know when the clock-tower bell rings.
Bong! Bong! Bong! Bong! Bong! Bong!'

Head tilted, I glare into his eyes.

Raleigh shudders
and quakes
then
crumples
to the
floor.

Bless him. I j
u
m
p
down.
Smirking inside – cats do excellent poker face – I pad over.
'You okay, Waltie?'
'Fifteeeeeen,' he says, short of breath.

I approach his nose, sniff, then move to his ear and raise my voice.
'You sure we can't do SIX?'

I flush my tail.
'SIX is SO much easier to remember.
I'm a cat, you see. Human time's not our thing. But SIX–'
'Fifteeeeeeeeen.'

I drop my tail and walk away.
'Oh, go on then. For you. Suppose so.'

He presses a hand to the tiles and clambers to his feet.
'I'm sure you must be somewhere else,' he gasps. 'But a last thing before you go.'

'Shoot.'

'The Tower is beautiful?' he says, steadying himself against the table.

I give the room a cursory glance.
'If you're a stone addict.'
'And tidy and clean?'

'Can't argue with that.'
'Then stop using our beautiful central lawns as a toilet.'

'Err– excuse me?'
'If it happens again–'

'What?'
'There was poo on the lawn outside the governor's house on Tower Green.
He won't tolerate it again. We're not a place for second chances.'

Hang on.
'I did nothing on the Tower Green lawns. I go elsewhere.
The garden down the bottom.'

'Then who did?'

FOURTEEN

When you need to go, you need to go. Poos don't wait, but when the litter tray's mid-clean and Chaplain's on the phone, you do. He's lucky I didn't drop it on the rug.

However, as the helpful and thoughtful cat I am – to him and this doggin' Court – I not only waited then – and waited while I sprinted across the Governor's precious lawns, under iron skies mooding rain – but got to my spot here in the secret garden's borders, and deposited it extra deep to remove any more ridiculous charges on a respectable cat's manners.

Something is off, though, for I have rooted and sniffed and dug through the black compost soil, and there's not a sign of the errant poo of Sir Walter's accusation.

I most definitely did it. Not one you forget when a young ghosty ex-queen is staring at you. My bet's a yobbo fox had it. They'll eat anything.

Tonight's deposit covered, I set for home when two mists appear. They form into the boys I saw running on my first night, still in their billowy night shirts.

The taller one clasps his hands.
'Master Thunderpaws.'

That name is getting around quick. But I like master. Politeness is an excellent start.

I put my tail up in welcome.
'Teufel actually. No matter. What's happening boys?'

His back stiffens.
'You're late. Sir Walter Raleigh awaits.'

'Am I? You his staff?'

'We are princes of the York dynasty. I'm Edward, this is Richard.
We are not staff.'

'Alright. It was a legitimate question.'

The younger one scowls me up and down.
'Do you want the guards?'

New humans need setting up right. Interaction guidelines. Golden rule, don't be a stroke-over.
'Bit busy at the moment.'

'It's not a request.'
His foot taps at the damp grass.

My tail wands.
'I'm ready when I'm ready. I need to clean.'
I nod down to highlight my scruffiness from digging.
'A cat's duty...'

'Nope, now,'
says the tall one.

'Oh, really?'
I pad to a tree and rake my claws in the bark. Plane trees are excellent scratch.
Now... Should I run, attack, be helpful?
Decisions, decisions...
Citizen said don't let anything slip.
'Guards you say?'

The tall one glances left.
He nods.

'Oh, go on then. Since it's you.'
I pull myself off the tree's flaky trunk and get back down to terra-firma.
'No need for the armoured idiots. Spikes up your bum from morons ain't pleasing. I'll come. What's this obsession with by-the-minute accuracy when you're all half dead and stuck for eternity, eh?'

The younger one glares.
'You are rather rude, cat.'

'So is pulling me from cleaning. But, come on.'

I go to where the older one, Edward, glanced, guessing that's where the guards are hiding in whatever place it is before they mist in. I stink out a cat fart, aiming high.

The short one grabs Edward's hand. 'Ew.'

With a tail flick, I get in front and lead us off.
Moody clouds blackening to anvils above and the sweet smell of cat farts below.

Oath?
I'll listen, but nah. Don't think so.

The two princes leave me at the entrance to Court and I pad in.
'Anyone home?'

Sir Walter is working by candlelight at the table.
The lions sleep by the bed.

Taking a wide berth I jump to his side. Spread over the table is a curly old map showing Earth with continents flattened out, and another with what look like star constellations.

'Late again,' he says.
'Time and tide wait for wanton cats, it seems.'
He puts down a quill, lifts a small note from the table and folds it into the breast of his tunic.

'Good evening to you too.'
I assess a good place to sit and decide on Africa.

'Off!'
He rolls up the maps, puts them with the scrolls, and steps away.
'We have a lot to prepare. A king needs you.
To be in service to Court, you need to say the oath, no more arguments.'

Citizen, that ghost cat, warned me about the oath.
'Suppose I say no?'

'Then our mutual acquaintances can...'

The lions rise, showing Teufel-size fangs.

Oh.
'When is it then, this oath?'

He lifts a hand through his hair.
'The Bishop has yet another announcement,
then Anne's confounded internet idea,
then Halloween and Bonfire Night
– autumn's always busy –
and then any other business.
That's you.'

'Charmed.'

'The last two merge.'

'They what?'

'Bonfire Night, the night of fireworks celebrating the death of the traitor Guy Fawkes,
and you. Your fates entwine. Bonfire Night is your night.'

I get to the edge of the table, tail beating the stack of scrolls. I ain't liking the sound
of this. That mouse mentioned Bonfire Night. I'm starting to think she wasn't all lies.

'Excuse me?'

'Presenting you to a light will save us. Those were the King's words.
At least, my interpretation. The Bishop heard them somewhat differently.
And therein lies your first problem.'

'My first?'

'Your first problem relates to a section of the King's words.
Devil wreak havoc and war. Black cat. Save us.'

Walter gazes through a window onto the nighted city.

'What does the definite full-stop pause between cat and save mean? Words and
punctuation are such tricky things in English, they really do change lives.
You may be trouble or salvation. Question two: what did the King say beneath a sneeze
that followed? Snippets from dreams are so fragmented.
Bonfire Night.
Light. *Midnight.*
Devil wreak havoc and war.
Black cat. Save us.
Sneeze. *Atishoo* if you will, *the light*, but I have an idea on that.
Shame his cat allergy flared up. We still feel and sense things as spirits.'

'Yo, Beardo. Wind back a moment.
What's all that devil wreak havoc and war malarkey?'

'Alas,' he sighs, 'that precise wording does also compound your problems.
It was said before, almost a thousand years ago, by another king, Edward the Confessor.
His court ignored that dream and would you believe, it came true.'

'The very same dream?'

He nods.

I'm being mugged here. Jane said smooth things over – not get dogged.
'What were the words?'

'The very same words. Court dismissed his royal message.
The country was invaded. Colonised.
Our riches and freedom taken. "Civilising us", they called it.'
He sweeps his misty hand at the view.
'Everything you see,
this building, every king and queen,
every tragedy and triumph since,
is because of ignoring that dream.
The Devil was William the Conqueror, the year 1066.
He wreaked havoc, fire and war until London surrendered.
Our whole future – all our potential and possibilities, gone.
We pivoted from our own independent destiny to his wish and whim.
His blood became our blood, our new royal line; the old ruling families wiped out.
A full takeover. White Tower was his first castle, a castle the like of which the English had never seen.'

'And this is now, somehow on me?'

He nods with sympathetic eyes.
'Indeed. We will not be invaded again.
Not on our watch. We have to act. The prophecy will be heeded.
It's down to you.'

I get up with my thinking tail on.
'So, if I've got this right,
you're obeying some perennially sleeping dude over there on that bed, because
he muttered something in a bad dream which you overheard a snippet of?'

Sir Walter nods. He feels at the pocket where he put the note, then tugs his cuffs.
'King Henry VI was a pious and noble man, alas not much suited to ruling.
Went mad several times. He was stabbed to death where we met yesterday.
Not the best of luck.'

'Aha, new information.'
My tail-tip swirls. I meet him eye-to-eye.

'So, if I've got this extra right,
you're obeying some perennially multiple-bonkers sleeping dude over there on that bed, because he muttered something in a bad dream, which a thousand years ago was muttered by a confessed multiple-bonkers sleeping dude in a bad dream, which someone else also overheard a snippet of?'

Walter nods. His hand pulls his beard and lingers.

'I don't believe this.
Who killed Sixy?'

'The Duke of Gloucester, who became King Richard III. It is believed he killed the two princes too.'

'The boys who brought me here?'

His lips purse as he tips a nod.
'Richard denied it, but they were in his care and never seen again.
He became King instead of Edward, the oldest one. All rather convenient.
The princes are very brave about it, they won't issue a word on the subject.'

There's a noise at the door. The guards enter carrying an extra table, candlesticks and linen. They set the table by the windows and begin lighting candles across the room.

'You sure about all this?'
I say, turning back to Sir Walter.

'You know more than kings, do you?'
he says, giving me constipated-bat face.

'Why not?'

He laughs an exasperated laugh.
'Show some respect.'

'I am and I do. But that doesn't mean I don't point out stupid.
Humans are way too good at it.'

He paces towards me.

'Everything in Court is protocol, Teufel. Awake, he's the senior Royal.
He must be obeyed as if he's the Lord himself.
Monarchs are celestially appointed, an expression of the divine.
We have no choice. You have no choice.'

'You have to believe him because he's appointed by God?'

Yes.'
He fiddles with his hair again.
'Look. Just think about it for a second.
It's a process. Protocol. All we've got to do is show you to some light.
On Bonfire Night at midnight. Which can't be hard. There are so many lights on
Bonfire Night. Job done. Dreams may come true, but the same one twice?
Not much chance of that. Then you can go about your business
having been part of a Royal moment. History being made.
You, as a cat. Imagine telling your grand-kittens that.
At the Tower of London. How lucky can a black cat be?
And we're lucky to have you present at this momentous moment.'

'I'm a prophetic black cat then?'

'Yes.'
He smiles.

'Here for luck?'
Can't be too bad, I suppose.

'You'll be quite safe, I'm sure. We are merely exercising extreme caution.
Precedent and protocol. To protect you. To protect us all. To protect Britain.'

'Hmmm.'

'A word of advice, though.
The Bishop. I'm not sure he likes anyone.'

'Don't worry. Bishops love me.'

A bustle of noise begins in the ante room.

Sir Walter's attention changes, the guards ready themselves.

Queen Bony must be arriving.
I bat a map to the floor. Sir Walter stoops to pick it up.

'Cat!'

There are heavy footsteps from the other side of the drape.

Sir Walter startles.
He fumbles the note out of his breast pocket,
shoves it in his mouth and chomps furiously.

'That's... the... Bishop.'

SIXTEEN

A big, bald ghost in a brown smock and gold oversize sunglasses waddles into the room hugging a book. Stony-faced Queen Anne follows in a red dress, with Lady Jane behind, smiling to herself in her sack.

Sir Walter gives me laser-eyes.

I return a narrow-eyed smile.

He places the map back on the table and whispers, 'Nothing on the note. Keep still and don't speak until spoken to.'

I offer no response.
Curled whiskers, flicking tail.
Nothing more.

As Sir Suck-Up bows to the queens, I slink off to the new table by the window, now resplendent with linen and candlesticks. Out of the way for the Bishop and his no doubt boring announcement (if it's anything like the ones the Chap reads to Mrs C, I'll be dozing in no time). Not interested in the internet, I'll perk up for mentions of Bonfire Night.

I leap onto the table and pass a pair of dimwit pigeons cooing outside on the window ledge – safe for now, plop-drops. A weave past the candlesticks on their doilies, I select a spot on the linen and settle down as the rest of the Royal procession marches in.

First are the two murdered princes, poor things. They come to my table.

'Move up,' says the younger one.

I lift and resettle. He reaches for a stroke.
'I'd rather you didn't.'

He glances to the older prince, who's adjusting his nightgown.
'Can we get a dog? Like a Rotti-Doberman-thing?'

'I'll ask the Bishop,' he says, not looking up.

Magnificat mists in on the far side.
She steps over the princes then waves her bum in my face as she passes.

'Do you mind?'

She plonks herself down.
'What?'

'Being so close. You're in my whiskers.'

'It's cosy.'
Her eyes track down my front.
'This is Court you know.'
Her tone is sharp. She nods to the dirt.

'Yeah, well. If those blonde bozos let me clean instead of getting all Swiss watch about meeting Walter, and he hadn't rattled on for 6,000 minutes, I'd have a chance.'
I lift myself up for licking duties.

'Not now. There are Royals present.'

'So?'

She flattens her ears, her misty fur prickles.

'Don't get pointy with me.'
I drop back down to paws tucked – proper tidy.
'No pleasing you lot...'

'For cat's sake, pay attention. Sit.'

'I am sitting!'

'Upright! Upright!'

I sit 'upright'.
Dogged by idiots left and right, I check the drapes to see what other doofuses are coming. Two tall women glide in wearing grey hooded capes, their heads bowed. The old woman who chased the princes runs in – still in her nightdress, and now it's a doggin' polar bear, dripping puddles as it lumbers by, dragging a chain.

'Who's that?'
I say, to Magnificat.

'Present from the king of Norway, eight hundred years back.
Name's Gnut. We call him Snowy because he never sees any.'

The polar bear lies by the fireplace away from the lions.

Back at the table, Queen Anne sits.
The Bishop brushes past Sir Walter and takes a seat beside her,
placing the
book down.
It's Chap's blue prisoner book – the gift from the Governor.

Has he stolen it?

Sir Walter lifts a stool from the table-end and fusses it to a new position.
Lady Jane stands against the back wall beyond Magnificat.
The Bishop gets up and brushes his smock down.

Shut-eye time for me.

'Right, you lot,' the Bishop says, lifting his gaze.
'Your Majesty, Lady Jane, ladies and gentlemen of Court. Welcome.
Busy agenda this evening. First, I'm having another state of emergency.
Proper one. All frivolous ghosting prohibited. No drifting visitations.
Or any other general haunting of the living:
Tower residents or tourists, I don't care.'
The princes sigh.
'There are suspicious activities that need extreme vigilance.'

I lift an eye.

The Bishop cranks a hand at the old lady.
'That means you, Margaret Pole.
No more midnight chases.
None of your other fun, either.'

The lady's face goes all moochy sulks.

'The Governor's wife is frazzled enough.
Extreme vigilance and my favourite activities –
prosecution and persecution.
Because Royals, ladies and gents:
among us, we have traitors.'

He steps to the centre of the room, lifts his sunglasses up,
and eyeballs the assembled ghosts.
'The Ladies of the Rods confirm it.'

Anne thuds her fist to the table and stands.
'Traitors! My watch. My Tower. You hear that?'

The
words
hang
like
a
carcass.

Walter fiddles with a quill while flitting glances to the grey ladies.
Their hoods lift, revealing faces of slab-grey nothing,
not a single feature.

I shoulder-bash Magnificat.
'What happened to them?'

She doesn't respond.

I shove again.
'Oi.'

'Shush... No one knows. They may be witches. They have strange powers.'

'I thought you lot hate witches?'

'Power is power.'

One of the women brings her hands together. In each is a small L-shaped rod.
She sweeps towards the Bishop holding them like pistols.

'Uh-oh,' says Magnificat.
'Truth detectors.'

'You what?'

'Dowsing rods. They point to truths or lies.
Divining they call it.'

I look to the timbered ceiling, lost for words.
'Astrology, rod-twiddling? What's next, dungeons and dragons? Ghouls?'

She doesn't reply. Her eyes are fixed on the Bishop.
He approaches the lady and smiles.
She and her companion bow, and he pivots back to the room.

He taps
the blue book
on the table.

'One-thousand five-hundred prisoners died here.
Six-thousand five-hundred survived. We have every name.
Has someone come back? Or... Is it one of you gone rogue?
I don't mind getting my old tools out from the cellar to find out.
Anyone for the rack, the scavenger's daughter?
We can have a two-for-one Torture Tuesday with
extra pain sauce.'

He stalks the room.

Observing this lot fearing up is fun. Prosecution and persecution are excellent.
It's like running back great mouse movies in your mind.

Anne presses her hands to the table, fingers crabbed over the oak.
'Has anyone seen anything?'

Her
black
eyes
land
on
me.

'You. What about you?'

'Me, Your Majesty?'
See, nailed that, didn't call her mood-butt or anything.

'Yes, you.'

'Tourists?' I say, getting to my paws.

'No. Ghosts you fool. Any others than those here.'

Head still, I slow-blink to add drama then give the room a quick scan.
'Not a soul. Now, there was a strange mouse–'

'Not rodents,' she says,
'who cares about vermin?'
Her eyes sweep across Court.
'Any of this lot acting weird?'

I swivel my eyes, adding on an ear-track left and right.
'Well...'

Sir Walter Wobble's face washes with panic, his eyes are pure mouse.

Just what was in that note?

Jane is watching her sneaker caps.
I could give up her rave plan. The queen's good books is a place to be.

'Back to you on that,' I say.
'Keep an eye out.'

Anne locks her arms and leans in.
'They are out there. Find them, or I'll be sipping souls in my gin.'
She fiddles a fingernail as she sits. 'Next agenda item. Next!'

The Bishop stands.
'Court, we come to Halloween.
Our night of divine prayer, saving us from the dead and the not so dead.'

Heads bow across the room.

'Our most solemn night. The modern world, these living people, ignore our pain
and loss. Laugh and jest with their lanterns, their tricks and their treats.
We souls, trapped between death and the great beyond – for no fault of our own –
pray for salvation and protection. The ravens will be locked up as usual.
We will remain safe from the underworld dangers, if we pray hard.
As guardians, we respect the ravens as always.
Hail the ravens.'

The room stands, even the Queen.
'Hail the ravens!'

If ever I need a reminder this lot are beyond bonkers – it's them and their attitude
to puffed-up crows.

'Danger is close,'
he continues.
'Traitors love evil's evening.
It sings sweet melodies to their darkened souls.
None of us should be tempted by the devil.
Witness his presence.
Feel the energy.
We know his power to hide in plain sight.
To pad with silent steps, his tail whipping at the night.
Prayer heals. Prayer protects.

We will strive extra hard this year minute by minute.
And there is great potential, for those who aren't traitors – one way or the other.
I hereby announce Sir Walter Raleigh has a plan for full death.
If successful, it will re-make his illustrious soul, and get us where we belong.
Heaven or Hell. God decides. Plans are finalised.
We – the famous ghosts – all immortalised for our great deeds;
we the ghosts of books, films and tourist attractions,
will no longer be stuck for eternity. No.
We will be released to the same hope and knowledge ordinary ghosts have.
The freedom to rise into the light
once the last memory of our lives has died with the dead.'

Lady Jane lifts a hand to her mouth.
'Without the destruction of culture,' she coughs.

'What was that?' Anne says.
She turns to the Bishop.
'You were saying, Edmund.'

'Amen,' he says. He shakes his head. 'Modern ways are not progress, Jane.
Walter, enlighten Court with this plan of yours that you hope will *save* us again.'

The Bishop sits. Heads lift. The mood changes. Lighter.

Sir Walter rises and claps his hands.
'Indeed, it is my belief that salvation may be soon.
I've studied and consulted the stars.
Calculated and extrapolated and sextanted–'

'Get on with it,' says Anne.

Walter fusses at a pocket.

'Assessing what the King said beneath his sneeze, I can announce, I am confident that
Bonfire Night is our release to the light with the arrival of this lucky black cat.'

Everyone grins.
Even Anne and the Bishop.

Release to the light? What's that mean?

'I'm hopeful, friends,' says Walter.
'Not one-hundred per cent certain. But hope should always be pursued.
Our dear King dreamed a great revelation. Midnight the light comes.'
He beams to the room.
'Momentous times, I'm almost sure.'

Anne's finger taps the table.
'But if it doesn't work, Walter. Destroying the internet continues!'

'Yes, Ma'am.'

She smooths her hair.
'Good. Books, TV, and radio. All of it. I want it gone.
If we don't do it soon, this technology stuff will be in brains.
Everything is escalating. We're doing the living a service!'

'I work day and night, Ma'am. It does require – how might I say – a certain degree of
global coordination. Removing every book, TV programme and radio story,
deleting this new-fangled net-a-ma-thingy
– wiping all human history and data is not the smallest of tasks.
I'm currently investigating fibre optics.
It appears that's what we're after.'

She nods a small acknowledgement.
'What about just the English stuff then?
Just mentions of us?'

'The books are everywhere, Ma'am.
All corners of the world, and as for the interweb...'

'My point exactly. Take it all down. They can build it again, when we're in Heaven.
We remove history, we get to be dead, released, you do get that, don't you?'

'We shouldn't do it,' says Jane.

'Quiet, child,' says the Queen, not even looking at her.
'Walter, you get it?'

He bows his head.
'I do, Ma'am.'

'Good. If it fails like your Cuban missile plan, I'm not going to be happy.'

I whisper to Mags.
'Cuban missiles?'

'Walter tried a nuclear war back in the 1960s but someone went chicken.
Stopped them hitting the button.'

'You can't just delete everything because you're tired,' says Jane.

The Queen glares.

Jane crosses her arms.
'Being seventeen for four-hundred years, that's what sucks.'

'It is the Queen's wish,' says the Bishop.

'Erm, why were you trying to create a thermonuclear war?' I say.

Magnificat whispers,
'If people remember you, you can't move on from being a ghost.'

I cough.
'So you can "move on?"'

She nods.
'Shush...'

'A little longer, Ma'am,' Sir Walter says.
'Let's get Bonfire Night out of the way, and the King's dream. Let's try with this cat,
I respectfully request.'

'What are you lot on? You lot been kissing dogs or something?'

Walter's stare is top-banana harsh.
'This is not your business. I told you.'

'Yes it is. My Chap and Mrs C like books, TV and everything.
Alien is on at the weekend. Nuclear war isn't friendly.
And if that's your idea of a good idea, you need some cat sense, pronto.'

A grey lady glides to the Bishop and whispers to his ear.

The Bishop glides to Sir Walter's ear and whispers.
The old man's face falls.
He nods and moves away.

'I have news,' says the Bishop.
He steps towards me, eyes set on fierce.
'Our ladies are of the view that the state of emergency is this cat.'

'Excuse me?'

The princes jump from the table. Magnificat too.

'You. The King's words said it. Black cat. Save us. Save *us from a* black cat.
I brought us together this morning to bear witness.
So Court sees the evil within us.

Witness his presence. Feel the energy.
We know his power to hide in plain sight.
To pad with silent steps, his tail whipping at the night.
It's you.'

He gets close, his super-smooth skin stinks of coconuts.

'Dog off, you nutbunk.'
I jump off the table and look up.
'Give me one single example of my evil. You lot need to calm down.
If your last attempt was nuclear war, someone's got to speak up.
I'm supposed to be here for your king. Teufel ain't happy.'

The faceless-rods woman wails to the ceiling, though she hasn't got a mouth.
The rods twitch and flick in her hands. Her head sways.
'Teufel, I remember that name...'

I peruse her slabby face.
'Never met you before, darling. Remember what?'

'From the last war. Those German spies we executed fifty years or so ago?
I'd see their hearts go pop and take a stroll on the battlements under the barrage
balloons and flying bombs. Teufel is the German word for the Devil!'

'And?'

She glides forward. The rods spin and cross,
then settle pointing at me.
Her face leans down.
'Our truth delivered to the Bishop. That you are the fire, havoc and war.'

The woman turns to the Queen.
'Your Majesty, I present the Devil incarnate.'

Her long hand points back at me.

'What are you on about, you gorm?'

She speeds around the room.
Wherever she turns, the rods track to me – she's twisting them!

'He's here, he's here!'
the words scream from her face.
'The Devil in traitor form.
Cast the Devil out.
He is among us.
Cast him out!'

Chants build across the room.

'Cast him out!

Cast him out!

Cast him out!'

The lions stir. Everyone stares; the Queen extra hard.

'You what?'
I stutter, my mouth sticky, dry. This is doggin' barmy!
I back into the table. My bum bashes the tablecloth.
Candlesticks crash above. Fabric singes and burns.

The other grey woman points.
'Fire! Fire! The Devil is here. Look!'

What now?
'Look? You haven't got eyes, you muppet!'

'Havoc and fire. Proof! Proof!'

'Will you stop with this Devil stuff?' I shout.

The polar bear stands, an iceberg rising. He slaps to me with powerful wet paws, reaches the table and plops the burning doily to a dull sodden char.

The other grey woman stabs at a map.
'A witch's cat, or the Devil himself! The stars say it! The stars say it!'

Court panics. Lions stand and roar.

'Shut it!'
snaps the Queen.

The beasts slump.
The Queen's ice fire eyes arrive on me – burning black.
She's enjoying this.

'I am not a witch's cat,' I plead. 'Nor am I the Devil. I'm a chaplain's cat. The name is a chaplain's sense of humour! And you lot need to get one – fast!'

The faceless rod woman starts again. 'Why does the Lord's servant call you the Devil? To warn the world of your truth. The full stop meant death!
The full stop meant death!'
She repeats the chant.
It builds around the room.

Ever have that feeling
you're falling
down a
never-
ending
hole?

'I don't know why he called me Teufel. Ask the Chap. I mean,
I muck about sometimes, but...'

One-Eye strikes his halberd to the floor and steps forward.
'Your Majesty, black cats are the Devil's familiar.
As true as rain. I saw him jump a window.'

What now?
'What's wrong with going through windows?'

One-Eye studies his metal armoured feet.
'Witches go through windows.'

I stomp at him.
'Witches go through windows? You're all bananas. Rods? Stars? If you care to see
– to acknowledge the actual truth – there's white on my toes and a white T-shape
on my front. Faint, but there, so shut your mouth!'

He refuses to lift his gaze.

No one moves.
The Queen tugs at her lip.
I don't like this one bit.

'We see nothing,' says One-Eye.

'Are you a liar, Cat?' calls the Bishop, his sunglasses now back on.
'Traitors lie.'

I check my front. The garden soil has obscured my white bits.

'You must have seen them. You must, you must. I am not the danger!
I'm sick of this. Your king wants me. Called me. That's why I am here! You need me.'

Court is silent and blank-faced. I stomp to the polar bear, ignore his growls and kick
the puddle around his paws. The mud washes away showing my white toes.
Next, I slap my chest in and swish it about, then pad back.
'See?'

I spin to show everyone.
'I ain't no devil. If you want help, show respect. I'll say your oath, but I wanna be Sir Teufel the Magnificent. No more doggin' Thunderpaws!'

The Queen bolts up and kicks her stool away.

Head down, she glides forward, her pace slow and deliberate.
A surging rage pulses the room.

Her face rises – she's grinning!
'This cat's got fire.'

The Bishop's head drops, he seems defeated.

The Queen winks at Sir Walter.

Phew.

She twirls to me, her face a dazzle of fun; broad smile and sparkle-dance eyes.
She crouches down.
'So you want to be recognised, do you?'

I nod, stunned.

'How about Keeper of the Stool in my Privy Council?'

Now I'm confused.
'A furniture storer?'
'Ha! Not quite. Walter, sword and Bible.'

Sir Walter fetches the Bible from the table and signals One-Eye to present his sword.

All ready, the Queen smiles, her voice light and joyful.
'Head down and paw on the Bible – very gently.
Magnificat will give you the words to repeat out loud.'

My mind flashes Citizen's warning about the oath, but he's not just been through all that and isn't about to be a knight. Besides, none of them know my actual plan.
I spin to find Magnifluff. She looks dazed, her eyes fixed to the ceiling as if she's trying to remember something. A head-bob of recognition and she quickens. I prepare myself.

Ha, I'm going to be a Privy!

I rearrange myself with a shuffle – back paws over each other,
make sure my balance is right, bow my head, lift a front paw to the Bible,
ready to repeat the words as they come. How exciting.

Magnificat whispers in my ear, and I punch out the words:
'Under the eyes of the Almighty, I do solemnly swear to give my life and my soul to the Royal Court of Albion...'

'Louder!' shouts the Queen.

'Serving my King, Queen and country as they so desire!'

Not too keen on that last bit if I'm honest, but what can I do?
'I will undertake any task or sacrifice in service of the Court...'

Pump through it, Teuf, you can ignore the content...

'Should I ever refuse, myself, my family and friends for every generation past, present and future, their souls, bones and flesh, may be tortured at the Court's will, and damned for eternity in the burning fires of the pit of hell and anything else they can think of, so help me God... Amen.'

Ahem, that was a tad excessive.

The sword touches my shoulders.
Anne returns the blade to Sir Walter and clasps her hands.
'Congratulations. You are now under sacred oath.
Arise, Sir Teufel the Magnificent, Keeper of the Stool.'

The whole Court applauds,
especially the Bishop, his own claps big and slow.

'You are free to go about your business until the light arrives,' Anne says.
'But not a whisker of trouble. And if you witness anything dodgy, you better tell me,
or I'll be having your tail off and everything else.
A Privy Council member does not mess about.'

'Of course, Ma'am.'

'Court dismissed,' says the Bishop.

Easy-peasy.

Magnificat's face is well-dogged.
'What are you up to?' she asks.

'Nothing. Why?'
Uncrossing my back paws, I stand.
What are *they* up to? That's the question.

SEVENTEEN

I leave Court sick with happiness and relief. What a bunch of pushovers. Not only did I pull it off, I'm ***Sir Teufel the Magnificent***! Always go big.

From Bloody Tower to the Inner Ward, I'm thick in thought. The terms of that oath – all that soul lynching – are well out of order, but when your back paws are crossed nothing counts, does it? With luck it will be ravens' hearts for breakfast soon.

Squawks start from over the old stone wall.

Doofus, you were thinking near their cages.

Still, what are they gonna do? Only birds. I keep going up the road. The squawks get louder. As the wall ends, I look back. The cages are in view. A man in grey overalls clambers out of one of them. What's his problem?

I can tell I'm not wanted. When you're a cat, that's like a wedding invite from your sister. You go. Game on, Mr Poop Shoveller, or whoever you are.
You're messing with a ***Sir*** now.

I abandon heading home and swerve through the railings onto the cool grass.

He steps towards me.

I step towards him.

The slow meeting of soon to be combatants.
We're like gunslingers from a western on Chap's telly.

Me, high-tailed.

Him all swing hips, tight-eyed swagger.
His fingers twitch above overall pockets.

He pulls out a gun!

What? You're a cleaner.
Nah, he wouldn't. Couldn't?

This is a game, chicken or something.
A Sir does not back down.
        No way.
          I pad on, eyes locked on the trigger.

He goes to squeeze!

I slam to the ground.

Crack!

A fast sound, but no bullet.
Opening my eyes, the so-and-so is smiling.

He pockets the gun and strides back to the cages.

Over his shoulders
come ravens.

He was the doggin' decoy!

My paws shoot the steps so fast I barely touch the stone. Darting the lawn, birds dive trying to land talons in my back.

Citizen's warning F L A S H E S in my head.

Claws in, I turn and bat the birds away.

We tumble, roll and crash over the grass – a bowling ball of beaks, talons and paws. After two last swipes at the largest raven, I free myself and jump for the kitchen windowsill.

Watching me, his face all exploding baboon, is the Governor.

You've got a problem too haven't you? My tail whips. I was being nice. Restrained. Armed lunatics out there. You should concentrate on them. *I bet you're a dog person.*

The Chaplain is behind him at the kitchen table. The Governor turns.
Chap's face falls death-grey. Or is it pukey-sick pink? He stands and makes for the door.
Excellent. He's letting me in.

I meet him on the steps and scurry past. I need water, a wound check and a long rest. Despite rewards, this place is proper work.

The Governor, arms crossed, leans against the worktop.
'This is not working, Chaplain. Battersea Dog's Home will take him.'

I glance up from my water bowl. Dogs?

'Toileting on the lawn, Chaplain. Now this. Unacceptable.
Battersea is a fine establishment.
I'm sure they'd find a home, soon enough.
Experts. He's rather substantial.
Might take a few months. A diet would help.'

What's he on about?

He reaches into the breast pocket of his suit.
'Number's on this card. Always liked dogs.'

He hands a tatty old Christmas card to the Chap.
'Damn handsome hound, that.'

What's a dog's home got to do with me? He's lost his brain cell.

While the Governor scratches his face, I get on the Chap's lap to offer moral support. My tail plays against his chest. He strokes my head and I drop in a couple of thigh claws in return, you know... Because I can.

'Governor,' says Chap,
'we can't put human rules and obligations on creatures.
The toileting is unusual. He's tidy on that front.
Never home-turf. Perhaps he was ill?'

The strokes continue. That was fast thinking on the poo, Chap. Quick. Agile. I like it.

His thumb runs along my spine.

Again, my claws flex at his thigh. His pain, my pleasure
– it's another cat thing – you want simplicity, get a mutt.
Head in the air, purring away, the pressure lifts.

Oi, don't stop.

He slaps my bum, pushing me to the floor.

I stare up from the flagstones, confused. His eyes are steel. I get it, I get it. Control.
He's showing the Governor control. Smart. I jump to the chair beside him.

'This is a royal palace, Chaplain,' the Governor says.
'Queen Elizabeth II's property. Respect is due.'

The Chaplain stands.
'Indeed.'

Excellent move from the Chap. That standing-up-to-get-them-leaving trick he uses.
Always works wonders when visitors are overstaying their welcome.
Super smart.

The Governor, flustered, steps to the window and looks out. Bit of a blood pressure issue, Govvie boy? Or is it being a moaning accusatory lying flump that does it?

He shakes his head.
'He can't invade buildings and rampage historical antiquities.
As for attacking ravens. That's the no-no of all no-nos.'

Calm down, grumpy-pumps.

'I warned you before he came. Cattus non gratis if he's up to that.
You're aware of their importance, and the legend.
They have names: Thor, Munin... you can tell who's who by the leg rings.'
He straightens the tea and sugar jars by the kettle, trailing a finger over the lids.

'I am aware,' says Chap. 'I'm sur– '

'The Tower will not crumble on my watch, nor will England fall.
Can you imagine the news stories?'

He's proper doolally, this one. Delirium or something. He names birds!
Gives them jewellery!

'The monarchy,' he continues, 'the country, our whole foundations.
The media will be at the lot.
Interviews. Heavens, documentaries.
What if, Chaplain? That's the question.'

He puts his hands to his face.
'What if your cat... Oh, I barely dare to think it.

I can't have the summit of my career,
my decades of service and duty to the Crown ruined by a fat black cat.'

Chaplain nods a fourth time.

A phone beeps.
The Governor reaches into his pocket and scans his mobile.
'The Ravenmaster...
Ballistic...
Had to fire his starter pistol.'

'Pistol?' says Chap.

'Uses it to scare foxes. Those birds are loved and cherished.
Blood biscuits. Raw flesh.
Everything except rotten meat, and that's only because of the tourists.
The birds are national treasures. Worshipped.'

Chaplain's waiting until it all spews out.
Expunged from the man's whining, whinging chest. That's it. True pro.

'I do understand, Governor. Things will calm down I'm sure.
I'll deliver a sharp word. Quite intelligent for a cat.'

I close my eyes. Too right – but less of the quite.
Suddenly I'm grabbed by my scruff and in Chap's arms.
He takes me to the cellar door, yanks it open and dumps me inside.

'I'll sort him out,' he says, tugging the light on and pulling the door shut.
'I'm joining my wife shopping. Can I show you out?'

What's in here about? Then I understand. He's showing control again. Smart man.
Almost as smart as me. And see where I am now? The cellar. Excellent result.

The mouse has to be here. Luck comes at least once a day. Mrs C and Chap gone. Loads of time. No one will hear your little-fur scream. Croaker time.

Might as well get the little ditch-dweller excited.
I scurry down.
'Time for mouse!' I shout, into the fresh blinking light.

She's on the dresser.
Munching one of my cat biscuits.
'Are you talking about me?' she says.

'Yes. You're mine,' I say, tail whipping.

'Actually, it's the other way round.'

'What?'

She rushes down the dresser. Sits right in front of me.
Offers me one of my own biscuits, half nibbled, right from inside her mouth.

I'm gobsmacked.

She clears her throat.
'I'm Mushika, Carrier of Gods,
and I have a problem.'

EIGHTEEN

The cellar full bright, I ready my pounce.
Then her words sink in.

'You what?'

The cocky-whisker-flicker remains calm.

'I need you, Thunderpaws.'

She's got guts, I'll give her that. But weird's normal here, you face it up.
The brave idiot edges closer.

I keep still, every fur frozen – for now.

Hard-staring me with big globe eyes, she bashes her ear.
'Now,' she says. 'You became a church cat after your mother's death
in a car accident, watched a lot of TV.
Correct?'

'Excuse me?'

'Is it true?'

I look around the cellar.
'Well, yes. They kept me in to protect me and I inherited my mother's job it seems,
but...'

'Seen *Star Wars*?'

'Of course. Chap's lap last Christmas.'

'Excellent. Set that as your frame of reference.
An empire's coming. Big looming power thing.'

'Oh, really?'

'Yep. My universe is run by a cat, called Zeus.'

'Your universe is run by a cat?'

She nods.

'There's more than one universe?'

'You think all those movies happen just beyond Mars?'

'And...?'

'Zeus is the death star of cats.
I need a Luke. It's you.'

'How stupid do you think I am?'

'You really want me to answer that?'
She glances to the steps.
'The future of your planet is at stake. Mine too, as it happens.
So, you're going to be Luke and I'm Leah, Han, Chewie and Yoda.
You're going to blast Zeus up!'
She smiles.

At least I think it's a smile. Mouse smiles aren't something you see a lot of as a cat.
Death Star cats? Cats named after Greek gods ruling other universes?
I mean, what dog-breath. I'll draw her in. Neck bite. Straight into the spinal cord.
Bye-bye mouse, hello flavour.

Cord is moreish. But something holds me back. A feeling.
'You're making this up, to keep me from eating you, aren't you?'

'The Oggle said you're all like this. Quite primitive. Who would make this up?'

'A weird-eyed mouse trying to cheat death. What's an Oggle?'

'I'll tell you later. And I'm not weird-eyed, I'm cat-eyed.
Can't you see?'

I ignore the ridiculous statement.
'There won't be a later.'
Distance calculations run through my head. Likely escape routes. Paw stops.
All calculated. At mice, I'm a pro.

'You couldn't catch me before, what's different now?'

That mind stuff again. My tail wands.
'You ain't sparkle-flashing around with your magic. And keep out of my head.'

'I don't need my tools. I've discovered protection within your very own laws.
This being a chaplain's house, I claim the right of sanctuary.
A hospitality across centuries that must be honoured.
You can't touch me. So, ha!'

She scuttles behind the dresser and comes back with another one of my biscuits.

'These are tasty.'

'Stop eating my food. What's sanctuary?'

'The ancient right by the laws of the Church
for protection within a sacred place.
Such as a chaplain's house. Protection that comes from
up there.'
She looks to the ceiling.

'You read?' I say.
'*Up there*.
What insane nonsense mouse are you?'

She taps her ear.
'I told you, I'm Mushika, Carrier of Gods. And 'tis true too.
Bible, Isaiah 11:6. Go see. And 65:25,
They shall not hurt nor destroy in all my holy mountain.'

A leap from a high drop will take her out. Distract her. Keep her chatting.

'A mouse that can read. This is funny. Come on... Tell me about holy mountains.'

'It's a metaphor. You don't know much do you?'

I head to the table, leap up and peer from the top, testing
my claws in the manky old wood.
'What's a metaphor?'

'A story. Symbolic. Where one thing represents another.'

I take a seat. Right above her.
'And an Oggle, what's them?'

She seems quite unruffled; she trusts this sacred law. Obviously hasn't met claw law
– a touch more power-based and rather flexible.

'The Oggle tells everything,' she says.
'Every universe and time.
A repository of facts
for every world.
Amazing really.
Quite the invention.'

'Bonkers. If sanctuary exists, or that Oogle thing, nothing applies to rodents.
The Bible's human. They need it. Not vermin.'

Mid-munch, she peeks up.
'Vermin is such a discriminatory term.
All deserve to live, to eat, to love.
Care to risk breaking sanctuary?
In a Royal chaplain's house,
in a Royal palace that's a thousand years old?
Under those eyes?' She glances up.

'Yes!'
Claws primed, I leap for the cocky imp.

The mouse bolts under the table.
'I can tell you about your dad!'

I land with a thump. My heart pounds.
I shove up to her, towering above.
'Dad? What do you know of Dad?'

She peeps out from behind the table leg.
'A lot, and I can find out more.'

'Dog poo, you can.'

'He is Gaius. The legendary Mau of the South Hams.
Descended from the first Roman cats.
A direct line from Egypt.
Met your mother one spring weekend,
at what was it,
the Winking Prawn?
Stole a whole mackerel from the kitchen...'

Busted.
I sit down. What the dog?
'How do you know that?'

'Do you promise not to kill me?'

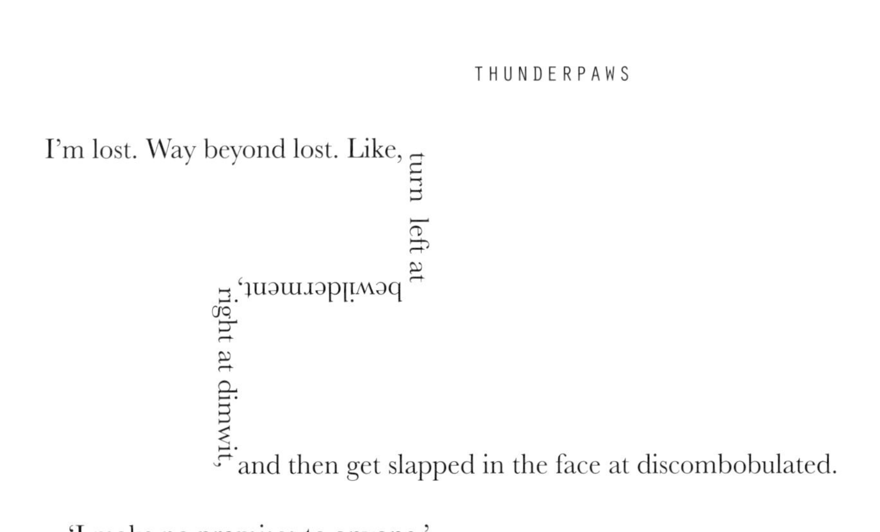

'I make no promises to anyone.'

'Well, if you stop being nasty to someone who's here to help your whole world,
I'll tell you what I know, and why I need your assistance.
By the way, to remind you, I hear everything you think.
You really need to behave.'

I daze at the wall, speechless.

She returns from the dresser with a strip of dried meat and flicks it across the floor.
'Try some of that. I'm here as a friend, you know.'

I lean forward and sniff.
A sweet mildness. Light, more than chicken, not as strong as pork.

'Now, Zeus,' she continues.
'He's a prince. Hero. Future king if he survives his parents and siblings.
Fearless.
His plan – as far as I can work out – is to go back in time
and make your world a better place, and I've got to stop him.
That's where you come in.'

I move the stringy meat in my mouth so I can speak.
'Enough with the brain ache. What's wrong with making here better?'

'He's a cat. The second most selfish species in existence.
But that's not the issue. You change things, other things change.
We need to stop him. He shouldn't be here.
Trust me.'

'Why here?'

'The Tower is an historical touch point. One of the world's mythical places.
Built on sacred ground.
So much has happened: the Holy Grail, the Raven King, Arthur.

The Oggle reveals all. Zeus is coming fifth of November, a powerful date for revolution.
He'll be passing through your time on the way to old time; history's down there.'
She gestures to the floor.
'Think of all he could change. Right under your paws.
History is like the rings of a tree, but vertical.'

'Ridiculous. I want more on Dad.'

'Later. I have to go.'

'Why?'

'I need to check on something, something from home.
You have much to learn, Thunderpaws.'

Another one and that doggin' name. Is nothing private?
'You'll go back using that sparkle thing?'

Her head taps up and down.

'How's it work?'

Mushika scampers right up under my nose. It's everything not to swipe a claw.
'Remember. I'm a carrier of gods. Elephant!'

With a spark of light, she is gone.

*

I circle the cellar. A carrier of gods? Another universe? Stop a death star? Luke?
Prevent a cat from making this world better?
Help a magical disappearing mouse who knows about Dad?

Not a single answer comes. Beyond a feeling I've been played. Again.
How does she do all this disappearing malarkiness, and doggin' brain-reading?
I need me one of them Oggles.

I chew the rest of her dried meat, which is rather scrumptious actually,
and find another slither under the dresser.

The Chap is hours. Finally, the cellar door tugs.

'Teufel.'

In the kitchen, Chap and Mrs C unload shopping.
I take a drink and review this morning's leftover food, terrine of salmon with whitebait.

A sniff confirms my suspicions. Five per cent dry is no use at all, so I watch them work.
Cats like to observe staff; watching them do chores soothes the mind. I'll see if I can
wrangle something fresh when they finish. Bit early, but persistent mews are a wonder.

Mrs C stacks boxes with cartoon cats on the side.
Next she tugs a blue cushion from a large bag. The cushion is similar to mine,
but flatter and striped; she replaces the sofa one by the cooker.

'Here you go.'

I lean across and sniff. All plastic. Yuck.

Mrs C heads for the hall.
The Chaplain loads tins on shelves.
Mrs C returns, gives me a head rub then picks up my food bowls – fresh and biscuit –
goes to the sink, opens the door underneath and dumps it all in the bin. Bowls washed,
she grabs a cartoon cat box, tugs the top and pulls out a slim grey pouch.

'The vet says they're super tasty, darling.'

My ears bolt. Vet? What's she been there for?
Nothing good ever comes from that monster.

The Chaplain closes the cupboard.
'I'm sure he'll love it.'

Examining the package, Mrs C touches her necklace.
'Expensive, but reduced calories and easy on the stomach.'

Chaplain sighs.

Ten seconds later, doom arrives.
The pouch contents, a grey lumpy sludge with the odour of wet cardboard,
is presented with all the pomp of Tuna à la Teuf.

Mrs C rubs my cheek as I edge forward.
'Nothing but the best. This will stop the sick.
Must be unsettling losing your home.'

I turn away in disgust. Tasty? How does a vet know that? Does she ever think in that
place? They'll sell you anything, vets. Rip-off bum-prodding violators they are,
the lot of them. I go to the stinky new cushion and sit facing the cooker.

This is diet nonsense again. She hasn't mentioned the word, but that's what it is. Fine.
I'll go raiding. Given or stolen, I don't mind. I wouldn't give that mulch to a dog.
I wonder if the Governor's got anything?

NINETEEN

An hour later, I'm on the new cushion, ravenous but determined not to show it.
Tail-tucked, steely "I don't give a dog's about you" indifference.
You got that Chap? Not one mouthful of that sludge will pass these fangs.

He's in the fridge arranging things.

Which brings an idea. A suck-up leg-snake never fails when Mrs C's out on business – his weakness facing feline charms alone is absolute. As I set off to manipulate, a ball of grinning ginger mist appears at the window.

Finally Citizen turns up. He signals to meet outside.

I rush to the Chaplain and weave through his legs.
'Miaow. Miaow.'

He shuts the fridge.
'Sorry, Teufel. No.'

'Miaow. Miaow.'

I scamper to the kitchen door.

'You're not going begging, either.' He leans over the bowls and points.
'Look! Food. Eat.'

You know, sometimes you want to slap humans. Just with something small, like a combine harvester or a bus. It's food, but not the food I want (hardly an unknown problem in cat-versus-human land). But – because I must – I go over and force every bit of this tepid wet-cardboard-smelling artificial whale poo, or whatever it is, down my gob and return to the door, wanting to retch but knowing it won't help me this time.

'Miaow. Miaow. Miaow.'

'Well done, Boy.'

Outside, a sun-kissed Tower is ablaze with tourists. I pad to the bottom step, puke, then look for Citizen.

He pokes out from behind a plant pot.
'You okay, mate? Hear Court got rough.'

'Of course I am,' I say, flushing my fur out.
'Rod-twiddling stargazing morons, the lot of them. I got what I wanted. Respect. You are now facing ***Sir Teufel the Magnificent***.'

He steps from behind the planters and gives me a once over.
'Sir Teufel, eh? So, you said the oath?'

'Nah, paws crossed. Don't count for diddly squat.
I'm a Sir with none of the obligations, thank you very much!'

'Our source said you almost fluffed it.'

I glance towards the Governor's house.
'They're lying. I did not.'

Who's his source?
He gets close.
'Not everything is as it seems at Court. Private plans linger and swirl.
The Bishop and Walter. They both want to be the Queen's only advisor.
You're a complication for both of them, which is good. But you've got troubles galore.
Troubles that don't go away with a pretty tap on the shoulder with a long knife, trust me.
You need to up your game, Big Boy.'

'What you on about?'

'You glanced right when you lied, touched your face. Lots of tells.
Body language can betray you in seconds here. The Tower is a trial and a test.
It's not playtime, not kitten school. Control yourself. You are being watched.
Always watched. Flicky eyes, blinks. It's all amateur. Amateur doesn't survive here.
That's what he said.'

I burp.
'Who?'

He turns away. 'Yew, what you been eating?'

'Poo-food. Who's this source? You got a spy?'

'Never mind. And burp in my face again, I'll kill you.
Don't you have manners in Devon?'

Why does everyone know my business? Where I'm from, and everything.

'Check yourself, fella. You're not exactly feline perfection.
You look well scraggy.'

He scratches at a black patch on his chest.
'Can't get it off. Stuck in my mist, bonded or something.
Anyway, we're off to the Turret of Justice. Time to meet my disciples.'

'You've got disciples?'

He grins, whiskers high.
'Worshipped like a messiah. Men so devoted, they lick my paws.'

'Get out of it. You mean staff? Nothing special about staff. Every cat's got humans.
Some's got too many – free ones they'd happily give away.'

He shakes his gingery head.
'Not like these. And not like the way I got them. Like the song goes,
I got the power.'

'Power?'

'Messages,' he says, peering up to the patchy bubble-pop sky,
'from up there. This mission is big. A voice in my head woke me up from a centuries-long slumber I didn't even know I was in. *Awake, Citizen, awake.* It said this collar would float onto my neck and reveal things I could never even dream.
Happened right there and then. Never had a collar. Amazing things.
Told me I would get revenge for my injustices.'

'What injustices?'

'So many you wouldn't believe. Anyway, it said men would come and
help. Serve me.'

'They're your posse?'

'They heard the voice, too. But only once. I had whole conversations.'

'From that collar?'
He's doggin' bonkers.

He glances at his chest. The bell hangs silent and still.
'Destiny gives what it gives. The voice told them to come to the Turret
of Justice. A leader would be waiting. To lead them to salvation through revenge.
And that was where I was told to wait.'

I sit back on the flagstone.
'So, you love a collar and it chats to you?'
Proper loonville.

'It knows everything, and check this out.'
He shakes his neck.
The collar bell tinkles.

'So?'

He shakes again.
The collar bell is silent.

'Woah... You did that?'

He nods.
'It's at my service and whim. As are the team. So careful as cat be.
The mission is big.'

'Where's this Turret of Justice then?'

He glances to White Tower.
'Up there. My leg's giving me grief, so I'll mist it. Meet me at the hole.'

'Where do you go? Between misting here and appearing there?'

His lips purse.
'Oh, no. No way. Universe's number two rule.
The living can't know what's beyond, not until you're there.'

'Come on... cat to cat?'

'No.' He mists away.

The Turret of Justice. Great name. And I'll be having some of that. All these cats and people telling me what to do and think. After a quick route scan, I decide to leg it. Details are overrated.

Around the back of White Tower, I slip under the huge staircase,
whiz past the struts and see Citizen waiting by the hole.

'Right,' he says. 'In we go.'

'In there?' I gasp.
A vision blasts my brain.
Giant leathery head.

Giant leathery head.
Cauldron.

A booming, swirling, echoing
scream of blackness and screams,
blackness and screams.

I try to shake it away.

Citizen appears puzzled.
'You okay?'

'Do we have to go in that way?'

'Yes.'

'Can we run? Fast?'

His whiskers twitch.
'Ah... Little Ease. Don't worry. We're not going in there. We'll shoot right by. Don't let fear in. Face it. Tell it to do one – dog off. Learn to live. You'll change your life forever. Ready?

One,
two,
three,
go!'

He
dips
into the tunnel,
misty tail fading into the black.

I look up, grab a lungful of air and race in. Passing Little Ease, giant head images flash in my mind, but I do it, I get past.

We come to a halt down the passage.

'Well done, mate,' says Citizen. 'See, not that bad. Follow me.'

The tunnel is long. A silent series of twists. Musty on the nose, grime under paw. Dead torch holders hang from the walls. At the end we reach a rusty iron door.

'Give me a sec,' he says, misting through the iron.

I sit waiting.
How good it must be to mist through things. Doors are the biggest pain.
Humans should be stationed at every one, just to pay for inventing them.

A few seconds later Citizen's grinning head pops through the iron.

'Stand back.'

The door groans open. Citizen hovers mid-air. Behind him is a solid brick wall.

'What now?

'Observe.'

He drops to the floor, turns and stares at the bricks. Two at the bottom begin to shuffle out, then a third. A halo of light opens around them.

'This is how they brought you to Little Ease.'

The bricks slide away and light fills the tunnel followed by an acidy tang.
Citizen points the direction with a paw, and bows.

'This way, Sir Magnificent.'

We come out into a small room. All white. Filled with mops and buckets. Shelves of bottles and tubs. A bench in the centre. He pops his head back through the hole, stares the door shut and pulls the bricks back into place.
Dogs, I wish I could do this stuff.

'The guards next,' says Citizen.

'One-Eye?' I ask.

'No. Not those idiots. Real ones in long-tailed suits. Stop the tourists clambering on horses or stealing muskets.'

'Horses and guns?'

'You'll see. Keep out of sight. If they catch you, you'll be out.'
He nods to steps opposite. 'We're going up there.'

They lead to a vast hall with tall arched windows and columns supporting a timbered ceiling. Tourists gaze at suits of armour. Some are on model horses, others in glass boxes; there's even a metal child. We tuck in by a column that smells of morning gravestones.

'Right,' says Citizen. 'Along that wall to the next hall. Stop at the display case on the left. Move low and fast when I say go. I'll meet you there.'

I set my shoulders, tail tucked. The cruise-missile cat ready to launch again.
A group of tourists move.

'Go!'

I bolt the hall and skid into the next room. The hall is as huge as the last. Packed with swirling displays of swords, axes, pistols and guns. Some arranged in magical dragon and demon patterns. It's the strangest thing I've ever seen.
Citizen appears at my side.

He signals to a spiral staircase in the far wall. I automatically get the plan. I wait for a break in the crowds and scoot. Up on the fourth step, out of view, in a few seconds he's by my side.

'Now,' he says, scratching his front. 'Upstairs you need to be modest. Best behaviour. Polite. Don't underestimate my team. I know how they are with me. I don't know how they'll be with you. You're just a cat. These are very powerful ghosts. Histories like you wouldn't believe.'
He hovers up a step.

'Can't I just swing in there? I'm a Sir now.'

'No.'

'And, what do you mean, modest?'

He turns.
'You know humans can be stupid?'

'Obviously.'

'As ghosts, they get annoyed quick, cat-like quick. A bit dysfunctional. And they don't all like felines. We weren't popular every century, it seems. Don't know why. You ending up in Little Ease proves the point. But don't worry, we'll get revenge on that.'

'Yeah, I still don't know what happened there.'

'You spoke truths. Silence and lies are simpler sometimes. Just be careful upstairs. Don't speak a truth because it's true. Understand? They are humans. Treat them like children.'

'What, swipe them?'

'No... Be forgiving... patient.'

I nod, though I'm not sure why I forgive anyone, never mind kids.
Citizen glides ahead. The spiral staircase is old and cold. A gloom-fest of darkness. We pass another floor and come to a black iron gate topped with spikes.

In the centre a small sign says: private

Citizen mists through the bars.
'Come on.'

Private is always an invitation. I leap up and haul myself over the spikes.
'Who am I meeting?' I say, catching up.

He stops and studies my demeanour.
'Well. There's Richard III. Very misunderstood in history our Richard Lots of lies told. A great king. Legend really. He's a new ghost like me.'

'New?'

'Just woken up. I was stuck in a wall trapped between two layers of bricks. Richard was under a car park in Leicester. Seems none of the local ghosts were interested in helping him wake, like no one helped me here. The collar woke me up. The message woke him and said come here.'

'You didn't know you were ghosts?'

'No. Richard's having a period of adjustment about being subordinate to a cat. But that's what the voice told him, so he must. He's tricky, but no human's trickier than a feline. I'm not worried about him or the other one.'

'Too right on tricks,' I say.

He's okay, this ginge. Proper. Real cat. I like him. That Richard. His name is familiar.

Citizen carries on up the steps.
'The other fella,' he says, 'he's just straight up helpful, always helpful. But you might need a leap of faith, at first.' He chuckles to himself. 'It took me a while.'

'In what way?'

'It's Guy Fawkes.'

My fur almost explodes.
'The Bonfire Night man? What kind of mad idiot are you? He's been hated for centuries. He's the only thing we agree with birds and dogs on. No way.'

I head back down the steps.

Citizen hovers after me.
'How do you think I blew up Little Ease? Staring at it? He's useful. An idiot but useful. There's a charm. You'll like him. He knows stuff. They're both useful.'

'Don't care,' I say, quickening my paws.

'Fireworks aren't his fault. You can't blame him for what people do centuries later. Once you get over his past, he's a dude. Bit weird, but a dude. He got tortured a lot. You know, sacrifice for the cause?'

I stop, turn and examine Citizen. He's sincere. Whiskers flat, ears up, tail steady.
'You, mate, are crackers!'

'Teufel . . . Sir. You don't know what you're leaving. Come and meet them. If they're not for you, you can go. Promise. It's gonna be love. Eventually.'

My whiskers settle. My tail stills. Heart eases. This place...
Somehow Citizen decides that's acceptance.

'Come,' he says. 'Trust me.'

The steps go on forever. Up and up.
We reach a landing.

'Here we are,' he whispers. 'The Turret of Justice.'

'Why are we whispering?'

'I want to see something.'

He peers into a square room, windows on every side. A tall, male ghost gazes out of a south window. Dressed in green with a purple-velvet hat, shiny black hair bobs to his shoulders, a leg playfully cocked back. Sat against the opposite wall in a dirty brown coat, knees to chest, is another ghost, face hidden under a wide-brimmed droopy grey hat. Before him, twisting and turning in the air is a metal scaffold clamp. A nut travels along the central bolt. Another set lies discarded on the floor by a table.

'It's so different,' says the man at the window, tapping his fingers against the stone frame.
'That building there. That's new. So much I don't recognise.'
He sniffs the windowpane.
'The energy's here though. Like a sweet spring rose.
Power. Death. Glory.
The things I did. And to live it again. To do again.
It's the bomb.
You do bombs, don't you?'
The man turns.

His face is almost angelic – a smooth powder-white with hard blue eyes fixed in a permanent stare. The eyes catch me behind Citizen.
It's like thunder rumbling in my soul. You're waiting for lightning. I turn away.

Citizen limps forward bringing me into full view.

'Practising hard, I see, Richard.'

TWENTY

Shaking off King Richard's stare, I follow Citizen into the Turret of Justice.
Richard glides from the window.

His scent is how I imagine war:
dark,
pungent,
burning,
and blood.

A smile opens across his face and the stench fades. He tucks his hair behind his ears.
'You've been a while,' he says to Citizen.
His eyes flick to me. 'So he's the one is he?'

Citizen's tail swirls.
'He is, Richard. This is Thunderpaws.'

Richard's face flickers. 'You call me Your Grace.
How many times do I have to tell you?'

Citizen hovers up and gets in his face.
'And how many times have I told you I'm a Scottish Londoner,
French-named cat, with direct messages from God you don't get, so good luck with that!'

Richard shakes his head and takes a step back.
Citizen floats to the table. He nods for me to join him. I jump up and twitch my gaze
between Richard and Fawkes. Richard gives me a wide-open smile.
'Mr Thunderpaws. Good name. Welcome.
Hope you're better mannered than this oaf. Pleased to make your acquaintance.'

His huge right arm comes forward. He tickles my chin, his mist cold.
I remember Citizen's advice and don't flinch, but will anyone ever keep to my proper
name? I try to get the polite bit right though.
'Hello, Your Grace. I do prefer Teufel, though, if you don't mind?'

His hand cups my head. There's a hint of pressure.
'Now, now, Cat. What nonsense. Thunderpaws is as fine as fine can be. And actually, no need for formalities. I was having Citizen on. We're a team of equals. And we're having absolutely delightful fun following this young fella, aren't we, Guy, even if he can't take a joke?

'That we are, Dickers,' says the man from under the hat. The scaffold clamp keeps turning before him.

Richard's eyes are locked on mine. He slaps his thighs.

'Yes. Yes. Perfect. So, I hear those Tudor dogs treated you dreadfully? Put you in that old pee-pot Little Ease. I used to love dumping people in there for a month or two. Tell me, is it still a dark hell? Has it got that gloop from the old toilets?'

I nod.
'Who are the Tudors?'

'Court, lad.' He leans against the window frame. 'That despicable lot of thin-blooded, double-crossing dung-munchers. The ones who jailed you. With us, you shall be a king.'

'A king?' My eyes flash to Citizen. He nods matter of factly.

Richard spins across the room, arms outstretched.
'Well, if not quite a king – 'cos that's my job – like one. Famous for eternity!' He comes to a stop in front of the table and squats before me.
'Tell me, Thunderpaws, does that sound fun? Do you want to be my best friend, my confidante, my personal cat? Smash up those stupid souls and create a bit of freedom and respect around here?'

'Erm, maybe.'

That thunderstorm stare flashes in his eyes then fades.
'What's the hesitancy? What did that fake lot of pompous pops say to you?'

'That I've got to help the King.'

He scrunches his lips.
'Well in that, they are right. But not that king. Not Henry. This one. Me. And certainly not as a sacrifice.'

'Sacrifice?'

My fake calm crumbles, legs flopping to the table.

Citizen twitches a relaxed confirmation.

Richard motions with his arms. 'Up now, lad. Pick yourself up.
This is good news – come on, stand.'

I haul myself up – when can sacrifice ever be a good word?

'I want to paint a picture,' he says. 'For this great cat Citizen's plan
will banish that disgraceful Court and those horrible ravens and make you a hero.'

'Me?'

'You.'
He gives a black-toothed smile.
'We want you to help us kill the ravens.'

Citizen licks his flank.

I return to Richard.
'Love to, truly. But aren't they dangerous?'

Head lopped to one side, his lips purse.
'Yes and no. They are dangerous for ghosts, not so much for you.
You're alive, you see. And you're a church cat. A fatal combination.'

'Fatal?'

He lifts his hand.
'Faithful. Apologies, mis-spoke.
I'm still getting used to words again. Six-hundred years on your own isn't easy.
For us ghosts, trapped between life and death, ravens are indeed dangerous.
We can't touch them.
Soul eaters.
Evil.
But you. A church cat has special powers over them.
That's why they are so worried by your presence. It's in case you find your power.
We have a plan that will trick the ravens – the tricksters of tricksters getting tricked,
just delightful and so deserving. Once I get my bag of secrets and let out some magic.
Some fang-and-claw magic of your own, and the world is yours.'

He comes closer.
'Can you do it?' Fiery twinkles of delight dance across his face.
'With a name like Thunderpaws, surely you've killed hundreds. Thousands!
A kindred spirit. Tell me. Can you? Do you want eternal fame?'

'Mum said I'd be like Dad one day. He's famous.'

Richard's face beams.
'Is he now?'

'Yep. A warrior.'

'I'd like him.'

He gives me another good tickle and jumps up.
'Excellent. I like good blood. Blood is everything.'

'And I have Royal feline lines. I am Mau and Siamese.'

'Fabulous.'

'And what do I get again, for helping Your Grace?'

He laughs.
'Fame, boy. What does everyone want but fame. All those dreams.
The food. The attention. Destiny.
Dare I say, the ladies...'

'But why will I be famous?'

His face stiffens; he checks the windows.
'Therein is a story. The ravens have a horrible grip
over this country, despite all their lies and crimes.
Did you know we were the most powerful nation in the world for a thousand years?
Our island of little grey people and drab food? And the ravens ruined it all.
And still, even after they mucked everything up, still they hold this nation,
still they claim we need them. Guy told me all about the lies.
Font of knowledge this man. I'm learning more every day.
So many new facts. So many new words. To be almost alive again is magic.'

He gestures at the man in the hat.

'A king called King Charles II decreed the ravens must stay. But I,
being from the best century ever, know what actually happened,
because the actual truth of the ravens is in my bag of secrets.'

'Bag of secrets?'

'It's where a king keeps his personal business. A leather pouch.
I'm looking for it at this moment, just for sentimental reasons, you understand.
I remember everything in it. Kings don't mess about.
Guy and I have dug around about these birds.
In something called the Second World War every one of them here died.

That alone proves their presence protecting this island is a lie.
Couldn't handle a little bang and pop. Dropped like peasants. Which is rather a secret.

The governor of the time installed new ravens all hush-hush.
I tell you, they are the reason this country lost everything. Our empire and powers.
Back to being a lonely grey rock in a cold grey sea, if with much better food.
I had curry in Leicester and whoosh, what a thing!'

He smiles, waving a hand over his mouth.

'The ravens should go forever. No more problems. We get our destiny back.
No more parading the lawns like they own the place.
They are darkness and death. We remove them and God shall return us to glory.
We rise again.
A world power.
The world power.
A Yorkist powerhouse! With curry and kebabs!
And you, Sir – you, Sir Thunderpaws of the Tower – will be famous beyond dreams.
Tell me young tom, are you in?'

I jump up and shuffle my whiskers.
'Does a dog lick its bits! Of course I'm in.'

'Excellent. The full secrets about the ravens are in my bag.
Might you have seen it somewhere?'

'Raleigh had a bag. On the table.'

'Did he now? That might be it. Brown leather with a leather tie?'

'That's the one.'

'Excellent. I want to start ticking a few things off my revenge list,
and I'm pretty sure it's in there.'

'You've got a list too?' I say.

He smiles super-wide.
'Of course. An absolute necessity as leader. And top of mine is anyone called Tudor, or
related to them. How does Citizen put it? I want to dog them up.
Smile in their faces going,
Dickie's back! And you've been Dickied.
All those grand old sayings from my slaying days.
Get this island back on its feet.
What do you say, Guy, one last big try?''

'Aye,' says the man beneath the hat, examining a long match.

'Up for it, Teufel?' says Citizen, pausing his clean.

I beam at him. 'Oh, you bet.'
I'll ignore the fact I haven't ever killed a single bird. But really, how hard can it be?
And, I have an idea on that.

Richard chuckles.
'Citizen, old boy. I like him, I like him.
Well done.'

A dull thunk. Metal hits stone.
The clamp hovering before Fawkes has dropped to the floor.
His hat lifts
revealing
a scarred face,
clouded eyes
and a
mangy
straggle beard.
He's not a pretty sight, yet somehow there's a bliss to him,
a calmness.
'How's it whiskering, Sparky?'

'Don't call me that,' says Citizen. 'This stuff still isn't coming off.'

'It was amazing though, wasn't it?' says Richard.

Citizen looks back.
'I told you before. Yes, flashy and bang-bang. Smelly. Loud.'

'It's not fair I couldn't be there.'

'I told you, we couldn't risk freaking this cat out.
His world is changing very fast.'

'I heard a tourist the other day describe soldiers as being in the industry of violence.
What a term. Beautiful. If I'd had bombs and good powder...'

Fawkes laughs.
'Good powder's sunshine and song, and the new mixes, eeh, what a kick.
I did warn you, Citizen.'

'You could have warned me twice, to make sure I listened.'

Fawkes tips his hat.
He reaches down, strikes the match against a box
and brings it to his face.
The flame dances against his cloud-eyes.
'Everyone knows be careful with matches.'

'Hello. I'm a cat.'

Fawkes blows the flame into a black swirl of smoke.
'Gets the voice of God. Knows all things. Can't handle matches.'
He lifts himself.
'You've got a war wound. Marks of the trade, my furry friend.'

Citizen humphs.

'Where did you find gunpowder?' I ask.

Fawkes sniffs at the smoke while itching his beard.
'The guards with the big black hats. Cellars here hold all sorts.'

Richard tips his velvet hat.
'We were told to come to this very room and assist
whoever was here. Found a ghost cat, would you believe.
How did you find yourself here, Mr Paws?'

'Well, Your Grace and Mr Guy Doggin' Fawkes...'

Richard laughs.

'I don't have much idea,' I say. 'One minute life was normal – well, as normal as normal can be when you're suddenly a locked-in house cat. My mum died, you see, hit by a car. And Mrs C worried it might happen to me. Wanted me safe. Kept me in for months.'

Richard frowns, all sad eyes.
'That's terrible. And your freedom lost, too. How tragic.
Loved ones are such a pull on the soul.'

'Thank you. Anyway, for a few weeks the house energies had changed,
and then strange men in overalls arrive. Placed everything in boxes. Turn up again
and take them all away. Chaplain shoves a tablet down my throat. Recognised the taste
straight away. One of those space-out sleeping pills from his writing desk
and then shoved me in the vet box.'

'There are tablets to sleep?' says Richard.

'Put you under for operations and things. Cats and sleep is no problem but when there are vets about with their knives and twisted dreams, things get feisty.'

Richard comes down to my level.
'The wonders of these modern times. Keeps them in his desk, you say?'

'Yep. A whole bottle. His cousin's a vet. Derek the Savage I call him.
And you won'teven believe where he lives: place called Catsgore. Says it all.
Vets poke, prod – no respect. Anyway, I'm caged in the car, fighting the tablet – yowling, banshee style – and I'm gonna beat it, then next minute I wake up here.'

Richard gets closer.
'And what unfortunate luck since you arrived.'
He strokes my head.
'Getting sucked into those Tudor plans. Black cats do have a time of it.
That Bishop has some very primitive old ideas. I thought my century needed progress, but where he's from...' He frowns and turns away. 'I mean, you, lovely you – as a sacrifice...'

'What do you mean?'

'Oh, their plans on Bonfire Night
are quite different from the explanation you received.
From what we've deduced, I expect fires and explosions.
You're very lucky we found out.'

'What?'

'A Tudor court should never be trusted. And the Bishop.
The things he used to do in your chaplain's cellar.
Quite the innovator. All manner of pain and torture.
Yes, you don't want to get boshed by Bishop Edmund Bosh'em Bonner.
We'll get you out of it somehow,
in return for a little favour and fame
beyond your wildest dreams.
It's a steal of a deal.'

'Oh, it is!'

He sighs and nudges his hair back.
'I'm glad you agree. Worry not.
You've got Dickie on your side now.
Life will be much better. There are some important rules, though.
You must tell no one about us. That is imperative.
Understand?'

'Okay.'

'Whatever you do, don't think about our plan near the ravens.
If they are close, they can, and will listen to your thoughts.
They are dangerous beyond measure.
Have been for millennia, since the birth of myth and time.
Intelligent and manipulative.
Remember, they've fooled this nation for centuries.'

'Citizen warned me. How close is safe?'

'Ten paces, I'd say.'

Richard smiles an easy, relaxed smile.
Down to earth, friendly.

Whatever I'm into here, friends are a help – especially if you've been set up.
'So what do I have to do? When's this plan?'

Richard steps back to the window and gazes out.
'Ah, that's the thing. We'll use the cover of Court's wicked evilness to do our own.
They'll be so busy on their sorry little business, they won't notice ours.
We strike at ten pm on Bonfire Night, two hours before them – to save you first.
Frankly, it's genius. My genius.'

'Excellent,' I say, getting to my paws. 'One thing will make it even better.'

He turns.
'What?'

'Citizen's collar.'

Citizen remains still, blank-faced.

Richard checks his fingernails.
'We all want that collar, Thunderpaws.
He wouldn't give it to me.
It's not that easy.'

'It speaks Cat, Dickie,' says Citizen. 'Not your language.
You wouldn't understand a word.'

'I speak Cat.'

I glance at Cit. He doesn't ooze happy, but I don't give a monkey's.
Cats aren't about others' happiness.

'Why do you want it?' says Richard.

'That bell is stealthy. Kill the ravens with extra speed. And gore. I'm thinking ninja.'

'Ninja?'

'Fighters. Move like ghosts. Black like me. Swish. Dead. You'd love them.'

Richard eases back.
'Now, don't get me wrong, I like the idea, but as I said, it's Citizen's and as you've seen he's rather attached to that collar. Besides, you're Thunderpaws – you shouldn't need trinkets. Not with our plan. We can discuss it later. For now, you'd better return home, so the Chaplain isn't wet with worry again. I hear he was a total loss when you were in Little Ease. You can find your way back down?'

'Sure.'
I smile at Richard, Fawkes and Citizen.

Still want that collar.

'Your Grace, gents, delighted to help. For this moment, I bid you farewell.'

I puff my fur, a dance tickling in my paws.
Famous like Dad. I knew all it needed was opportunity. I pad for the door.

'Oh, one thing,' calls Richard.

I check back.
'Yep?'

His eyes are black. Suddenly I'm mid-air.
My sides crush. Intense pain stabs my ribs.

He strides towards me, stench blasting my nostrils, so close his lip-cracks are rivers.
His mouth comes to my ear, the words s l o w a n d l o n g.
'Your Chaplain and his adorable wife will be killed at the stroke of midnight,
any night, for the smallest error.
You tell someone. They're dead.
Late for a meeting.
Dead.
Lie to me.
Dead.
You, too. Got that?'

I nod my head.

'Make no mistake, Cat. Working for a king can be deadly work.'

I'm dropped to the floor.

He smiles, his eyes blue again.
'Now off you go. Toodle pip. Fawkes, tell me again about World War I.
Gas, you say?'

I run for the door.

Citizen chases me down the spiral staircase.

'Te
u
f
e
l!

H
a
n
g

o
n!'

'Wait!' cries Citizen.

I pull up by an alcove on the spiralling staircase.

He flies the corner and tumbles to a stop.

Tail high, I glare at him.
'Nice, you said. What was that?'

'That is Richard. Violence and deference were the only rules in the fifteenth century.'

'We're a team, he said.'

'I did warn you.'

'When was I impolite, then? When did I say the wrong truth?'

'They do what they want. You saw it with Anne. Arrogant. Deference is a drug. We are a team. Richard was joking and see how nice Guy was?'

'Whatever.'

He hovers close.
'York gave you a tiny rib-crush. You're supposed to be Thunderpaws. You've done that to a hundred birds!'

'That's not the point.'

He bundles me into the alcove.
Suddenly, I'm head down a hole. A long way down I see grass.
Fresh air drifts up my nostrils.

'This is a long drop toilet, Teufel. Old school. The clue's in the name. It's a loooong way. Want to find out? I'm not sure landing on your paws will *help. Cat up.*'

I'm tossed back into the stairwell.

'Fine,' I gasp.

'Stop doggin' about and don't make me run.'

'Okay.'

Citizen floats to me, his ragged ears low and soft.
'Look, sorry...'
He nudges my head.

It feels weird – spongy. Like mouse brain when you've crunched the skull too hard.

'This isn't easy, Teufel. You need to get with the game.'

He hovers back a few feet,
floats mid-air and starts to slowly spin, staring at me.

'Remember the goal.
Remember the goal.
The birds dead
and you
the most famous cat
in history.
You want the fame.
You play the game.
Remember the goal.'

'Yeah.' I look down the spiralling stairs.
Remember the goal.

'Good,' he says. He stops the spin, comes down and pats my shoulder. 'No more messing about. How about food? When did you last eat? A full belly will improve things no end, settle the nerves. More prawns?'

'No.'

'Chicken?'

'Chicken. And cheese.
Salty, I like that Cheshire stuff.'

'No problem. The New Armouries cafe beneath the old hospital block will do us nicely. We'll leave by the main exit, doesn't matter if the guards see you now.'

Despite the guards' sheep-herding impressions we make it out. From the parade square we head down past the hospital for the New Armouries cafe. Citizen leads me up some steps to a side door, and a few minutes later hovers out a chunk of white Cheshire cheese and a piece of red tandoori-chicken breast, whiffing like a chilli factory.
He dumps them on the step.

'What am I supposed to do with all that?' I ask. 'They're huge.
And that's gonna be hot!'

'Chicken. Redded up, but it's definitely chicken. And cheese. What am I supposed to do, bring a knife and condiments, for Sir Teufel the Doggin' Choosy? Thought you'd be grateful?'

'I am. Thanks.'

'Now,' he says. 'Back to the plan. We need best behaviour, with Court, the Governor, the ravens, everyone.'

'Yeah,' I say, sniffing the cheese but deciding on chicken.
Like Chap, I've got a taste for fire.

'We need information. Court's plan for Halloween specifically. Magnificat will know. I want you to find out.'

'Shouldn't be too hard.'
I secure the spicy, red breast with a claw, fang it and yank with a full head-tug.

'Remember, you're their sacrifice. She will misdirect you. Lie. You know how to see lies?'

I nod, chewing. It's alright this. Charred skin is yum...

'You can listen for them, too. Chat first. Observe her normal responses. Then get on with your real questions, monitor any changes from her earlier behaviours. Get it?'

I nod again.

'Do her pupils change when she smiles? Paw to her face? That can be lying. Glancing right, too.'

Talk about details. I take a break from chewing.
'You sure about all this? What if it's just being cat?'

'Another thing. Sucker up to the ravens.'

I spit out the chicken.
'What?'

His whiskers curl in confirmation.

This might be a chance.
'Give me the collar. I'll think about it.'

'Shut up about my collar. You'll find Magnificat on a roof by Byward Tower, the Tower's main entrance. It's her special place.'

'And?'

'Off you go. She was there earlier.' He reviews the sky. 'Weather's holding, she won't have moved. And take some of that.'
He motions to the food.

'Do I have to?'

'Richard will be happy, and you love the Chap and Mrs C. It's a test.'

My tail taps the wall of the step.
'What's that supposed to mean?'

'Don't play stupid – you know what it means.
You prefer your Chaplain alive. And Mrs C.
The planning meeting is at six. Bring good news.
Tower of Justice. Six o'clock. Don't be late.
Toodle pip.
Oh, and our spy will be watching. See ya!'

'Wait!' I shout.

He stops, half misted.
'What?'

'What's your view on mice?'

'Sly little critters. Mad. All kinds of stories. Why?'

'Nothing much, but views on mice are an insight to character.'

He dips his ripped-up ears.
'You're weird. See you at six.'

Through the gates onto Water Lane, the Tower's entrance is far in the distance. Citizen said Magnificat's on a roof somewhere, so I get on the outer wall's battlements and head down.

A dip and weave past tourists admiring the Thames, a few jumps and leaps, and I face a wall. Muted music drifts over the top. I work a way up and drop down.

Magnificat doesn't notice. She's on her back, splayed over a blue cushion, head swinging between the cups of Lady Jane's headphones.

My blue cushion!
There's movement on a high roof.

A flash of white.

The polar bear is peering beady black eyes at me, snarling cat-ripping fangs.

So you're the spy are you? Okay whitey. Let's play things black.

Positioned in line with Magnificat, fur shuffled and whiskers tidied, I'm ready.
'Magnificat. Oh, Magnificat.'

No response.

'MAGNIFICAT!'

She's up like a rat, startled eyes.
'What are you doing here?'

I glance to the cushion.
'What's that doing here?'

Her claws test the fabric.
'Being comfy. Why?'

'Why is it here?'

'Liked it.'

My own claws cut at stone.
'That's my house. My things.'

She steps off the cushion and into my face.
'Your house? You've been here four minutes. I do what I want.
Take what I want. This is my Tower.'
Her head turns to an alcove stuffed with toys, trinkets, an upturned cage.
'We liberate things.
Jane, Anne, the Bishop, Sir Walter.
A hobby to pass the centuries.
The small and the...'

She gestures over my shoulder. Across the river is a long warship. All camouflage greys, funnels and big guns.

'Shut up...'

'Why not? They've teased Sir Walter since 1971 with that. You don't tease an Aries. We can't nick a World War II cruiser, obviously. But you know, move it a bit. We love boats. Freak a few officials. Get someone sacked. Anyway, why are you here? And how did you find me? This is my private spot, my refuge.'

'Oh, I've been searching e v e r y where...' I raise a paw to my face. 'This is, like, the nine millionth place. I'm worried about this Groom of the Stool thing. How will I know what to do?'

'Care of royal poo and pee is a true honour.'

My fur shivers. No way will I catch poo.
I'd be like those weirdos in parks following dogs. And human poo is evil.
And what do I do with pee?

Magnificat's tail flicks.
'Yep, up close and stinky with the monarch.
You keep their toilet and their secrets.
It used to be a stool over a bucket. You'll be the first in a hundred years.
You should be proud.'

'The queen's gonna wipe her wotsits with my fur?'

'You're not toilet paper, no.
The title is honorary now, it's being close to the queen.'

'Phew. Secrets? Are they in a bag, at all?'

'What are you on about, Teufel?'

'You know, a bag with secrets.'

'You ask too many questions.'

My claws relax, but I can't. I need Fawkes and Richard's information.

'So what's happening tomorrow, Halloween?'

Her eyes narrow, searching mine for meaning.
'Why?'

'Well, if I'm to help the Queen – '

She shakes her head,
tail and everything else. 'Sorry. Black cat on Halloween?
Witches? No chance.
Have you looked at yourself?'

What's she insulting now?
'I'm spotless,' I say.

'A large black cat with white on its chest.
You might be a Sith; soul stealers
from the time of Arthur. Siths are tricksters...'

What's she on?
'Why do you believe all this myth nonsense?'

'You're asking a ghost?'

'So, I can't come?'

She turns to the Thames.
'No. Maybe December...'

December – ? My fur shudders.

'...When you've proved yourself.
I have a part in mind for the Christmas play: Arthur.'

'The legend?'

'Yes. *The Life and Death of King John*. You're his nephew. Anne loves a play.'

'Can I have my cushion back?'

'No.'

I don't know what to say.

She sits in the silence in total comfort.

I've got to think of something, Richard and Fawkes are gonna...
'Do you get trick-or-treaters?'

'What?'

'You know, kids?'

'You think a knock down there on the gate works when we hold the Crown Jewels?
Halloween may be a four-hundred-year-old tradition, but no one gets in here after
hours, whatever the night. Why?'

'Curious.'

Fear scratches. Fawkes and Richard will
– No.
I can't think about that.
I have to get this information.

'Well, I've got to go. Mrs C's not well. A last question.'

She flushes her tail. 'What?'

'I need to whisper.'

She rolls her eyes and shuffles closer. Even annoyed cats love secrets.
I need to make sure the bear can't hear, or lip read.

'Why are there lions and a bear here?'

'There was a zoo. It's at Regent's Park now.
Anne likes to watch the bear fight the chain as he swims.'

'And the lions?'

'Hundreds over the years. They threw them dogs as snacks.'

'Not all bad then?'

'Some dogs are okay. Our three lions represent the lions on the Royal coat of arms.
Although they should be leopards. Someone got confused way back.'

'Fascinating. Well, I better get home to Mrs C, but I'll see you soon.'

She stands back.
'Why did I have to whisper?'

'Practice, for keeping stool, innit.'

Her whiskers twitch irritation.
'Innit? So you're slanging it up like a Londoner now,
some Hackney rude-boy?'

'Halloween a bit of a party?'

'It's important, Teufel. There are ceremonies and discussions before prayer.
We are not about masks, fancy dress and woo-woo.'

I shrug my shoulders.
'Don't know, do I?'

But I do now. Well – enough to blag it anyway. And with that I leave.
No sign of the bear, but Halloween information secured for Richard and Fawkes,
the Chap and Mrs C are safe.

Now Act Two: the ravens.

*

A fact of life is that birds are always where you don't want them.
Crows together are called a murder. Which is what I'd love to do now (even though
I can't) to the two largest ravens, who are high on the battlements above the garden,
ruining my privacy. Ravens together are called an unkindness.
Sometimes words are perfect.

I push one out, though. Grey and stinky. Usually I love my poo, but this one is so gross
I can't even bury it – that diet rubbish has to go. Cleansed and prepped for what's next
– be nice, Teufel, nice, nice, nice – I head up to the inner Tower. Do I find ravens, or let
them find me? I decide to double up. If good is the goal, be better.

Part One. I sit on the chapel lawn and close my eyes.

Sure enough, a screeching caw. The thump of air.
A raven lands. I open my eyes. Baldrick.

As ever, Mr Young Stupid and Inquisitive, ten feet away, eyes flicking.
Never learns.
Here we go.
I flip on my back, splay my legs and force out a purr. Yo, Dull Boy. A new friend. Come.

He cocks his head, sniffs and hops forward.
At three feet, he stops, sniffs again then flies to a railing.

I roll and purr, roll and purr.

He comes back.

This time, nearer. It's a struggle not to claw him into the raven equivalent of chicken nuggets. But I don't. I think little fluffy clouds and sunshine, fluffy clouds and sunshine.

When he waddles off, I prepare for Part Two.

The Ravenmaster fills a water bowl. Munin and Thor are on the Roman wall above, eyes on my every step. Thor's feet scrape the stone. Idiot hasn't the brains to find a decent scratch-post.

Tail down, I ignore their stares and make a diagonal for the farthest cage.

The Ravenmaster steps to the lawn with a proper mood face – I'm surprised he's not fingering his gun again.

My tail plays in the steel as I approach. Cage by cage. Chin caressing the wire.
His expression is static.

I'm at his legs.
Rub, rub, rub.
'Miaow.'

He huffs away. I rub again. Again he moves.
With a flop, I repeat the Baldrick roll and expose my stomach.

He doesn't react beyond widening his eyes, and that'll do me.
Humans are rubbish at emotions – always a tell. He's on side.

I get up and stroll for the White Tower's stairs, job done.
It's busy, this knight-of-the-realm, future-world-star business.

Next, the planning meeting.

‘Oi! *Oi*!’

My eyes lift. Citizen is before me. We’re under the stairs.

I struggle up and yawn.
‘Oi? – I’m the Groom of the Stool, if you please.’

The night’s dark and so is he. He’s covered in black again. This time, flaky stuff.

‘Do you ever clean?’

‘Never mind me. You done?’

I stretch and ease out a yawn.

‘Yep. Suckered up Magnificat. That fat youngster, Baldrick – we’re best mates. Munin and Thor are so chilled we’ve got Scrabble booked, and the Ravenmaster gave me a stroke. All set.’

‘So, you’re ready?’

‘You bet.’

‘Then let’s go.’

After a few shakes, Citizen is ginger again and we enter the Turret of Justice – all dust and grime gone. Richard and Fawkes are juggling clamps in the middle of the room.

Take the lead, Teuf. Drive the conversation. Firm. Business-like.

Richard turns our way.
‘Croeso, Thunderpaws.’

'Excuse me?'

The clamps still mid-air. He smiles.

'Welsh, Boyo. Always keep learning. So, what's the intelligence on Halloween?'

I stride in.
'They meet for midnight prayers and pray until dawn. Magnificat refused to say at first, but I crafted it out. Dropped a casual "by-the-way" in at the end, pro-style, and boom. I watched; no lies.'

Richard beams. 'Excellent. He learns fast, Mr Fawkes.'

Citizen nods beside me.

I jump up to the table.
'So, what's the plan?'

Fawkes's clamp falls with a clatter.
He comes to the table, drops to his knees
and gets eye-to-eye. His face is rutted with scars,
those blue-clouded eyes unreadable.

He sighs.

'Ah, Bonfire Night, Teufel. The annual reminder of my failure to blow up the Royals and their corrupt, political friends, who dare call themselves politicians, will at last become the night I planned. Our one last, big try, as Dickster said.'

His face melds into a grin, blue-cloud eyes blasting with shooting stars.

'Rockets will fire their songs and flashing wonder, and our dear ravens will be distracted and therefore vulnerable to our little plan.'

Citizen jumps up to the table. He slides in front of me.
Richard crouches opposite Guy. I'm surrounded by grinning ghosts.

'Mr Paws,' Richard says. 'They will cower like doomed children.
Or – let's say in your world – mice.'

Citizen stabs his paw at the table.
'That's when we strike.'

Fawkes jumps to his feet, followed by Richard, who makes for a window and tiptoes to look down through the glass.

View checked, he leans against the wall, hands behind his back.
'Every mind has two weaknesses, Teufel: temptation and greed. Your Tower raven is no
different, except these birds don't know theirs. But I do.
Deep in their soul, through thousands of generations, is the love of just slightly off meat
– on the touch of rotten. Death is part of their connection to the underworld.
The meat protects and nurtures them, bonds them even.
The Tower doesn't allow it because of the tourists, and that's what we'll exploit.'

My fur fizzes.
'We're going to feed them to death?'

Richard tucks his hair behind his ears
and glides over.

'In a way, yes. They will be crazy for it, for sure. That heady scent dancing
in their nostrils. We'll lay a trail of meat from their cages
to White Tower's staircase and there we'll crash a scaffold on them.'

'A scaffold?'

He points to the window.
'Outside, you'll see. Citizen's been on paintwork destruction duties.
The Governor's such a perfectionist, the stairs will be repainted before dawn,
and that means scaffold. And the best bit – as a present for you – we plan to do the same
thing every night until the fifth of November, until he's stark raving bonkers.
Our original plan was Bonfire Night only, but we like you, and we know you don't like
him, so we decided to start early. I love giving officials grief.'

'You've done that, for me?'

Richard nods.
'Yep. Citizen's idea.'

Citizen is licking his back.

'I'm touched,' I say.

He stops licking and meets my eye. 'No problem.'

'And we're giving you his collar,' says Richard.

Citizen stops. 'What?'

'Now, now, Sparky. Give it to him. For the mission.'
Richard gestures encouragement with his hands.

Citizen's fire-face softens. He rolls his eyes. Shakes his head.
'Okay. But he'd better not damage it, and it's only for the mission. I want it back straight after.'

Fawkes unties the collar and hovers it over to me. Swapping them in seconds, the fit is perfect. Citizen declines mine.

I give my body a full-on twist.
The bell tinkles.
'How do I silence it?'

Citizen pads towards me. 'Close your eyes and think silence.'

I close my eyes, think silence and shudder my fur again. Not a sound.
'Wow. Nice. Very nice.'

Citizen glares at me.
'Don't try asking it questions. You don't have the power.'

'It answers questions?'

'It can if you've got the password. At least, for me. But you're living. It will smash your brain to pudding soup. Mess with the frequencies. Or I will. I want it back right after, and don't tell anyone about it, either.'

'Of course,' I say, feeling more brainy already.
And when I'm more famous than a king..
'What's the plan for Bonfire Night?' I say.

Richard looks over to the clamps.
'We've practised with the scaffold brackets. We'll remove the core supports, loosen the rest and the whole thing will crash.
The ravens will be so wild for the meat, they won't see it coming.
As you say, **boom**!'

'And my job?'

'The scaffold might not hit every bird. So you follow in with the claw and fang thing – now the super silent version. It's the simplest of plans. And we have protection for you.'

'Protection?'

'Yes, you're going to have a bit of meat, so you take up the scent.
The ravens in their delirium will think it's one of their family coming to the rescue.
When actually it will be the dance of Teufel the Magnificent's claws and paws.
The fangs of fate frolicking their necks. Just delightful.'

'Excellent. Bolts on the raven cages, you thought about them?'

'Yep. Do them from a distance. Checked and tested.'

'And when the ravens are dead?'

'I'll take over from Anne. Stop this stupid – what do they call it – internet plan of hers.
I've only just woken up to ghosting, and I tell you, boy, I like it!
My second coming is not being bust by Tudors.
I'll restore some manners to this place and give it a proper tidy up.
She did the same when she came along – can't complain, it's what Royals do.
Then together, you and I shall see England rise.
Me and you, Mr Paws.
And the genius is that the scaffold fall is cover for what you get up to.
It will all be the workmen's fault.
You, my friend, will be – how do they say – off scot-free.
When we once again rule the world,
I will reveal to the globe your crucial contribution.
The press will be mad for you. I'll make sure of it.
For there are some poor trapped souls I want to save,
who are involved with the actual truth of these ravens.
And when the world knows – you shall be a star!
Famous beyond any cat ever known.
As long as you don't mess anything up.
But you love Mr and Mrs C, so I know you won't make any mistakes.'

Gulp.

'You want to keep them safe.
Be the catalyst of our great rising,
the phoenix leaving the ashes of mediocrity.'

'Catalyst... I like it.'

He clasps his hands.
'Now, to mark your induction,
we've arranged a celebration behind
Waterloo Barracks at midnight.
Will you see us there?'

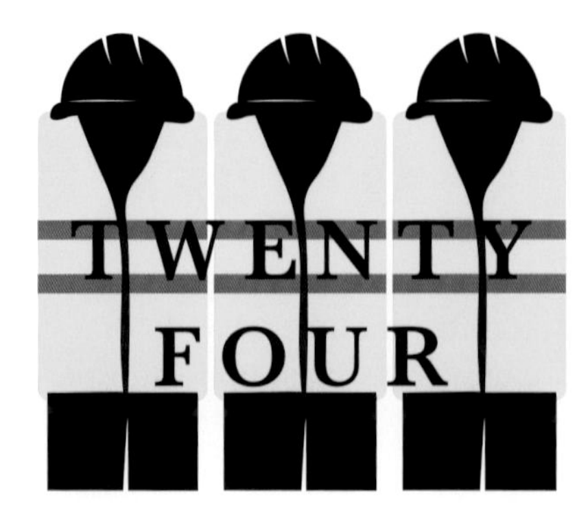

A celebration for me. That Richard does have a soft side.

I think the word *silence* and skip down through White Tower all smiles as the bell remains noiseless. This is gonna be so easy.

Out under the stairs, a whiplash wind races the Tower. Above, the staircase is clamped with scaffold. On the lawn, workmen in yellow jackets stand braced in a line, gazing at the structure.

The Governor is there, fighting his hair while arguing with a pear-shaped man in a long coat. The man shakes his head. A huddle-shouldered Chaplain appears to be the silent referee.

No one's happy. I'll slink for home.

The Ravenmaster prepares the night's roost while the birds wait on the grass.
Thor and Munin track my path.

Steady, Teuf. Steady.
Clean thoughts.

Baldrick flies overhead.

I meet the Ravenmaster's watchful eye to show my peaceful intent.
Off home, mate. That way. He returns to his rake.

A blunt force thumps my back. I bolt forward.

Baldrick bumbles past, his right wing splayed.
He hobbles to the cages, dragging his wing
Short repeated calls shrill from his bill.

He hops in circles. The other ravens rush over. That wing's out as if it's broken!

No, no, no. This is a fix! A stitch-up!

The Ravenmaster races to gather him.
Baldrick scurries away,
adding deep rasping calls to the
short shrills.

This is not good. What to do?
Out of here and fast. I lift a paw to go.

Fingers lunge at my collar. I'm dragged up.
'That's it!'

Windpipe crushing. I know that rage.
The Governor.

He grabs my scruff and I hang in the darkness until I'm turned to face his frenzy.

'You are gone!'

Save me, Chap! The baboon is at me!
Held forward, I'm stomped towards the Chaplain.

'Attacked Baldrick. You saw it!'

Thor and Munin swoop past. The Governor's foot *s l i p s* .
We jolt and skid.

Only just upright, the Governor storms back and checks the spot.
A long slide of grey poo is smeared across the grass.

'Out of my Tower! Now!'

I'm thrust to the Chaplain, hugged to his shoulder and marched for home.
From a cage roof, Thor and Munin flap their wings and caw.

Baldrick flies up to join them.

There's nothing wrong with the lying flick tail!
And nothing wrong with the evidence.
I'd recognise that poo anywhere, even if it wasn't me.

The poo was the ravens' revenge.

TWENTY FIVE

I'm caged on the kitchen table, my heart broken, lungs on fire.

My most desperate yowl, a slowed-down baby's scream amped to eleven,
does
nothing.

Chaplain grimaces by the sink.
'Teufel, shush.'

He sighs.
'What happened, eh, boy?'

Mrs C is sullen and grey.
'We can't do this.'

The Chaplain lifts his glasses, cups his face.
'No choice, love. Let the Governor calm down, I'll collect him in a few days.
Make some phone calls.'

Couple of days! I claw at the cage door. You'll be dead if I leave here!
Dead!
Let me out! Let me out!

'YEOWL! YEOWL!'

Chap glances over as he heads for the kettle.
'He's changed. Cats don't settle sometimes. I worried about this.
Always too independent. Perhaps we shouldn't have kept him in?'

Mrs C rubs a mark on the table, her eyes red and wet.
'Can't we lock him in here?'

Chap's head sweeps no.
'The Governor's furious. If he's onto the Bishop, we'll be off, too.'

'A mouser,' Mrs C says,
'all his years
and now he won't leave birds alone.
I don't understand.'

'Nor do I.'

She looks across.
'It's as if he's trying to tell us something.'

'YEOWL! YEOWL!'

The Chaplain walks over.
'Stop it, Teufel. You'll do yourself an injury.'

He puts a hand to Mrs C's shoulder.
'I'll drive him after a cuppa. Give the Governor his victory.'

Victory! You'll be killed, you fools, no!

No!

A light flashes by the cellar door. It's Mushika.
'Teufel, what have you done? Why are you leaving?'

TWENTY SIX

A red-haired young woman in a blue smock and vet perfume – disinfectant and evil – smiles as she slides the bolt across my metal cage.

'There you go, Toofull. Nice and high, so you can see all your new friends. We'll introduce you tomorrow.'

She taps my nose through the steel bars, then leaves through a glass door, hitting the light switch as she goes.
'Night-night, Munchkins.'

The narrow room glows green from an emergency-exit sign above the door. I face a wall of imprisoned cats. Two tabbies on the top row, then down through the furs, each bored or sleeping.

A clock shows 10.02pm.

In two hours I'll be late for King Richard, and the Chaplain and Mrs C will be dead.

'Oi! You lot. Wake up.'

A few eyes open and close, other cats turn their backs.

'Oi! This is important. I've got to escape. Lives are at stake. Human lives.'

A feral ginger yawns his bust-up yellow teeth.

'We ain't interested. Stories. Always stories. You're the twelfth this week. Heard it all. Your loved ones are gone. Shut them eyes and that gob. We don't do noise past ten.'

'This is an emergency. I'm on a king's business. My owners will die!'

A swirling curve of caramel and cream reveals a Siamese,
ice-blue eyes
set on full scorn.
'Die of heartbreak because big ole Humpty Dumpty got lost.
Dog poo. You ain't cute,
barely handsome,
no pedigree...'

I push my head at the cage.
'I am to be famous!'

Her tail drops. She laughs.
'Of course you are.'

'There must be a way out!' I say, pressing against the wire.

Lower down, a head cone lifts.
'Ain't been an escape in years,'
says a gorm-eyed calico within.
'Brother, they've been locking us up here since 1883.'

'You lot are useless! Useless.'

I retreat into my box's gloom, turn and charge the cage door with a body slam.

'Oi!' the Siamese calls. 'No noise past ten!'

I pull back, brace, charge and smash again. Shoulders bludgeon and crash.

I charge and slam.

Charge and slam. Fat my dog. I'm a chunky-hunky muscle bucket!

The Siamese glares.
'You can't do that! It's locked, you fool!'

'Watch me, sludge face.'

I THUMP the back of the cage, turn and surge. And this time it begins.

A TREMOR. VIBRATION. BOLTS SHIFT. UP. FLAT PACK
MOVEMENT. METAL CREAKS. FLAT PACK DOWN.

Another charge. Another slam. Another ram bam. And pop. Fixings release. It BEGINS.

Tip. Top. I charge and slide. Charge and slide. The angle arrives. Hello gravity.

My face slides into the falling steel. Across the cages, cats startle and scramble. Everyone but the seal-tip Siamese, her ice-blue stare sparkling rage. The cage above mine strikes their stack. A sharp jangled thud.

I face her.
'Hi! Time to be helpful.'

Her expression is pure nothingness.

Nose shoved against the steel, I twitch my ears to the bolt.
'Bash that and let me out. I told you. A king's business.'

Her pupils flex.
'This is a queen's country, but go on then, Twinkles... love a bit of hunk.'

Her slender paw reaches through the bars and lifts the bolt up and across.

The door falls open.
I slap down like dropped washing.

Claws testing the hard floor, I look around. Now what?

'Ha-ha,' she says. 'They'll do you tomorrow...'

Whatever.
The room is walls, examination tables, dispensers, metal cupboards, cages.
Classic vet. I jump to a table and study the door. Heavy. Safety-wire glass.
A fat L-shaped handle. That will do. Simple.
I leap at the handle and bash it as I fall. Practically bounce off the thing.
Door doesn't budge a mouse's whisker. What the fox? I have this technique down at home and they go and use a door from a battleship or something. Doggin' vets.

'You need more oomph, chunky-lunks,' says a straggly kitten, all ears and eyes.

'Dog off.'

I jump back to the table and look again. Nothing. This is a disaster. Just the door.
Thick, heavy, wire-protected. A small blue baseball cap bobs past the bottom panes.
I launch at the glass and splat.
'Magsi!'

Magnificat turns. Her face is a scowly mood slap. I slide down the glass.
'Stand back,' she gruffs, her tail whipping.

I shuffle back.

She mists through, fur so sharp it could stab me.
'The places you drag me. Come on.'

'A ghost!' says someone behind me. 'Ghosts can open things.
Let us out, Darling. Come on. Please...'

Magnificat bristles to the cat's cage, a fellow black-and-white.
'I'm not your darling and this isn't a prison. Trust me, I know.
It happens, that this idiot fur lump is needed elsewhere. A king's business.'

I smile to the Siamese.
'See?'

The Siamese curls away.
'Careful out there,' she calls. The words sing and swing like her tail.
'You won't beat the triple lock.'

Triple-what – ? But more important things are on my mind. I turn to Magnificat.
'Fur lump?'

Her tail wands.
'For getting you out of this mess, I can call you what I want. Follow me.'

She's right. It's an absolute result. Because I will be on time for Richard;
the Chap and Mrs C can sleep on, and Magnifiwander, Court and being sacrificed
in a light on Bonfire Night can do one!

I smile.
'Of course. I am terribly grateful. No more issues, I promise.'

Magnificat turns away, shaking her head.
She looks to the door and swings it open with one quick stare.

Man, the things ghosts get to do.

I swish my tail and shuffle my shoulders with a little yeah-baby wiggle.
Tail-up, future up.
With a last smile, I turn back to the caged cats.

'See you, losers!'

We fast-paw corridors, twist and turn, until Magnificat brings us to a fire exit.
I jump up, bash the bar and it swings out. Triple-locked, what? Don't think so...

Across a yard, through some railings and we're on a cold, industrial road. Thick grey
clouds leather the sky. The odd person brisks the pavements, vehicles grumble.

A train rattle-chugs a bridge.
Something is off.
'Where are we? I can't... I can't sense anything.'

'That's the Battersea lock.' Magnificat nods to the railway bridge.
'We're in a triangle of iron. Tracks every side. The iron blocks our homing compass.
It took me four hours to find you and I know the way. The Tower's down there,
I think...'

'Four hours! I need to be back by midnight.'

She lifts a paw.
'Why?'

'Because,' I look up at the blackening cloud, 'the weather is dog-poop,
and I'm not staying out in it. Today's been bad enough. Chap goes to bed at midnight.
I want to be wrapped up, duvet, warm hands, and everything.'

There. She'll fall for that.

'Oh, you're not going home.'

My tail wands.
'Excuse me?'

'You left the Tower. Disobeyed a Royal instruction. That's treason.
A capital crime.'

'I didn't leave. I was taken. That's no crime.'

'Reasons are immaterial. Crime is crime.'

'Only if you're caught. I'm a cat. We don't do guilt!'
I sit down. 'It's midnight, or, I go on my own.'

Her cap bobs as she laughs.
She stares down the street.
'Down there is zombie land. The marshes of Nine Elms. Good luck.
The safe way, my way, is Battersea Bridge. Up river.
And that's four hours at least.'

'At least!'

She gets eye-to-eye close.
'Yes. And when we get back, you say nothing. This didn't happen.

If the Governor sees you, anyone, our plans are over.
You do exactly what I say.
I'm putting you in hiding until I can straighten this out.
With luck, we should be back for the first prayer break at 2am.'
She swooshes her tail, turns and sets for the bridge.

I catch up and trot by her side.
'I'll hide myself.
How's that?'

'Nope,' she says, lifting her nose away. 'Don't trust you.'

'Come on.' I try to give her a nudge, but she keeps her stride.
'I didn't leave. I didn't attack Baldrick. Those birds set me up. Catists, the lot of them.
This isn't fair, Magsi. It was discrimination!'
I get in front of her. 'I was on my way back. I was just doing the door.'

'Of course you were.'

I turn and sniff better air, then follow in silence.

The
view
of
her
bum
isn't great,
but it's better
than being
moaned at.
We cross
a
road.

'Er, why are we going this way?'

She
doesn't
look
back.

'This isn't the way. It's that way, the road we just passed.'

Her bum stops.
Tail flicking.

She turns. Her face is fire.
'I told you, our senses don't work here. You can't trust what you feel.'

'I'm telling you. The river is down there. I can sniff it. The Thames leads to the Tower. I'm an estuary cat. I know river-sea smells.'

She bristles at me.

'I'm a London cat. For four hundred years. You...
can't...
go...
down...
there...'

'Fine then.'
I sit down.

She stomps towards some shops.

I go and catch up.

Magnificat halts. Her head lifts. She sniffs at the air.
'Maybe, it's not down here.'

'Told you.'

Ahead are more bridges. More trains chug.
'Isn't there somewhere nice? You know, pleasant and green? Not all this grim?'

'I'm protecting you from pleasant and green. Down there is Battersea Park.
But we need to go around it.'

'No wonder it took you four doggin' hours. Straight lines, Magsi.
Come on. Simple stuff. Basics.'

I set off under the bridges. A few paces the other side and my head clears instantly.
Hello certainty, my old friend. Really, things are easy. Simple.
When you actually know what you're doing.

A bus rumbles past. I call back to Magnificat.
'Chop-chop. That the park?' I nod to over a roundabout. Huge gates guard trees.

'Yes,' she replies. 'And it's dangerous.'

I take a quick scratch.
'Dangerous? It's a park. What's in there, killer squirrels?'

'The Two Charlies' Ghost Hunting Club. That's what's in there.
Charles Dickens and Charles Darwin come every night
from Westminster Abbey. But it's not the hunters
you need to watch.
It's what hunts.'

'I can outrun, outsmart, out-everything anything. I'll protect you, Magsi.'

'It's you who needs protecting.'

'Nonsense. I'm going in.'

'Teufel!'
Magnificat's still on the other side of the bushes.
She mists in, her face all, you know–

'So,' I say, 'where we going?'

She nods to a set of rosebeds,
petals ebbing on the soil.
'Through there and left. If you really want to do this.'

I go right.

'Teufel...!'

'The Tower is this way. I can smell the river. My magnets are up.'

'That way is the hunting club, Teufel.'

I stop.

She stands by low railings.
'Giant armoured rats. Super-giant bouncing ones.
Six-foot birds faster than a bullet. Poison dart frogs!
It's not good. That's what I've been told.'

My eyes go on a big roll.
'Someone's been telling you stories, Magnificat.'

'There's a zoo, down there. The hunting club get them out. A petting zoo–'

'A petting zoo? I'm going to be attacked by what, a maraude of flop-head rabbits? Bouncing lambs? An army of hamsters?'

'Concentrate, I'm telling you. Ears on watch.'

'Whatever.'
I trot off, in a direction that happens to be following her, because I don't have a choice. This could be Timbuktu and I wouldn't have a clue. The path follows a lake,
trees lining the banks. The odd fox scratches its bark, the occasional *bump in the night*, but otherwise it's quiet.

Magnificat fast-paces, high tail, ears on swivel.
At least she isn't slow.
Can't abide a slow padder.

She stops.

'We're coming to the jungle. Extra careful. It's a favourite hunting ground.'

'Of course. The jungle. They've been telling you porkies, Mags. Dog-pooping you. It's a wind up.'

She stares, proper serious.
'The monkeys like a bit of cat.
And if they're on the giant birds, big problems. The local cats were very specific.'

'The local cats are having you on!'

Around the next corner, smells change. Trees morph. Leaves spike. Trunks thick.
The air hangs warm. No monsters. No cat-hunting zoo army.
It's a bit jungly, if you really squint.

She stops at a side path curling into gloom – heavy trees laden the sides.
'Down here is our safe way to the river.
Anything happens on the field, run to the far trees. You got that?'

'Deffo.' I humour her.

She enters in stealth mode.

Creep. Creep. Still. Still. Paw. Paw.

We go through. And surprise-surprise. Yawn. Yawn. Nada.
The odd scurrying noise in the trees, city bumps and thumps but otherwise, zilch.

Mags stops.

Before us is an open field dappled in a camouflage of moonlight. Wind sweeps our eyes. Just out from the wood, in a circle of tarmac, is an old wooden pavilion shaped like a thick cross with gabled roofs. No outer walls, just stilts and benches against the inner walls. Tufts of smoke lift over the roof from the far side.

Mags sniffs.
'Dogs – the Club are here. We need to get to those far trees.'

I whisper. 'What are we up against? The whole zoo?
Kid goats, lambs and everything?'

'I told you, it's not that type of petting zoo.'

'What other types are there?'

A punch of musk swirls in the wind.
A quick scratching, tap-tap.
From the pavilion's right side,
head down on the sniff, comes a giant armour-shelled rat.
Seen them on Chap's telly.
An armabrillo or something.
Smell a flea at fifty paces, but couldn't see an elephant in a tutu. We're downwind.

For now.

I whisper again. 'Mags. We need to break the scent.'
I prime my legs and leap towards the left side of the pavilion.
Paws back on tarmac, I scoot under the benches to further block scent and sight.

Mags mists in. The armadillo keeps tracking the tarmac. It hits the broken trail.
Ha – gotcha.

You got the armour, but you're still doofus stupid. It scuttles towards the woods.
A pocket of smoke wafts over our heads – hot, sooty and sweet.

'Where are they?' a man's voice says.

A whimper follows. Another. A slight snore. A dog snore... Doggin' hell.
I get under the bench closest to their section.

'Does it matter?' says another man. 'Having a play, probably. A good feed.
Here, have another. This one's almost perfect, a goo-fest...'

With me at ground level and Mags hovering above, we ease our heads around the corner. Two elderly male ghosts lie on benches, head to head. One bald with a big white beard. The other younger with black tufty hair. Both are stroking lambs dozing on their chest. Between them in a shopping trolley is a barbecue, the coals glowing hot orange and white. The younger ghost is poking a stick through the trolley toasting marshmallows. Beneath the benches, giant wolfhounds sleep, paws tip-tapping dreams. The lambs are resting, content.

Except...

They're not lambs. They're dogs.

Doggin' Bedlington terriers.
Fanged, white blizzards.

That's what we called them in Salcombe.

Trickiest, fastest, dogs ever.

I pull back. Magnificat follows.

I whisper, 'Your local cats didn't mention doggin' dogs?'

'Oh, they did,' she says, matter of factly.
'The Charlies pick a lock or two on the way,
bring a few locals who don't get walked much.
Do races, bets and games.
The dogs get the leftovers and exercise. Win-win.
This park is a definite no-no for cats, night and day.'

'Didn't you think to tell me?'

'I did. **You** said you can outrun any dog.'

'Not doggin' sight hounds! Nor gangster Bedlingtons. I'm chunky not hunky!'

I edge my head around the corner and check again.
The shagster wolfhounds are tied to the bench legs. That's a few seconds.
The Bedlingtons are not.

Dogs... Dogs...

They're dozing. No one's looking our way. No lights. Moon is pretty covered. If I can get out onto the field into the dark. The smoke might hide any scent.

'Err, Teufel.'

'What?
... I'm thinking.'

'The packed rat is back.'

'So. He's useless.'

'He's brought his friends.'

I turn.

Oh my freakin' whiskers! Breaking from the trees are giant birds!

Fat bald legs! Heads like beaks on sticks! That's doggin' emus! And riding on their necks are white-moustached monkeys! This is a world-class shuffle of doggin' hassle.

'Run!' shouts Magnificat. 'The trees over there! They won't leave the park. Run!'

We bolt onto the path. Doggin' London!

'Ooh, look,' the older man shouts. 'Ginger, Milo. Food, boys!'

I check the pack. Hounds scramble under benches. Heads hit wood, leads strain.
The Bedlingtons leap and begin to chase. Leads unclip. I look to Magnificat.
She just mists off!

Vanishes!
Leaves me for dog food.
Again!

Low-backed, panicking, I speed for the trees. They're so far away they might as well be Christmas. The giant birds are closing, dogs racing to catch up – I'm doomed.
Monkeys howl delight. They're fast. Real fast. Faster than me. I pound and pound.

More thumps boom. The sounds are the birds. Beaks the size of my head. Brain-pickers.
Monkeys wail and scream. Brain-suckers! Closer. Snaps. Bites.
All drooling for flesh and blood.

Push, Teufel, push!

The emus and dogs come together. And the trees are too far.
My brain switches fight and flight. It panics and I collapse – don't give up, don't!

The zoo pack zooms and booms.

I need to run, but can't. Fear is killing me before the fangs do. I'm over. The killers bound towards me.

Magnificat blasts in, three times her normal size.

Hovering mid-air, hissing like a barrel of snakes on fire!
How the– ?

The pack freaks and splits. Yelping, they race back towards the pavilion.
I tremble and shake, then collapse and roll laughing to the skies,
'Yes! Yes!'

Magnifisave mists in above me.

'We haven't got time. Run. Run!'

I stagger up and chase after her.
'That was amazing...'

I pant.
'How'd you– '

'You spread your mist. Hurts like every fur being plucked at once.
You're a proper pain, Teufel.'

'Hang on! That wasn't me.'

We hit the trees, and with no sign of the pack, Mags eases the pace down. A weave through the railings and we're out onto a residential street. Vehicles head for an iron suspension bridge lit across the river. I take a moment to recover and sit.

'The other side,' she says. 'Move.'

'Wait. I'm dogged. This is hard work.'

'Yeah, and my fur being ripped up to save yours is what?
You're the one in a rush...'

She's right. Perhaps when Richard and Fawkes do their thing, I'll spare her.
A quiet word. Maybe.

I follow her onto the bridge. The footpath is weird, bumpy and undulating.

'So what's the plan?'

She jumps to the guard rail and peers down to the river.
'We're going to use one of those.'

I leap to her side.
Out from the bank, a pier is lined with barges and boats. Most have lights on.

'That's Cadogan Pier, and we're stealing a boat.'

'Steal a boat? Water! You're bananas, Magnificat! Dog-bits bananas.'

A great iron gangplank arms down to the pier. More bridge than walkway, the pier at the end is lined with boats both sides. Each one is gigantic.

'You want duvets by midnight,' says Magnificat. 'It's a boat. I'm expert. Studied them for decades. Hit a button, pull a lever. Go. Always wanted a play.'

My whiskers fizz idiocy.

'A play? You're a cat. Paws not hands, Doofus, and a slight issue with size. That's complicated, naval navigatory machinery down there!'

'Nonsense.' Her catnip eyes lift to the sky. 'Ghosts are part of the universal energy. I go through things, move things, touch things. Control things. Walter's told me all about shippies and I crossed the Thames in one once. Driving is a dream.'

'It's steering. You steer boats!'

For dog's sake. But I don't have a choice, I have to be on time for Richard.

'You better not dog this up, Magnificat. And I am not getting wet!'

She hovers down to the footpath and we get off the bridge. Past a red telephone box, down to a promenade, tall globe streetlights dot the river wall. The gangplank has its own steps. Fences, spikes and railings block the entrance. A big dog-off – go away.

But the cat way is always open.

A railing squiggle, a push and a squeeze and I'm through. Down the gangplank, out on the pier, the water laps and the wind whips. Up close, the impossibility of Magnificat's plan is obvious; the boats are beasts. More like houses than anything. But at the end, tied between a big grey boat and a scruffy brown one, a wooden speedboat gleams under a cream cover, a blue skull-and-crossbones flag hangs on the stern.

'That'll do,' says Magnificat. 'Seen these...'
She stares at the tarpaulin cover, which unties and begins to lift towards the pier.
'Jump in, shipmate!'

'Can't we catch a bus?'

She glares at me. 'In.'

I accept the inevitable and leap to the passenger seat. Claws in the white leather, happy like a cat in a speedboat, I turn to Magnifipirate. My stomach sinks. The demented moggie flips her cap, dumps the tarpaulin on the deck, furls the mooring rope and jumps to the captain's seat. We drift to the river's flow.

She peers forward from the backrest, studying the console.
'Now what?'

'You said you knew!'

I clamber onto the back of my seat. The console is full of dials, switches and knobs.
We slip further into the current. Magnifidumbbot gawps at the controls.
Nothing happens.

We swirl in eddies.

'Do something, Magnificat!'

'Shush. Electrical stuff's hard.'

She hovers off the seat, gets right up to the console and bashes it with a paw.
A roar of engine.
Splutters and kicks.
The boat quakes and shakes.
Streams of water jet from the back.

'And you, baby,' she says, 'must be the throttle!'

She yanks a black stick. The boat smashes over the water then spins in circles.

'The wheel, Magnificat! Control the wheel!'

She laughs hovering back to the seat. 'Isn't this fun!'

Turning to the console, she steadies the wheel, adjusts the throttle
and the boat eases, rotating to face downriver.
Wind in fur, her demented eyes meet mine.
'Tower of London here we come!'

A double kick of speed and thrust. Riding the tide, claws gripped, ears down.
The keel bounces as we whizz the water, surging towards boats lumbering upstream with slow flashing lights. I'm wet and cold, but starting to enjoy it!

We swoop and arc as the river bends. The huge golden Gothic towers of Parliament and Big Ben rise into view, gleaming against the black river and star-dotted sky. The most famous clock in the world strikes eleven. Long bongs bound across the water.
The engine roars behind us, wake tumbling and churning.

'How long?' I shout.

'Four miles.' Magnificat beams. 'There in a jiffy.'

'How will I get in?'

'Gap in the spikes,' shouts Mags. 'Traitors' Gate.
Bang this baby up, and jump, easy. No locks, no walls, nothing.'

As the final Big Ben bong booms, blue lights flash on the river. Another boat, chunkier than ours, crests over the water, churning foam as it speeds. They're in an awful rush.

Blue lights are the emergency services.

'Err Mags! That's the police!'

She slams the throttle and races us at them.

'What are you doing?'

She doesn't reply.

The police siren wails.
Blue lights beam and flash.
Police in high-vis jackets crouch at the bow.
Steadying themselves – they're aiming machine guns!

'They've got guns, Magnificat, guns!'

'Relax. It's just the Feds.'

'Feds? Relax? Are you mad?'

'STOP, POLICE!' cracks a loud-hailer.
**'METROPOLITAN POLICE.
THIS IS A RESTRICTED AREA.
WE WILL FIRE.'**

The helmsman lifts a window in the cockpit. The boat slams and slaps.
The police on the bow level their barrels to the guard rail.

'Mags!!!!'

'They're in a tin can, Teuf. Watch!'

Magnificat spins the wheel.
Weaves us left and right,
then straight at them again!

She shouts over the bow.
'Chicken time, chickens!'

I scream at the wet, cold air.
'You don't play chicken with officers of the law, Magnificat!'

We surge forward.
A policeman sweeps his gun over his shoulder. Reaches down.
Fiddles with something. Lifts a long black pipe.

'Mags! Mags! He's got a doggin' *bazooka*! He's gonna take the boat out!'

The long black tube aims straight at my head.

Mags bangs the throttle.
'They can't if we're up their nostrils!'

'THIS IS A LETHAL FORCE AREA!'
shouts the helmsman.
'LETHAL FORCE WILL BE APPLIED!'

We bounce and bounce at the boat. Magnificat's gone mad. We're so close I can see the bazooka officer's stare. He lifts a switch. Mags slams the wheel. The police boat churns right. With a thump of throttle, we rise and scoot, smashing down the river.

'Yeah, baby!' cries Magnificat.

Level with Parliament, I look back to the police. Chasing down the river is another boat speeding the tide.

'ERR Mags, a long black boat's coming! It's FAST and full of coppers dressed in proper black, army business!!!'

Magnifispeed yanks the throttle down. The boat screams. Skimming and skipping the surface. Their boat is fast, too. Super fast. Rocketing. A searchlight buffets the water.

Bright light blasts my eyes.

'OFFICERS WILL FIRE! STOP THE BOAT! STOP THE BOAT!'

Mags ducks, swinging the wheel.
She swerves us at bridges, barges, cruise boats,
anything to stop the commandos taking a shot.
Central London flies by. The river bends.
Finally, the Tower comes into view.
A last bridge, we sweep past the long grey bulk
of battleship cruiser *HMS Belfast*, and cut across
the river's flow aiming straight at Traitors' Gate.
More police boats charge from under Tower Bridge.

Magnificat laughs.

Then I see the gate. There isn't one. Just a big wall.

'It's blocked up, Magnificat! Stop the boat! Stop the boat!'

Magnificat sees the bricked-up wharf and swings the wheel left.
Heading straight at a long pier. The police boats are closing. Sirens wail.

Mags aims for the gap between the shore and the pier.
'You're gonna have to jump, Teufel!'

'Jump? How did you miss this huge, great, big stone wall, Magnificat!'

'I was looking out, wasn't I, out to the river. You moderns. So fixed about details!'

'Jump where?'

'There!'

An inlet is cut into the wharf. Submerged steps lead to the top. But there's a gate.
A big spiked gate half in the water, and I've got no idea how deep the water is.
We're dogged. More dogged than a dog. And we're at crash speed plus ten.
Mags keeps the boat straight. I'm flying through the air, tumbling over the gate's spikes.
She's doggin' chucked me!

I land splat into cold river water. Magnificat hovers over me, landing on the first dry step
as the boat crunches and scrapes down the wall. Police boats swarm in.

'There you go, boys, go play stick.'

Police jump to the steps. They clamber the iron gate towards the spikes.

'Run!' says Magnificat.

We scramble up. There's another gate at the top. Smaller. I can manage this one. My paws touch the iron and she chucks me again! I land on the top step.
'Will you stop with that!'

Dripping wet. Cold. We tuck under a bench. Confused police search the empty wharf.

The size of the Tower's walls make me feel like a flea.

'What now? I mean, how can I get in? You're not going...' the thought of flying over the huge walls...

Her ears drop.
'I can't. Too worn out. Can't mist the gates either. Way too heavy.
I used all my misting energy in the park.
All the windows are alarmed.' Eyes on paws, she sits. 'There's only one option: Elvis.'

'Elvis?'

'The ruler of underground London.'

'Why you so worried?'

'He's a pouch rat from Bethnal Green. Grew up with a Pitbull.'

'So? A rat's a mouse with attitude and better teeth, nothing more. I can take him.'

'He's the same size as you.'

'Oh.'

TWENTY NINE

The police lights on the river still and the sirens slow. Up on the wharf our problems mount. The Tower's entrance is guarded by four towers, two, very big locked gates and a moat. Magnificat's face isn't exactly full of promise either.

'There's a secret tunnel at St Dunstan's,' she says, 'it's an abandoned church where Elvis preaches.'

I shake stinky river water from my ears.
'He's a preacher?'

She nods.
'The rats adore him. He's brought dignity and hope. From Parliament to east of the Tower.'

'A rat rules that?'

'Underground, yes.'

Weird.

'He might not be there though, right? And a preacher's all peace and love?'

'Eyes everywhere. If we're lucky, he'll be mid-sermon and their attention will be on him. If not...' She shakes her head.

'Come on then,' I say, checking up and down the wharf.
'Let's go meet, Ratty-watty. Where to?'

Magnificat gestures to a roadway leading up into the city. A small road tracks off between large, office blocks.

'Down there.'

We pad the lonely street, hugging close to the walls. Not a soul or sound, except the hum of streetlights guarding the night. The road ends by a cluster of trees and bushes. Over a big sweeping road, up a smaller one, more offices, until a huge Gothic spire pierces the night.

The white spire stands like a starship waiting to launch. Walls gripped in tumbles of ivy. Riots of vegetation crowding the stone. Wind drifts from the river rustling leaves. The church is railed off.

'It's almost as old as the Tower,' says Magnificat.
'Burned in the Great Fire of 1666, then bombed in the last war.
Now, inside, be super quiet, super serious. Not like Battersea.'

'Gotcha.'

She's so cautious... A rat's a rat. As big as me is a ridiculous exaggeration.
I trot across the road, suck in my chest and get about squeezing through the railings.

'Teufel!' she hisses. 'For dog's sake! Not there.'

'What?'

'Ssssh...'

It's a rat, not a monster. I can outrun them, out-think them, out-fight them, out-bite them. Proved it countless times...

High-nosed, she sets off up the street then stops at a gate. Catching up, there's a path with steps leading to a stone porch. The arch framed in carvings, dappled with ivy and moss. I squeeze through the railings at the gate's side and Magnificat edges forward, ears and eyes twitching for rat. She heads around the back of the nave. And that's where I see them. Rat bums and tails sat in lines along four huge tracery windows.

'Brothers. Sisters,'
a voice booms from inside.

'Elvis,' whispers Magnificat.

A raised bed along the nave, creates an almost sunken path. We drop our tails and slip past the rat-bum windows.

'We gather to believe,' the voice continues. 'They say,
to seek solace and comfort. I say dogs to all that!
We gather each night, my friends.
Until you truly smell the joy of life.
The art and revenge of a good steal.'

Past a statue. Tight in the shadows, there's an arched doorway into the nave.

The church is now a garden. Trees weave through windows, ivy trails over mullions. On the far side, a big circle of benches is covered in rats. In the middle of the circle on a raised platform, a giant golden-brown rat sports an ear-to-ear grin.

Magnificat is whisker close.
'Inside,' she whispers, 'in the bushes, straight away. Follow me.
The tunnel is behind a planter. We go at his next words.'

'I say, why—' the rat booms.

Mags slips in behind the first bush.

Claws tucked, tail low, head down, I follow.

She mists over the leaves, soil and sticks. I place each paw with care, feeling for noise.

'Again,' the rat says, 'and again until you believe.
You are loved! Spit fear like bad kebab.
Lose names like flea heads.
Never hold words of hurt.
We are life not vermin.
Life is love.
Their right. Our right.
Their blood is our blood. Cats. Dogs. Humans.
Seagulls. We claim dignity. What is ours and theirs.
We take treasure my friends, until they do unto others!
Together!'

'Together!' the congregation cries.

'Together!' he repeats.

What an over-eared over-worded tosspot. A rat heaves a plastic bottle of milky liquid to him. He lifts it with ease and takes a long raised gulp.

'What's that?' I whisper.

'Protein drink,' says Magnificat. 'That's why he's so bulky.
Works out three hours a day.'

A neck's a neck. Teeth in and they're all dead.
'I reckon I could take him.'

'That's two-hundred rats, City of London rats, Teufel.
He controls a thousand. More.
They will be on you in seconds. Dead in a minute.'

'Dog bits.'

'Yes bits. Follow me. We need to get to the tunnel.'

Magnificat gets behind the ivy-covered planter and floats into the hole. I got business. I leap on top, give the rats a full-on go-wah hissing-scare-fest and they fall out the window.

In a second I'm facing Elvis and the other rodent muppets.
'Yo, verms!'

Rats turn.
Mouths drop.
Big bozo Elvis
leaps from
the
bin.

'Teufel!' I hear Magnificat call.

'Chill. It's puffed up mices. This needs to be done.'

I turn to the now-charging rodents, shuffle my shoulders and give them some proper Teufel knowledge.
'As good as cats!
You ain't good enough to eat my poo!
You're a bunch of
garbage-head,
stinky, whisker-flicker
trash-buckets!
Jog on!'

I get up on my hind legs and stand tall. 'Who are ya! Who are ya!'

Rats pile at me.
I drop down and turn. Magnificat is gone. I leap down the hole.

It's
a
big
black
drop.

I land with a slap and splash.

Magnificat
is already a long way down the tunnel.

'Ease up!' I call, getting my bearings in the drippy wet. 'It'll take them ages.
They can't land like cats.'

'Don't bet on it!' she calls.

A sudden plop, plop, plop. Rats thump into the tunnel. Oh, doggin' hell.

I race after Magnificat. A flash of white as she turns left.
We sprint under circles of light. The scamper, scratch and snap of rats builds.
Another tunnel, tiny. My paws drag in stinky mud. A sluice gate. Blocking the way.

A dead end!

A tight grid of thick iron! The rats are closing. What's she done? I'll be torn to bits!
Magnificat stares at the gate. She's going to hover it up!

Come on gate! Lift! Lift!

Behind us, rats jump and tumble. A wall of stink-teeth and angry eyes.
The gate creaks up. We bundle under and Mags slams it shut.

I collapse on the floor, rats snap, mouths poking through the iron.
Elvis appears above them, black eyes filled with rage.

I stand, pad to the gate, spin around, lift my tail and pump a fat, noisy fart in his face.
'Have that!'

Out from the secret tunnel, Magnificat is by the hospital block, fur out, high-tailed.
'You are puerile.'

I pull myself out from the hole and lean into a stretch.
'What's that mean?'

'Childish.'
She stares at the bricks and mists them back into place.

What I am, Magsi is a genius. I'm back by midnight, saved, and you don't have a clue!

'Nah.' I say. 'Gave an idiot from an idiot species what for. A cat's a cat. You should remember that. You try to be too human.'

She rolls her eyes and sets off for the parade ground.

Crossing the square, Waterloo's clock shows 11.40.
Perfect. Plenty of time.

'This way,' she says, heading towards the bottom gates. 'Once you're in hiding, you don't move. No going home. No, *I'm bored, I'll take a wander.*'

I catch her up.
'Gotcha. I'm grateful for back there. Truly. Thanks.'

'Prayers finish at 6am on the first. I'll come for you then. You stay all night and all tomorrow. You got that?'

'Got it. Stay put.'

We drop from Salt Tower's battlements and head left into the Outer Ward. A row of cottages are built into the Tower's curtain wall. She points to a staircase.

'Up those steps. Left, up again. You'll see a box. That's where you hide. The Yeomen don't go up in winter, so you should be okay. Keep your guard up.'

'Thanks, Magnificat.'
I keep eye contact so she feels the recognition.

'See you on the first,' she says.

And with that she mists off to prayers. Up the stone stairs, in a far corner of the flat roof, is a cardboard box tucked by a wall. Two chicken thighs and a water dish sit outside and a blanket inside. Bonus. I turn and set off for Richard and Fawkes.

The Tower is black and deserted. Clear sky, windy, but lovely. Solid autumn atmosphere. Waterloo's clock shows a tick before midnight.
Stepping off the parade square, I check my paws. They're a bit stinky from the tunnel. Should I clean for a king?

BONG... BONG... Midnight's chimes begin.

Richard said don't be late.

Around the next corner I'm hit by a slap of wind. And on that wind is Richard's mooding stench – pungent burning blood. I edge forward and ease my head around the stone. Richard and Fawkes are sat on a bench, the King with his feet up on a bin, Guy picking his teeth with a match.

'Time is a precise thing this century, is it not Fawkes?' says Richard.

'It is,' nods Fawkes. 'Minute to minute.'

'I am a king, am I not?'

'You are.'

'Then where is this cat?'

'You could choose a sword while we wait?'

'Dandy!'

Richard swings his feet off the bin.
Fawkes gets up and pops around a corner.
He returns with a collection of swords and daggers hovering in the swirly shape of a winged serpent.

'Any of this lot any good?'

Richard studies the collection.
'Nothing Kingy, Fawkes. Where's the oomph? No. Not good.
Do better. I can't go into battle with a peasant's metal stick. I want something big.'

I step into view.
'Hello, Your Grace.'

'Finally,' says Richard, irritation writ across his face. 'Where have you been?'

'I was attacked, Your Grace. On the way, just now.
Two giant rats arguing about the princes you killed.'

Richard looks to the sky.

'I was straight in. Took them out! Dead, Your Grace. They were disgracing your
honour. It was messy, stinky, dangerous but fun. Had time to clean my mouth,
and that's all – couldn't be speaking with blood dripping from my fangs, Your Grace.
My sincere apologies for not being spotless and absolutely on time! Smell these...'
I offer a paw for a whiff.

He lifts his nose forward, but declines an inhale.

I drop my head and peek up, all super-meek.

His face is white, and bone still.
Richard turns to Fawkes.
'What do you say, Guy?
Do we forgive kitty for being late?'

'What are the swords for?' I ask, to change the subject.

Richard's eyebrows climb his forehead. 'We have a small complication.
Apparently, even when injured, if the ravens smell a cat, they may
be able to suck you into the underworld.
Never know what's down there. I'm picking a sword, so I can help if needed.
A back-up plan – not without some sacrifice and risk on my own part I might add,
young cat. Ghosts don't mess with ravens. Killing them remains your job.
As I said, we'll cloak you in their scent.
It's a classic hunting trick.'

'I've got to smell of bird?'

He laughs. 'No, not quite. We wouldn't inflict that on you.
You will smell of death, if you remember?'

'Charming.'

'That is, you will smell of the food leading them to the scaffold. Rotting meat.
It's a little whiffy, but a soldier's life is sacrifice. Trying now, means we won't waste a
second on Bonfire Night. No surprises. Any good British soldier knows the Five Ps.

Proper **p**lanning **p**revents **p**iddly **p**erformance.

This is proper planning. We protect you then by protecting you now. Mr Fawkes...'

Fawkes stoops behind a buttress and hovers back a saucer of stinky, squidgy stuff. Mince, if I'm not mistaken. I pad forward and micro-sniff, keeping my distance. The odour is big and blunt, like dog farts.

'I'm not eating that.'

'Your Chaplain will tell you,
who dares wins.'

'My Chaplain tells me all sorts. And I'm telling you like I tell him. Do one.
I'm not touching it. How do you know he was in the SAS?'

'I do my research, cattie. And you need to up your game.
You're a warrior's son. A knight. And if you want to be a Sir under me.
Have true fame. You practise now and get that down.
Be a professional.'

I micro-sniff the mince again.

Richard comes close.
He leans down.
'Look, it's not bad. More on the turn than fully rancid.'
He dips a finger, lifts some sauce to his mouth. Gives it a suck.
'My army would call that leftovers.
No chicken korma but it's not going to kill you.'
He stands.
'Give it a good nosh. Get used to it.
No surprises. We can't waste a second on the night.'

Needs must. I suppose.
I take a chunk and yank it down my throat with a gulp. Pure yuk.
But at least it doesn't need a chew. The stench is worse than the taste.

Richard sniffs my face.
'We need it on your breath. Stinky. Take more.'

I keep my nose closed and gulp at the mince. As he said, sacrifice.
I won't be accused of not being good enough.

Can't believe I'm doing this for someone who thinks chicken korma is spicy.
He needs a Chap curry, madras his ass, bhuna this kahuna.

Richard sits and slaps his thighs.
'Now, cat, let me tell you a story of logistics, shopping and a surprise.'

I look at him gone out. This is going to be special.

'When you're a king leading soldiers into battle and war,
what you really are is a preserver of goods.
You need to look after your supply line.'
He puts his feet back up on the bin.
'There are hard things and soft things to look after.
The softs are flesh, food and water, and the like.
The hard is your supplies, weapons and sneaky surprises.
And look what I found.'

He leans behind the bench and rattles a small bottle at me
– Derek the vet's sleeping tablets.

'So delightful and small. Tiny! Tiny and tasteless.
It turns out there are things called chemists all over cities now.
And when you can go through doors and turn locks,
all manner of ghosty things come into your path.
Fawkes has taught me so much.
You can get a whole bag full of human versions of these.
Sleeping tablets. A whole Tower full.
We wouldn't want any unexpected interventions from the Governor,
the Yeoman or soldiers during our plan.
So the beer and tea of this fine establishment,
will be getting a little extra spice for our adventure.
Security guards, too.
The Tower will be ours
for playtime.'

Richard comes down to my level again.
'Now. Here's the surprise.
We're going to do a deed of great good, while we're at it.
Did you know there's a prison of poor trapped souls
underneath the ravens' cages?
A friend of mine, Bran, is down there.
And you probably won't believe this, but...
what's the modern parlance.
Yes... there are moms down there too.'

'Moms?'

'Yes. Hundreds and hundreds.
We're going to release them all, using a magic word.
What is it again, Mr Fawkes?'

'The word is Dod, Dickie. Welsh for come.'

'You're going to save moms?'

Richard nods.
'We are. Everyone down there. Can't just save your mate, can you?
We're going to get this country back on proper, moral high ground.'

'With a magic word?'

He tilts his head and smiles.
'I'll have my enemies ripped up by hunting dogs.
Hundreds of them. And those that really annoy me,
I'll execute on Tower Green.
Revenge needs spectacle.
A bit of emotion.'
He reaches down and scratches my chin.
'So better behave, eh, little cat? Or your Chap and Mrs Chap might get chopped.'

'Chopped?'

He makes a slicing gesture across his neck and gestures to the greens.
Eyes back on me, his bulging arm comes forward.
'Now, your earlier lateness is forgiven, but tomorrow no more mistakes...'

His fingers close in a pinching motion.

I feel my ribs crush.

'If you are one second late, my vengeance will be total. Understand?
I'm really not one for lateness. Never mind twice.'

I wheeze.
'Tomorrow?'

'Yes. Twenty-four hours from now, the tick of midnight, the plan will be executed.'

'Not Bonfire Night?'

'We brought it forward. That a problem?

'No– ' I cough.

'Halloween is much better for everyone. Trick *and* treat.'

The pressure on my chest releases. And with an intake of breath comes doubt.

Richard has a satisfied grin.
'Now, not a word to anyone.
Be at the scaffold at a quarter to midnight.
Bring your best fangs and claws. See you there.
We will be monstrous!'

With that, he and Fawkes mist away.

I wander back into the silent square. Dickie Boy's up to something, I know it.
If I do what they say, the ravens will be dead. If I make a mistake, I'll be dead,
and the Chap and Mrs C. If I don't do what Dickie says, we're all dead anyway.
But if I succeed, I'm a hero.

A hero for what? And to whom?

The Governor will want me dead if I do succeed. That's for sure.
And the Ravenmaster. There's a common theme in all this.

Me dead.

Richard is proper tricky, he'd make a good cat.

My choice between life and death?
My choice, Dickie boy?
Is you.
Dead.

I've got twenty-four hours. How do you kill a ghost?

Through the Tower's shadows, I paw and ponder.

Nothing comes.

Over the battlements to my hideout, I clamber in and clean.
Washing is peaceful, soothing, repetitive. I start on my paws.
A sweet feeling hits me, a warmth in my stomach. The sensation spreads into my head.
Queasy. A sensation that's familiar.

My eyes droop.
That mince!

Richard's drugged me, too. Trick or treat.

*

I wake, groggy and confused in the crook of night. All is still.
Outside the box, light is coming.

No – that's wrong. Light's going. The darkness is growing. This is evening! He lied about the date so I'd have no time to change my mind, and drugged me so there's even less time to plan a way out!

Think, Teufel! Think!

I shake myself awake. I don't know how, but I'm getting out of this. I'm doing over Richard and Fawkes, saving Chaplain and Mrs C, the country, and continuing my reputation as a charming, loving, honest cat!

What might work? I could ask Citizen's collar.
But how? He said that to silence the bell you just think it.
Is it the same with questions? Do I just ask? He said don't, though.
Said it will smash my brain. A smashed brain will help no one.

The mouse! That Oggle of hers. That knows everything, and she can use it.
I find her. She asks. It answers. I do. Simple.

I've just got to find her: cross the Tower, enter the house and cellar with no one seeing me. With a silent bell some of it is possible. Then I think. Nah. Dogs. You're the Teuf, be **bold**.

Out on Water Lane, cleaners heave black bags into industrial-sized bins.
The first entrance to the Inner Tower is closed. Down the lane, tourists stream for the main exit. I slip behind a cannon and sharpen my claws on a tree. The next entrance is directly by the raven cages – that's a no-no. I need a fat wall between them and my mind. That means the gate under Bloody Tower. That will do it.

I speed through tourists, skirt Wakefield Tower's circular wall and dip under the portcullis.

Right, Teufel, empty your brain before the raven cages.

Mouse hearts. I concentrate on mouse hearts, nothing but gorgeous mouse hearts, hot and steamy. Past the cages, up the big steps and across the green, the Governor's house is ablaze with lights. Outside a soldier stands to attention. This might work.

I stroll up to his shiny black boots and stare up like I want supper.
He makes a flicker of eye contact. Nothing more.

Go on! Scuttle in and tell the Governor that terrible cat's back.
He doesn't move.
Chop-chop.
I'm illegal. An invader. Banished! Arrest me! Nothing.

Okay. More direct.

I swirl his legs. Giving him a proper fur dump. Nothing. Not even a kick. Hopeless.

I leave him and jump to the Governor's window for a more direct approach. He's there. On his phone, of course. His back to me. Turn, Govvie boy, turn!

He does. The phone drops to the floor. Bingo. I jump down and sprint for home.
Through the kitchen window, the Chaplain's reading a book at the table,
while Mrs C skims the evening paper. I paw and mew at the glass.

Chaplain's face goes white with shock. Mrs C, too. I paw again.
Come on! It's me, not Jesus. Door open, I'm tight in the Chaplain's arms.
'Teufel! Teufel! I mean how? How...?'

I fight for the floor but he won't let go.

Thud.

Thud.

Thud. The door knocker knocks. Governor time.

The Chaplain, always a sharp cookie, and aware I'm not the world's most subtle cat, dumps me into the cellar while brushing frantically at his top.

He slams the door shut. Right on plan.

In the gloom, I hear the Governor.

'That cat was at my window, Chaplain.'

'You saw me take him to Battersea, Governor.'

Smart – a truth that cannot be denied.

I stare into the darkness of the cellar and scurry down the steps.

'Oi, Mushface. You down here? Slight problem with your plan.'

Mushika smiles from under the broken dresser, a chunk of cat biscuit in her mouth.

'You are pushing sanctuary way too far, mouse!'

'Excuse me?' she says, crumbs tumbling to the floor.
She comes and sits before me.

'Every time I see you, you're eating my food!'

'It's food. Not your food. This is your problem?'

I glance back to the steps.
'Well, no. I might have got wrapped up in something. But it's not my fault.'

'Such as?'

'There's been a double cross. I was lied to. You can help fix it.
I want that Oggle thing of yours.'

'My Oggle? You don't know Oggles.' She picks up a crumb and nibbles.
'What's happened?'

I circle, lost in the cellar walls.

'Those Court ghosts said they'll show me to a light on November fifth to save the world. Well, I'm suspicious, right from the off. Bonfire Night and these barbarians used to throw cats into fire! Fur-melting, flesh-bubbling fire! That's what I heard a yeoman say. Sir Wally Wonker Raleigh's all, *they have to do it because a king shouted it from his dream,* and they have to obey everything a king says. *But it's just a dream and dreams don't come true. But, but...*'

I get close and tower over her. She stays still.

'What if they're lying? Everyone lies here. What if they're really going to sacrifice me? Burn me up! Then these other ghosts come along, they're nice, tell me Court are a bunch of liars and they'll help make me famous–'

Her chewing stops.
'Who are these other ghosts?'

'Does it matter? What matters, is that to save my soul, I might be involved in a plan to bring down the whole country. This lot of ghosts want to kill the ravens at midnight. Say it will raise the nation back to her glory and bust the Court. But the Governor says, if the ravens are dead, the country will fall. I don't know. But I do know this –
I'll be killed either way, along with the Chap and Mrs Chap, and I'll get the blame for everything! You gotta help me out!'

Mushika ponders the grimy slabs of the cellar floor. The floor!

I'm in more danger than any cat ever and she's studying grit and muck!
My tail whips. Is she dim or something?

At last, she makes eye contact.
'Well, the logical solution is to sacrifice yourself
and your owners for your country.
Don't help, and die all the same. Simple.'

'I'm a cat. That ain't happening. I don't do sacrifice.
You're lucky I'm even doing responsibility!'

She scurries back to the dresser.
'If logic's not for you, how should I help?'

That better not be for more biscuits.

'I like to finish off with this,' she says, dropping some
jerky strip to the stone.

I go over and claw a piece from her.
'That Oggle thing! You said it knows everything. Ask it how to protect London.'

'Why?'

'Because,' I say, gnawing at the jerky. 'I don't trust ghosts, that's why.'

'I say again,
who?'

'An evil-eyed, lizard-armed geezer with a sideline in smooth talk. Richard III they call him, and Guy Fawkes. Your Oggle will know him. Oh, and another lying little toad called Citizen, but I reckon he'll be killed, because if they're going to do me, they'll definitely do him, so don't worry.'

'About a toad?'

'No. He's a ginger tom.'

She puts down her jerky.

'Oh, dear.
You've got yourself involved with some powerful ghosts, Teufel. I know King Richard and Guy Fawkes. Not sure I can help. I'm a little–'

'Look here, Mushface– '

'Relax. I was joking. Of course I'll help.'
She brushes her whiskers and bustles to the centre of the cellar.
'You're on track, Teufel. Don't worry. This is all excellent news.'

'What are you on about now?'

'Well...' Her whiskers flutter as she looks up.
'You said earlier, you want fame.
Fame's arrived. This is it.'

'Stop talking riddles.'

'That light on November fifth is real. That's your destiny.
Remember the cat, Zeus? Mr Death Star I first mentioned?'

'Vaguely.'
So much has happened since I arrived, I'm surprised I remember my own name.

'That's who's in the light,' Mush says. 'You're going after him. To stop his crazy idea. Only a cat can tackle a cat, that was my thinking. And I chose you. You want to be admired like your mum and dad, you want excitement. Here you are. I present to you... responsibility.'

'You what?' *Is there one inch of this place that isn't full of dingbats and dunderheads?* 'You're bonkers. Dog off. I just want friends! To be loved.'

'You're always loved, Teufel, even when you're a cat.
Now you can be the hero you always dreamed. It's an amazing opportunity.'

I stomp at her.
'This is not my idea of fame! You are what you believe.'

'No. You are what you deliver. It's better to make it than fake it.'

'Where's that Oggle thing?'

'Back in my universe. I access it through here.'
She fiddles with her ear and plucks out a small orb.

The ball hovers before us, tumbling – sparkling blue, white and yellow.

'That?'

'Yep. All the answers in every universe. So, what's the question?'

'Two things I want to know. What can save London? And how do you kill ghosts?'

The Oggle flashes red and blue, then flickers.
Sparks dance in her eyes.

'The answers are coming. The answers are coming.'

'Well, hurry!'

'Okay, they're here.' She closes her eyes. 'Here we go. What can save London? A thing called the RAF. They did a fabulous job in the 1940s, apparently... The Thames Barrier, somewhere outside London. That any use? Bit newer...'

Her eyes open, but since my stare resembles a gone-out gorilla's, they shut again, sharpish.

'Or, if we want to go back. Gunpowder. That helped in the Great Fire of 1666.'
She gives me a nervous peek. 'Any of that do?'

I stumble sick.
'A bluss-fussering pile of nonsense! That's what that is. What about ghosts? How do you kill them? Try that.'

She studies the globe. Again her eyes burst with tiny stars.
'Not much coming through... To tackle them, they feed off fear, so being nice is a suggestion. You could do an exorcism and they might leave? Or burn sage.'

'Burn herbs! Burn herbs! That Oggle's a vegan cat! Useless.
Check again! Again! Again!'

'Oooh, I've found it. How to kill ghosts. The answer is...'
Her eyes return to normal.
'Oh, dear. The connection's gone.'

The globe dims to a soft pearl. She tucks the orb back in her ear.

'What do you think we should do?'

I turn away in a huff.
Dumping it on me.
Charming.

I rack my brain, but nothing comes up, until, until, until... Magnificat!

'You can leave here, right?'

Mushika smiles.

'Find Magnificat. You know her: fat-whiskered, black and white, proper attitude. She knows London. Don't tell her why, mind. Drag her from the prayer meeting and bring her here. Say I need her. Urgent. Code word *stool* – I'll wait.'

Mushika nods.
'Stool.'

In a flash of light she's gone.
She'd better be quick.
I pad up the steps and put my ear to the door.

'We'll leave him tonight, love,' says the Chaplain. 'I'll drive him to
Catsgore in the morning.
Derek and Doris are trusted hands.
Who better than a vet?
Their Jack Russells love cats.'

A vet!
You're putting me with a vet, with terriers, in a place called Catsgore!
Can things be any worse? I pad back down, slump at the jerky and comfort-eat the whole lot, then throw up.

Mushika is hours. My mind flashes on her: lost, arrested or killed. She's taking too long.
Finally, a spark flares by the dresser. She sits on the floor, beaming.

I stomp over.
'Where've you been: Australia?'

She gets up on her hind legs and lifts out a paw.
Magnificat mists in next to it, rubbing an eye.
Mushika puts out her other paw.
Another mist forms. Doggin' Citizen! Frazzled,
tight-whiskered, ears back, tail a-flick.

'What's he doing here?'

'You said he'd be killed. He needed to know. Took me ages to find him.
The more of us the better, that's what I figured. Explaining everything, he's definitely
been double-crossed. He's on our side now. He's a lawyer's cat. We can trust him.'

A grin spreads across her face – she's enjoying this!

Magnificat shakes her whiskers.
'Erm, what's going on? Why was I dragged from prayer by a
mouse using a code word?'
She twitches at Citizen.
'And who's that?'

Mushika shoots up the table leg and sits above us, paws up.
'Now, this is exciting. So, the thing is, our darling Teufel's got himself involved
in a plot with Richard III, Guy Fawkes and Citizen here. But it seems Citizen is being
lied to, too. Not part of my plan, but life's challenges are adventures.'

Magnificat scowls.
'Plan?'

M

I flick my tail.
'Nothing to do with me.'

Mushika nods.
'Yes. Teufel's going into the light for me.'

Magnificat's jaw drops.
'How do you know about the light?'

'I planted it in King Henry's dream. *Woo... fire, havoc and war.* You're not the only ones who can play in dreams.'

'You? A mouse?'

'I, a mouse. A mouse who knows all your history.'

Magnificat laughs. But the laugh is nervous. Like it might be true.
'So, you're saying, idiot brain here
is in a plot with two of the most powerful ghosts in the country.
They're the traitorous energy Court's been feeling?'
She turns to me, her glare brutal.
'That's proper treason!'

Mushika scurries back down the table leg.

Citizen steps forward.
'Richard and Fawkes work for me. It's my plot. And I want my collar back, Teufel.'

I barge at him. A fight won't save Mr and Mrs C, but it will feel good.

Mushika gets between us.
'There isn't time for squabbles.'

'Dog off!' I say, but back away, shuffling my fur down...
I'm so doing him later.

Citizen faces Magnificat.
'Since Richard has other plans, the fox shall become the lion.'

I'm beyond puzzled.
'But why?'

'Because my owner was imprisoned here for nothing. Because I died here for nothing. I want revenge.'

Magnificat prowls forward, her tail up.
'My owner was imprisoned, too. When are you from?'

'Eighteen sixty-seven.'

'I'm sixteen hundred and one. Why haven't I seen you?'

'He buried me inside a wall in Beauchamp Tower
to guard against evil spirits. Stuffed by a democratic republican! Spiritual cavity cat insulation after a lifetime with the miserable pen-pusher. How do you get a decent eternity from that?'

Magnificat cocks her head.
'Why didn't you mist it?'

'I didn't know about misting. There weren't any ghosts, in the four inches of wall I was in, to tell me about it. And the woodlice say nothing to no one, arrogant little rocks.'

Mushika jumps up and down.
'Can we focus on the matter at hand, please? How to escape this mess. Magnificat, you're the Tower guru. How can we stop Richard and Fawkes?'

Magnificat's tail curls and flicks as her whiskers tighten.
'I'm not sure you can.'

'There must be something?' Mushika says. 'What about Raleigh; the guards?'

Magnificat shakes her head.
'More bluster than bludgeon, all of them. And ghost powers don't work on other ghosts. We need something bigger. Much bigger. What do they call them, now? Gog and Magog, the giant guardians of London, but no one's seen them for a thousand years. Raven King, same problem – lost for millennia. Making Big Ben chime thirteen times, that's supposed to raise the Trafalgar Square lions. They'd be strong enough. But how do you make a clock strike thirteen?'

'You change the strike wheel,' I say.
Everyone gorm-eyes me.

'You what?' says Magnificat.

'The strike wheel determines how long the bell strikes. The larger the gap between the grooves, the longer the bell chimes. If we block the groove after the twelfth, which is the first groove, the bell will move over and strike a thirteenth time.'

Mushika scurries to my paws.
'You sure?'

'Yes. I watched Chap build that wooden one on the mantelpiece.
He carved loads before getting one right.'

Magnificat gruffs.
'So, what you're saying is that we go to Big Ben, which is miles away, and at the stroke of midnight, with a clock we've never seen, which is higher than a mountain top and probably bigger than a house, we stick something in and ta-da! Big Ben chimes thirteen?'

'Clocks are clocks.'

Her head drops. 'We'll need Elvis.'

My heart follows her head.

'Who's Elvis?' ask Mushika and Citizen.

Magnificat's fur bristles.
'Elvis rules the Thames between here and Westminster. Knows everything and everywhere. He'll know how to get in Big Ben, and I bet he can find whatever we need to make it strike thirteen, too.
However, there's a rather larger problem.'

Mushika stares.
'Which is?'

'Thundermouth, care to explain?' says Magnificat.

Everyone's eyes fall on me.
'He's a rat! I told him to do one, as any self-respecting cat would.'

Citizen's giving me proper cat disgust 'you're an idiot' glare-eyes.

'You included!' I shout.
'You've all manipulated me. I've been nothing but honest and friendly since I got here. But I'll tell you this, if kowtowing to a rat is the only way to beat Richard and Fawkes, I'll do it. I will raise those lions!
Now, are we doing this or not?'

Citizen attends a scratch.
'And how are you going to persuade this giant rat?'

I haven't thought of that.

'We need perfume,' says Magnificat.
'Lots of perfume. And fast.'

Waterloo clock booms eleven big bongs.

Magnificat's look suggests stupid before I even ask.
'How will perfume help?'

'The sewer pong kills Elvis's pride every day,' she says. 'But they're safe down there It's a home. If we can find enough nice smells, as a trade, and explain why, he just might help. We need what? Directions and metal? That can't cost much.'

Mushika's little hand scratches at my paw.
'Perfumes galore upstairs.'

I stare down.
'Is there anywhere you haven't been in *MY* house?'

'Our house is lovely,' she smiles. 'And I have other news. For now, it's up to you. There's a message from home in the Oggle. I have to go. Good luck!'

She disappears. Leaves us!

'A vanishing mouse,' says Citizen. 'How the–?'

Magnificat's tail flicks.
'What devil juice is that thing?'

'You lot mist,' I say, 'she does something similar, I think.
We don't have time. Come on!'

At the top of the cellar, the kitchen is silent. Magnificat stares the doorknob open and we creak out. In the hall, past TV light flickering from the lounge, we race up the stairs. On the bedroom dresser, like a mini glass city are eleven bottles of perfume.

'Got a box?' says Magnificat.

'Under the bed,' I say.

Citizen pushes out a shoebox and flips it, sending old photographs sliding across the floor. Magnificat glides the perfumes down.

'Take them to the sluice gate,' she says. 'You know it?'

Citizen nods.

'We'll get Elvis. Be quick.'

Downstairs and out through the kitchen window, Waterloo's clock ticks towards the quarter-hour. Doggin' time. Slow when you watch, fast when you don't.

'Around the back,' says Magnificat. 'We need to keep you out of sight.'

We weave through the shadows, past the chapel and over a wall. At the secret passage, Magnificat slides the bricks out.

'In you go.'

After tunnels of drippy dark and stinky stinks, we reach the sluice gate.

Magnificat mists her head through the iron and shouts.
'London is in danger! Fetch Elvis!'

From the silent gloom, tiny splashes fade into the distance.

She pulls back.
'Now, we wait.'

'Wait? How long? The clock is ticking. Ticking!'

'Elvis won't be long. His spies are everywhere.'

Minutes pass. Walls drip. Gloops gloop. Plops plop. Smells party in your nostrils. A galloping sound crashes up the tunnel. Elvis thunders to us. Long, brown face, black eyes, high ears, pink nose and full cheeks. Through a drain shaft we hear Waterloo's clock strike the quarter hour.

'What a nerve!' Elvis bellows.
'Disturb my sermon! Insult me, fart at me, and
now call me like a common dog!'
He pushes at the gate, snarling, long, yellow teeth.
'My guard said danger. What nonsense is this? We should fight!
Come here and fight, cat! Try someone your own size.'

'I'm not here to fight,' I say, 'though I could... I need your help, fast.'

He grabs the iron.
'You cats think you are kings!
Fight, then. We'll see who needs help, fast.'

Magnificat comes to my side.
'Elvis, my name is Magnificat. He's a fool and rude. Stupid. But we do need you.
The whole country is in danger, not only London. I know you love our city.'

The rat's anger seems to ease.
'Sister. With you I have no problem. You are passed,
beyond life, praise the Lord.
We have seen you watching. Ghosts are all over this city.
Yet this cat,' he pauses and hisses at me like an angry tom, 'who
treats others as less than himself.
Tell me what should I do? Why should I help this... dog!'

Huffing sounds behind us.

'Because we have these,' says Citizen.
He clunks the shoebox to the floor.

Elvis's nose twitches.
'What *this* is this? And who are you?'

'Scents,' says Magnificat. 'Citizen's brought eleven wonderful Eau du Parfum and
Eau de Toilette from the finest perfumeries of Paris, just for you!'

Elvis pulls his head back.
'What use are women's scents!
The ladies love me. I don't need presents.'
He shakes his long nose and turns away,
scaly tail flicking the gate as he leaves.

'Great plan, Magsi,' I whisper.

'Elvis, please!' Magnificat calls. 'This is to save London. Your London. Our London!'

'We have men's scents, too!' calls Citizen.

Elvis's head turns.
'You do?'

'We do!'

Elvis swaggers back.
'Show me.'

Citizen tips the box over. Chaplain's bathroom aftershaves fall out with the perfumes. Genius!

'A black one,' says Citizen, 'a red one and a blue!'

'Let me sniff,' Elvis says.

Citizen hovers over the black one and sprays a burst towards the gate.

Elvis's nose twizzles in the spicy, woody mist.
'This, I like! We can maybe begin to deal. But,' his eyes narrow,
'why only three? I like things in hundreds.'

'This is all he had,' Citizen says.

'Then there is no help.'
Elvis steps back.

'We'll find you more after,' pleads Magnificat, 'promise. Hundreds.
It's practically all men here.'

'And what help do you need for this pitiful trade?'

'We need lots of metal,' I say. 'Flat pieces of strong metal. Delivered to Big Ben.'

He leers at me dog-like, then turns to Magnificat.
'Why?'

Magnificat gets to the gate.
'Bad ghosts have a plan to kill the Tower's ravens at midnight. If we can make Big Ben
chime thirteen times it will raise The Lions of Trafalgar who can save them.
The ravens protect Britain. The lions protect London.
We want you to help protect both.'

'You want a rat to help set giant cats loose in London?'

'Yes.'

His nose scrunches.
'Hmmm. Do you think I'm a fool?'

I step in.
'There's no time for you deciding what is and isn't true.
Can you find the metal or not?'

'Of course I can find metal. This is my city.'

'The lions will stop the bad ghosts,' Magnificat says.

'And you promise big cats will be no issue for super handsome big rat?'

'Absolutely,' says Magnificat. 'They protect all Londoners. You're London. You are a Londoner. That's the rule.'

Elvis ponders, sniffing at the new fragrant air.
'But if these bad ghosts will kill the ravens at midnight,
and you are at Big Ben at midnight, the ravens die.
Who's the fool?'

'They need this idiot to do it,' says Magnificat, swiping a paw at me.
'When they see he's not there, they will have to plan again. That's our opportunity.'

My fur bristles.
'I am not an idiot.'

'Hmmm,' says Elvis. 'I am not helping him.
And there is too much hope in your plan.
But a handsome rat will bring some help to save London.
Leave this gate open and I will assist.
Where are these ravens? We have never been inside the Tower.'

Citizen flicks his head back.
'Down there, until the dead end. You'll see bricks with the mortar gone.
Shove those out and you can get through. White Tower's down the slope. Can't miss it.
The bricks are–'

'You lot! This is a saving my life moment, thank you! Can we do less details?
More action. He doesn't need a tour. We're dithering! Midnight is coming.'

Elvis growls at me.
'Details deliver destiny, fool.
And if you even think of double-crossing me,
destiny will be me chewing on your soul, eight days a week!
Get to Big Ben, and maybe I won't fight you.'

'You and whose army?'

'Mine.' Elvis scowls into the tunnel.

'Oh, Stinger!'

Hundreds of eyes appear in the gloom.

A grubby, white rat with pink eyes scurries forward.

'Yes, Pastor.'

'Tell Nick the Nicker. We need metal.
Lots of flat metal for this idiot.
As much as he has. All sizes. Strong stuff. To Big Ben.
Use the main sewer, and fast.
Go!'

'The big sewer?' says Stinger. 'Do I have to?'
He seems nervous.

'Rat up. I have told you a thousand times, it's only water.
Meet at Big Ben, fast as you can. That door by the left.
You know it?'

Stinger nods and splashes away into the dark.

'How do we get there?' I ask, remembering the boat. 'It's miles.'

Elvis studies us.
'The sewer is faster than that tin-can tube thing and no stops.
You swim strong and hard?'

We shake our heads.

'You run hard and fast for a long time?'

We shake our heads.

'Your problem, not mine.'

Magnificat's eyes sparkle. There's that demented boat grin.
'We'll get a taxi!'

Magnificat and Citizen haul up the sluice gate, ready for Elvis later. And I stand there, paws in gunk, wishing I was in Devon, a normal vicar's cat. But then I remember, I am my mother's son, Gauis's son. A believer in myself. A warrior. And time runs.

'That's Elvis sorted,' says Magnificat. 'Now a cab.'

Outside the Tower up the roadway, is a dual carriageway.
Paws on pavement, I point out the next obvious insanity.

'How do we stop a taxi? You better have this planned out, Magnificat.'

'Of course I do. You sit there,' she indicates to the kerb, 'and don't move. Act like you're waiting for food. One will stop. Stick their noses in anything, cabbies.'

'Really?'

'Comes with the job. They get bored. Remember, black beetle shape, yellow light on top. That's what you want.'

I'm not sure I trust her, but what can I do? I sit by the kerb and she disappears into the shadows with Citizen. Which is all fine and dandy for them, because they're not being blasted with exhaust fumes and roars from every vehicle in London, except a London cab!

From over the Tower walls, Waterloo clock strikes half eleven.
In thirty minutes, Chap and Mrs C will be dead. Unless I get a move on.

'We need to get going,' I shout.
'I'm getting poisoned here. This is useless!'

Magnificat pokes out from the bushes.
'Welcome to London. A queue of one is a dream. Wait. Best of British!'

In a whoosh and a roar, two lights blind up the road. I get excited. But it's motorbikes and they zoom past. Staring back down the road. Tootling along is a stocky black-beetle shape. The hump of a London taxi, the For Hire sign a glorious yellow.

'Stare at the road,' calls Magnificat. 'Don't look at the cab!'

What's she on about now?
'Why?' I call.

'Just do it!'

I do as she says. The taxi trundles past. Goes straight down the carriageway.

I stomp over to Magnificat.
'Why did you say that? Why?'

She comes onto the pavement. Her face a droop.
'It was a great plan. I know cabbies.'

Citizen joins us. He nudges Magnificat's shoulder and tracks his eyes up the road.
The cab's reversing!

'What do I do?' I say.

'The window will come down,' says Mags. 'Jump through. Straight into the back and sit expectantly. Classic perplex-a-human cat stuff and leave the rest to me.'

She pulls Citizen back into the bushes.

That's no detail at all. But I do as she says and sit waiting for the cab. The taxi finishes reversing. The passenger window glides down.

A driver – bald, pink-faced, with thick brown glasses,
leans across the wheel, scratching his stubble.
'On your jack, little fella?'

I walk over, and as instructed leap through the window and clamber for the back-seat.

The driver cranks his head around.
'You can't be in here, geeze. I've got fares to get.'

Magnificat and Citizen mist in by my side. I turn to Magnificat.
'And?'

'Stare him out,' she answers. 'Confusing humans for fun. Know it?'

Of course I know it.
'Then what?'

'Watch.'

She nods to Citizen. From my peripheral vision, I see him stare at a switch in the cab door. A light above it turns red. The driver's face puzzles.

His voice booms.
'You ain't gonna ask for Battersea, are ya?'

The switch has activated the intercom. I keep up my stare.
Magnificat mists off somewhere. The driver's eyes, blue and kind, sit in a squidgy pillow of pink skin – he likes his pies this one. Suddenly, he turns ghost-white.
Eyes horrified. Sweat trickles his cheeks.

Citizen starts to purr.
'She's artful.' He gives me a nudge. 'What do you think?'

I'm confused. I guess it's Magnificat.
'What's she doing?'

'She's in his head. Shouting. He thinks it's you.'

The driver turns back to the road,
hands locked to the steering wheel.
'Big Ben, right you are. Shouldn't take a jiffy, Sir.'
He slams the accelerator.

The engine thumps and grunts.

I slide into the seat.
Magnificat reappears.

Citizen gleams.
'Very smart. You're good.'

She nods.
'Fastest taxi in history coming up.'

'What did you say?' I ask.

Citizen laughs.
'She said, *They call me the Devil.*
Big Ben in three minutes, please.
Black's a wonderful colour for Halloween.'

'How far is it?' I ask.

'Two and a bit miles,' says Magnificat, licking a paw.
The taxi crunches gears. We scream down the street. Offices blur.
Into a tunnel, the engine thunders and growls.

Back out, Thames
to the left,
moored ships shutter through the trees
we *z o o m* red lights, bounce
kerbs, ride pavements,
everything to get past other vehicles.

The river curves and Big Ben comes into view. The Gothic tower and its white clocks. The Houses of Parliament beneath, all spires and turrets. The taxi takes a right, a left and skids to a stop by Big Ben. Magnificat mists the door and we jump out as the taxi screeches away.

Above, a clock face shows 11.42.

My eyes dart.
'Where's the entrance?'

'No idea,' says Mags, scanning the wall of spiked railings.

I leap up, squeeze through a gap and drop to the other side.
Magnificat and Citizen follow.

Citizen sets off left.
'Elvis said this way.'

We find an entrance hall with a wooden door.
A sign in precise, white lettering says,

CLOCK TOWER

Black iron protects the lock.

Citizen looks up.
'What now?'

'We wait,' says Magnificat.

'We don't have time,' I say. 'You sure he'll turn up? This is a rat.'

'He's a Londoner,' she says.

'You da cats?' a scraggy voice scratches.

THIRTY SIX

The rat poking around the far corner of the Clock Tower's entrance hall is grey, ear torn, and silver whiskered.

'I said: you da cats?'

'No,' I say, 'we're elephants.'

He steps out and totters forward.
'Less of the sarcasm. Can't see so much.
I'm Nicker. Got a delivery for ya. Metal plate?'

'Yes!' says Magnificat, rushing to him.

Onto his hindquarters, he lifts his hands up.
'Let me present – the world's finest steel.
My Sheffield collection! Boys!'

He collapses down and coughs. As he does, a mischief of rats tumbles into the entrance hall. Over, under and around. Black rats, brown rats, greys and whites. A forest of twitchy whiskers and snaky tails. Wedged in mouths are pieces of steel plate: thick steel, thin steel, larger bits are being dragged. Seething rats cover the floor.

'Dump 'em here?' Nicker says.

'No.' I gesture to the door. 'In and up.'

He gazes to the buttressed ceiling.
'You mean all the cattin' way to the top of this cattin' tower?'

'Yep!'

He shakes his head.
'Sorry. Steel to Big Ben. That was the job. Job done.
No mention of stairs, and I bet there ain't a lift.'

'Of course there's a lift,' I say. 'No human's gonna climb that. They're idiots, but not that idiot.'

'I ain't convinced,' he says.
'Now, if you've got cheese. A mountain.
We can talk.'

'But,' says Magnificat, 'Big Ben is up there! The bell of the clock is Big Ben.
This is the clock tower. You've not finished the job.'

'You got proof of that?' says the rat. 'Everyone knows this is Big Ben.
Common parlance, as they say.'

Huge rings sing above us. The clock striking the quarter bells of 11.45.

'It's a national emergency!' says Magnificat.

'Not my problem.
Boys. Drop your loads.'

Metal hits stone.

'Clear da path!' thunders a voice. 'Clear da path!'

Rats part. Elvis bounds through, drenched in sewer-stink and spicy-woody aftershave.

'That was quick!' I say.

He laughs a hearty, rat laugh.
'Sewer's super-fast if you are a king swimmer!'
He surveys the dropped metal.
'What is the problem here, Nicker?'

Nicker startles.
'No problem, boss. Just, waiting.'

Nicker turns to the rats.
'Lads! Pick up your loads. No resting. Cheese later, cheese later.'

'Now,' says Elvis, turning to us, 'what do we do?
How will Mr Stinky Bottom Attitude here,
save our world with this steel?'

I ignore his insult.
'We're going up.'

Elvis strides over to the door.
Pushes with one hand, then two, then headbutts it.
'Locked!'

Citizen pads over.
'Not when you're a ghost.'

'Stand back,' says Magnificat.

They both focus on the keyhole.
A click and the door swings open.

Elvis's eyes dance with delight.
'You can do that to locks?'

Citizen curls his tail.
'Yep.'

'We're running out of time, folks!' I say.

Elvis turns to his rats.
'Boys! Up!'

They pick up their loads and pile into the Clock Tower. Inside, through another door, tight stone steps track up, floor by floor. Everyone's whiskers droop peering into the vertical abyss.

'Hundreds of steps!' a rat says.

'Move!' booms Elvis. 'No complaining!'

I leap for the first step. Rats follow, metal in mouth.
Citizen and Mags float up the void in the middle.

'We'll do the door,' says Citizen as he passes.

I signal okay and race up.

'What are we searching for?' says Magnificat.

'A cogged wheel.'

She nods and they shoot up the chamber.
A few moments later, Magnificat calls,
'Found it!'

Elvis bellows.
'Up, my friends! Up!'

The rats haul faster and faster. Another four storeys, we reach Citizen and Magnificat. They are slumped, crest-fallen.

'So,' I pant.

They swing the door open.
Down a set
of
steps, in a plain square room, is an iron clock
the size of a van!

Above the timepiece, a huge beam goes through walls to drive the clock faces. High windows show bits of each one. Black-iron hands coming together on all sides of London. The minute hands tick closer to midnight. But I can't see how close we are. The clock mechanism, also black iron, is behind a guard rail. A maze of wheels and cogs, levers and rods – all different sizes. It's sixty-three million times more complicated than Chap's wooden one!
I can't see where it starts or stops.

A massive clank and clatter. Rats drop steel to stone. Wheezing and puffing trying to recover from the stairs. I step through the seething mass of fur. Clock parts move.

Tick. Tock. Tick. Tock. Tick. Tock.

I leap to the railing and, with a twist, jump for the big beam above. I hang there half-on, half-off, pulling myself higher, dragging every muscle, every snack and biscuit onto the beam. Finally I make it.

I get up and look down on the workings. There must be twenty wheels! Chaplain's had five. What am I going to do? Through the windows the clock faces move on.
Another minute ticks by. Gone. Two are left.

Magnificat appears next to me.
'Well?'

'I'm looking!'

Among all the iron levers, cogs and barrels are three brass wheels.
The back one shows numbers for seconds around the rim.
The two at the front, hours and minutes. The seconds wheel surges on. It's fast. I'm sure it's fast. The minute wheel ticks again.

ONE MINUTE

Wheels and cogs.
So many! What am I looking for? Cogs.

There are big cog wheels. Small ones. I need one that looks different.
I can't see it. I can't see it. The clock ticks forward again.
Frantic, I check the other side of the beam. Nothing. I lean forward, peering under.

Below, rats watch.

And there I see it.

In from the left, in front of two large cog wheels, is a smaller one with different placed gaps around the circle.

'That's it. That's the strike wheel!'

I leap from the beam and scoot under the guard rail.
The clock shudders and whirs. A paddle near the ceiling spins.

Midnight is moments away.

'Magnificat, Citizen, here now!' I scream above the din.

Elvis shouts to the rats.
'Present metal!'

The wheezing rats grab their steel. Held high in their mouths, across backs, in little hands. I scan the rodents. These pieces. Nothing is right! Too big. Too thick. Too small. Wait – that – that one there. There!

'You,' I shout. 'No. Not you. You. You! That must fit.'

The grey rat lifts its piece, scurries forward. Drops it at my paws.
'Mags, C – hover it up now!'

Magnificat and C focus on the steel. It jiggles towards the clock.
'Jam it in the smallest gap on that wheel. Cover the edge and don't let go!'

Up close, it doesn't fit!

SECONDS LEFT. SECONDS!
BIG BEN STARTS ITS QUARTER BELLS MELODY.

'Drop it! Drop it!' I scream.

I barge through the rats, scanning every mouth. There! I swipe a piece from a young rat and with a swoop of paw, bash it up to Citizen and Magnificat. They grab it with a hover and shove it into the wheel. Citizen grimaces. Magnificat strains. The metal hovers and it fits.

It fits!

'Don't move!' I cry. 'If it falls we're done for!'

The clock goes mad. Paddles on the ceiling rotate. Iron whirs and clacks. A lever wedged in the strike wheel lifts. The piece falls!

'Magnificat! Hold that steel!'

And then it comes. The huge fur-shaking, soul-rattling boom as Big Ben strikes! A long *BONG!* blasts the room. Mags and C almost burst getting the steel back in place.

BONG!

Other steel drops everywhere as rats cover their ears.

BONG!

Mine scream in pain.

BONG! BONG!

The lever tracks towards the steel.

The steel wobbles.
'Hold it! Hold it!'

BONG! BONG!

Mags and Citizen crumble, but they keep their gaze on the metal. Only Elvis stands.

'Keep that steel!' I cry.

But Mags and C can't hear now. The noise is too loud. Too frequent.

BONG! BONG! BONG!

The steel wobbles. The steel will fall.

BONG!

They're losing hold, and two more strikes to go.

BONG!

That's the twelfth! The lever hits. The steel stutters.

My friend's eyes bulge like popcorn.

The metal quivers. At the final second. It will fall.
It is falling.
Hold it my friends, hold it! Please. Citizen launches at the metal. The lever scrapes across. It drags slow and shuddery over the steel right at Citizen's face and–

A thirteenth Big Ben bong bounds across the room.

B O N G !

We did it! Magnificat and Citizen fall in a crumpled heap of wobbly mist. The steel clanks on the floor, the clock whirs and clicks. Rats stare and then everything is quiet except the tick-tock rhythm of the rimless spoke wheel.

I stagger to my paws, ears ringing like wedding bells.
Elvis stands like nothing happened.

'We've done it!' I cry.

Elvis laughs.
'Now, for my boys.'

'Boys?'

'The lions of Africa!'

THIRTY SEVEN

Hundreds of feet above, the long, black hand of Big Ben's north face sweeps to six minutes past midnight. The rats have left, except Elvis.

I turn to Magnificat.
'Why aren't they here? They're giant lions. What are they doing, catching a bus? We're in trouble here. No lions! No nothing!'

She signals to a grand, wide road.
'Less than a mile, down there. They'll be here.'

There's nothing but tall buildings and distant traffic.
Red double-decker buses pass a stone column, black taxis queue. We're doomed.

Elvis thumps over the lawn after Citizen. Above the buses, the air ripples and shifts – a hazy black churns. Something's there.
Two shapes, black and molten, flow over the taxis. Another two above the buses.

Four gigantic black lions – their skin liquid metal.

I shout across the grass.
'Citizen! Elvis! Get your tails here, now!'

Magnificat grins. Polishes her whiskers.
'Told you.'

Elvis evil-eyes Citizen as they return. Citizen doesn't seem to give a dog's bum.
'Hurry up, will you!' I shout.

The lions pass in a swoosh. Big, swept manes, tails high, fat paws.
Coats a shimmery carbon.
Cats are the best.
I pump myself for the landing.

Twenty feet tall, they touch down with the grace and power of ballet stars. Taut and strong, ripped muscles. The lions rub cheeks, heads high, then sit facing Big Ben, bushy tails flicking. Elvis drums his back feet and starts to dance.

I sprint to the lions.
'Boys!'

No response.

They can't hear. I get in front of them and shout up.
'Boys!'

The nearest sneers down, rolls his eyes,
and returns to staring at the clock tower.

'Oi!' I call.

He looks again. An explosion of noise smashes my face.
He roars, 'Oi? You oi a lion of Trafalgar? Shoo titch! National emergency.'

I stand firm.
'I'm the one who called you.'

The lions' noses twitch with disgust.
'We,' the middle one gruffs, 'are summoned by Royals only.
Not pandered wimps, who wouldn't know an elephant from a meerkat!'

'I made Big Ben strike!'

'Hyena farts, you did. Off with you.'

Magnificat races over.
'Gentlemen, Queen Elizabeth II is in danger, and I can assure you he rang the bell.'
She steps forward, high-pawed, tail up like they are personal acquaintances.

Citizen and Elvis follow.

The lions stare down. 'The Queen?'

'Yes,' says Mags. 'I am of King Henry VI's Court at the present Tower;
and from Queen Elizabeth I's reign.'

The lions stand, puff their manes and flex their claws.
'Right you are, then. That's proper history. So, who's the problem?'

'The ghosts of Richard III and Guy Fawkes are at the Tower, trying to kill the ravens.
They die, the country falls. It's a legend as true as your own.
Or at least, we think. We need you to mash 'em up!'
She squeals with excitement.

'Mash 'em up?' the furthest lion puzzles.
She floats up to his face. 'Smash them to smithereens!'

'Two piddly human ghosts won't be anything at all.
I'm George, pleased to meet you,
that's Edward, Henry and Charles.
That Dickie Dick's a proper bad 'un.
Shakespeare said it all. We'll have him good.'

Magnificat's fur flushes, whiskers beam.
'I was a friend of Willy's. I'm Magnificat. That's Teufel, Citizen; the rat is Elvis.'

'Cats and a rat, strange, but... Welcome aboard.' He nods to his back.

The other lions dip and offer their backs too. I clamber up Edward, and do a claw test on his carbony metal skin. Before my tips are even in, the lions leap. I hang on, claws deep as we soar into the night, whooshing by Big Ben and over Westminster Bridge.

Magnificat is on George, smiling her whiskers off.
'This is better than the boat!'

Citizen is buried in his lion's mane, head down. Meanwhile, Elvis is doing a one-rat conga on his. We follow railway tracks over South London as, in the distance, Tower Bridge shines. The Tower's next door. We'll be there in moments.

I shout to Citizen.
'This will be easy! These lions are awesome!'

His face appears, then buries back in the lion's neck. We swoop over a cathedral, past *HMS Belfast* and across the Thames.

Magnificat scrambles to her lion's ear.
'There!' she shouts. 'Come in low. You see the pier, and the trees?'

The lion nods.

'To the right is Traitors' Gate.
Land on the roof, spring to the circular one, that's Wakefield Tower.
From there we drop to Tower Green, right by the ravens. Showtime!'

The lion roars. All four dive. We touch off the wharf, leap over Traitors' Gate and land on the roof of Wakefield Tower.

Below, on the green beneath White Tower, the ravens lie fallen by a line of rotten meat at the staircase. Above, Fawkes is loosening scaffold clamps, while Richard III stands smiling on a chunk of upturned rock to the right of the ravens' cages. He's in full combat armour and a weird gold-and-black hat. He's gazing into a black hole, one hand behind his back, the other playing with his hair.

We're just in time.

Then it all goes horribly wrong.

THIRTY EIGHT

Richard takes a step back on the rock. From the hole, comes a swarming torrent of ghouls. They soar and spiral into the sky. Grey-scarred faces, burnt scalps, they lurch left and right. Twisted arms tipped with spirals of horn fingernails slash and grab at the night.

Magnificat screams from her lion.
'What are they?'

I go for casual. 'Richard mentioned a pit.'

'The pit! That's a state secret!'

'Releasing moms didn't seem that bad?'

Her face is rage and fear.
'Teufel! You idiot! You gullible, stupid, stupid idiot! They're not moms.
That's the Monsters of Men! MOM. The Monsters of Men!'

I'm about to explain when the lions jump. My claws slam back into Edward's mane but we don't even land. Mid-air, the ghouls attack.

Hideous faces rage and scream; nails *stab*, teeth snap.

The lions swipe with thick, black paws. Elvis clambers up his lion's neck and joins in. But the ghouls keep coming. More and more. Over us. Under us. It's a torrent of evil and hate. The brave lions spin and spin. Smash and smash, ghoul after ghoul. But slowly and surely, they are being overpowered. I hang upside down on Edward, a ghoul clambers at me. Gnarled, void eyes; ragged, stick arms grasp and grope, its twisted hornlike nails break off to daggers. The ghoul lurches and swipes for my head.

With no choice, I fall. I tumble through the air and crash to the grass.

On the lawn, winded, helpless, broken, I gaze through the mist. Richard jumps up and down on the rock. He laughs as more ghouls soar, each more scarred and scorched than the last.

It's like they're from deeper in the ground, from deeper in pain and torment. And now they are free. Free and hungry for flesh and revenge.

Fawkes is at White Tower's door. He reaches to his hat and pulls two long sticks from behind the feather. Matches. Big matches. Huge, super-long matches. Firework matches! He must have gunpowder.

I scramble to the fallen ravens. They look dead. But Baldrick's chest quivers.
He's just alive.

The others, too. But above them is the scaffold. And above the scaffold are the lions and my friends. And the lions are losing and my friends can do no more.

With a thud, Magnificat falls to my right. Her cap tumbles away. She doesn't move.

Citizen falls. He smacks the ground, too.

I look for Elvis. He's still fighting, but three ghouls attack and he too falls. He hits the lawn hard, rolls, and with a glance at the doomed lions, legs it!
Deserts us! Saving his life! Doggin' rats!

The energy above changes. **Dark, heavy menace**.
'Magnificat!' I shout, 'Move! Move!'

Magnificat tries to stumble up. I race over and bundle her out of the way as George crashes down. Our breaths heave. George is still. Citizen drags himself through the mist. Edward falls behind him. Henry. Then Charles. The lions are slabs of black shadow. Flat, motionless.

Above, the ghouls soar. Screaming victory. More join in. The moonlight goes. Covered in a grey blanket of death.

I lie frozen in shock, shattered, a living corpse. Magnificat grabs her cap then huddles with Citizen. Richard sweeps from the rock and hovers over us.

'Hello little kitties,' he says. 'And traitor, Citizen. Nippy isn't it? Warming up later.'
He nods at me. 'Mr Tinklepaws, thank you...'

From behind his back, he brings a brown leather pouch and shakes it at me.
'The lovely bag of secrets. Terribly grateful you knew who had it. I wrote you a little ditty. Shall we sing a song? It's especially for you and your friends...
you'll know the tune.'

Richard looks over to the ravens.

'Four and twenty blackbirds baked in a pie.
If you haven't got enough, add some cats to die.'

He smiles at the fallen lions, then at me. 'I need a bigger dish.'

I try to stand, but my body won't work – until I make it.
'Dog off, stink breath!' I say, wobbling on my paws.
I get up higher, onto my hind legs.
'Who are ya?' I shout, but collapse down.

Magnificat and Citizen stagger up.

Richard gazes into the spiral swarm of ghouling ghouls.
'Now, who to pick? Who's really, really fun?'

'Do one, Tudor!' I cry. That's all I can muster. If I die, I die being rude.

Richard turns to White Tower and shouts at Fawkes.
'Get down here and find Bran, will you. He's not out.
Black holes of death are not a king's work!'

Fawkes points to his feet, I'm guessing at the gunpowder.

'Even your team defy you,' I say. 'You child-murdering lump of twisted dog poo on sick! I'd rather die than be like you.'

Richard sneers and lifts his face away.
'I'm just a king. It's what we do.'
He turns back, glaring at me.
'And you will die. A thousand times! Thank you for everything, but you lose!
Everyone always does to a king.
Now, it's time to finish these ravens with a little show. I present, Mr Guy Fawkes!'
He turns to the staircase.
'As they say in those new, magical picture shows! The stage is yours, Sir! Light 'em up!'

Richard swoops to Fawkes who brings the matches above his head and strikes them.
Nothing happens. He tries again. They won't spark. He tries them against the wall.
Nothing.
Safety matches! Ha!

Richard glances up to the ghouls.
'Just a minute, lovelies.'

The monsters swirl with a collective, droning, snake-like hiss.

'Soon coming,' he says. 'Boys and girls. Soon coming.'

'What's coming?' says Citizen.

Guy drops the matches. He yanks at the doors with both hands. They won't open. Double ha!

'What's happening?' I say to Magnificat.

'Magnetic locks.
Here and Waterloo Barracks. They need more force. You can't just mist it.
Too much value inside. The Tower doesn't rely on old keys.'

'What do they want from inside?' says Citizen.

'I don't know,' I say.

Citizen touches my shoulder.
'Look!'

The lions are rising! They stagger up, shake their heads and leap to the sky. Into the ghouls, they swipe and swipe. Ghouls descend from the hissing cloud, get struck and tumble to the lawn, gnarled faces slashed with terror. The lions bash and bash. More ghouls fall. The lions are winning! But the full cloud descends. And it's a swarm of stabbing, biting hate. A lion crashes to the ground. The next, the next, the next.

'Brothers!' a voice booms.

From beyond White Tower's staircase comes Elvis, followed by a wall of rats!

'Retaliate! Retaliate!' he cries.

Rats are coming from all sides of the lawn. Elvis has brought hundreds, thousands! They swarm the ghouls on the ground, leaping and biting. The ghouls bash them away, but rat after rat comes back for more. Other rats race up the scaffolding, hunting Fawkes and Richard, who are both yanking at the doors. Richard boots a clump of rats away and swoops back to the hole. He hovers above the pit and peers in. Then he starts to laugh maniacally.

He gets close, right to the edge, pulls his hands to his mouth and whistles.
Then he clambers into the hole.

Magnificat scrambles to me.
'If Bran's down there and he gets him, we're done for.'

'Bran?'

'The head of a king. A head that can control the dead. Every ghost in the world.
You give him a command and he does it. He's been lost for centuries.
Buried somewhere. From a tribe of Welsh giants.'

'Richard was learning Welsh.' I gulp. 'The word for come.'

Richard rises from the hole. Straight-backed, hands playing with his black-and-gold hat.
He's sitting on something black.

'He's on Bran!' I scream.

'That's no giant!' says Magnificat.

A long snout lifts out of the hole. Crusted in grime. Yellow snakelike eyes open.

'That's St George's dragon!' she says.

The dragon snaps, coughs and screeches. It begins to unfurl massive wings.

'Who?'

'From the Crusades. I told you the Monsters of Men are down there.
Every monster ever dreamed is in that hole. That's what the ravens protect us from.
There are locks across the world. It's all in the bag of secrets.'

'You looked inside?'

'Of course!'

The dragon rises into the night. Clawed wings extend. Spiked tail whips.
It hisses and coughs. Shaking and flapping, the grime falls, revealing red scales.
It tries to shake Richard off.

Richard kicks its eyes.
'Fawkes!' he shouts. 'Your powder. I've found a light!'

Fawkes races over waving his hands.
His grin demented, like he's meeting a long-lost friend.

Richard calls to him.
'Who needs a ghoul remote control when you've got a dragon, eh?'

'Dickie!' cries Fawkes. 'Go easy. That's no way to treat a dragon!'

'Shove off, fool. I'm king of all beasts. God appointed!'
He kicks the dragon's head and points at us.

'Look, Beaky, food! Eat! Toast!'

'What now?' says Citizen.

'If they've got a dragon,' says Magnificat, 'we need that head. We need Bran. He can control the Monsters of Men.'

'You mean, go into the pit?' says Citizen.

'No,' I say. 'There was a head behind Little Ease. It was huge. Moaning. Has to be Bran.'

'What?' says Magnificat.

'When you locked me up that time, Citizen blasted me out. Trying to escape, I ran into a giant head in a pot. If that's not Bran my name is Dickie Dog Features! What place has two giant's heads?'

But I need a back-up plan too. I look to Citizen.
'Go to the Armouries kitchen and get me chilli. As much as you can, you got that?'

'Chilli?' he says, puzzled.

'Yes. Chilli powder. Smells like that red chicken but way stronger. You won't miss it. Just smell. Red, fiery, hot. In a jar, or something.'

He nods and races off for the Armouries kitchen.

'What are you doing?' says Magnificat.

'No time to explain. We need to get that head.'

I push into the hole beneath White Tower's staircase. Magnificat follows into the black. Out of the tunnel into the passage, we stand by Little Ease's smashed door.

'Bran is in there!' I whisper. 'Down the back.'

'Go on, then,' she says. 'Get in. Don't look in his eyes. He's like a Medusa, but sucks on souls. He'll be hungry, too.'

'Great.'

At the back of the cell we enter the gap created by Citizen's explosion. Through more darkness, it's there. Tilted on its side. The cauldron.

'Drag it, Mags.'

She stares at the cauldron.
Her paws step back in unison.
The pot doesn't move.
She stares harder.
'Come on...'

It moves a fraction. Shuffles and scrapes. Inside, there's a groan. I shove from the side. Bran grunts.

'Shush, Baba,' says Mags. 'Freedom and snacks are coming!'

Mags strains, trying to gain momentum with the cauldron. Finally, it begins to move. She tugs like a rugby star. I push from the sides and we drag it through Little Ease, through the smashed doorway and out into the tunnel. Facing the hole that leads out of White Tower, there's no way the cauldron will fit.

'You're going to have to drag it out the front,' I say.
'Down the corridor and up through the tower.'
I stare down the tunnel.

'Nah,' she says, gazing into the ceiling. 'They experimented with indoor toilets.'

'You what?'

She stares the cauldron upright. There's a thud. Bran falls inside.
'Ugggarrrh.'

'Get on,' says Mags.

'On? On what?'

'The rim of the pot.'

'We're going up through a toilet?'

'Yeah. But it's dry... I think.'

Mags lifts the cauldron's handle. I leap onto the rim, balancing my paws away from Bran. This isn't going to be pretty, but there's no choice.

There are shuffling noises beneath me. A snapping sound.
Teeth snapping.

'Mags! He's after my bum!'

'Don't look, T! Don't look!'

Bran tries to reach and bite. He smells like bad cheese. Above me, Magnificat heaves and puffs. Up through the dark knobbly shaft we go.

The smell of old...

I leap off as we come out. We're not far from the main entrance.
Mags huffs and puffs the cauldron to the doors.
They're still holding.
I whisper to Mags.
'If Fawkes can't open them... how can we?'

Mags creeps up and listens against the wood. From the other side we can hear Fawkes.

'Come, my lovely,' he says. 'Over here. Lovely powder...'

Magnificat nods to the wall by the door. A green button. The emergency-exit button.
She removes her battered baseball cap and pulls out the red plastic lighter.
Genius!

'I'm going big,' she whispers, 'blow the powder, then Fawkes. Boom time. You ready?'

I nod.

'Hit the green button when I say, and stay behind the wall.'

The pot by her side, she expands to super-size, then nods. I hit the button.
The doors spring open.

'Boo!' shouts Magnificat. She hovers the gunpowder into the air, sparks the lighter and leaps away.

The spark hits powder and

BOOM!

A flash of light. Cries and shrieks. We look out through swirling grey smoke...

Magnificat, working super hard, hovers the cauldron up and we step out onto White Tower's staircase. The scene is chaos. Clouds of smoke. Fawkes gone who knows where – vaporised? Richard face down in the grass. The dragon nearby stamping its feet, angry. It seems to be jealous of the explosion. Coughing. Trying to find fire. Rats swarm over ghouls swarming over lions who are broken, staggering, their bodies near collapse. Richard gets up, first to his hands, then standing. He fixes his helmet and starts to laugh at us. Again maniacally.

What now?

I check left, right, up, down.

Nothing.

My ears track back. A whooshing sound. A growing whooshing. Mags and I turn.

From inside White Tower, flying towards our heads are hundreds of swords and daggers!

'Run,' I cry. 'Run!'

Magnificat fumbles down the steps, hovering the cauldron while weapons rocket up into the hands of the ghouls.

'What the dog, now?' I say, from the bottom of the steps.

The final weapon exits White Tower. A huge, shining sword. It arrows to Richard. He catches it with one hand, takes a full grip and, whirling it around his head, walks towards us.

'This do?' shouts Citizen. He's coming down the path hovering a large white tub above his head. 'Definitely stinks.'

I hurtle to him and sniff as he puts the tub down.

Sharp. Raw. Red. That's chilli!

'What's the plan?' says Magnificat, hovering the cauldron down. Bran grunts inside.

'You better have one, Teufel.'

I look to Richard. He's directing ghouls to the rats with his sword. Making swipes. It's going to be a massacre.

'Citizen,' I shout. 'Tell Elvis to get his army out of here, now! Strategic retreat. No buts. It's an order! Mags, put the tub in with Bran.'

'He's not going to be happy,' she says.

'He can lump it.'

Magnificat puts the tub in the pot, and I jump on the rim.

'Right, playtime.'

Bran is beneath me. Dark leather scalp. Eyes facing iron.
I settle my claws into his skin. He growls. I dig deeper.
He groans again.
Richard steps forward. Wheeling his sword.

Citizen races back. 'Playtime?'

'Swings and roundabouts,' I say. 'What goes around, comes around. Heard of those? Ready for a ride?'

'No,' they say, in unison.

'You're going to swing a cat. Me. The tub and Bran. Do exactly what I say, fast.'

'Have you gone mad?' says Magnificat.

'Citizen,' I say, 'open the tub a tiny bit, one side.'

Citizen stares the lid open. A pungent smash of chilli leaks from the gap.

'Now, hover the cauldron up and swing us in big circles.
We're gonna play bash a king!'

We lift into the sky.
'Now,' I say. 'Spin. Spin!'

The cauldron turns.

'Faster! We're going to whack him.'
Fat grins cover their faces as they finally get the plan.

The cauldron spins quicker and quicker.

Richard walks towards us, big sword swinging. He swirls in and out of view.
Each rotation he's closer. He steps past lions, past ravens and rats – ignoring all.
Smiling and swinging. Smiling and swinging – only wanting war. But you don't war with dogged-off cats!

Closer. My heart races. Dizziness spins.
His sword matches our speeding orbit.
Bran groans and groans.

'More,' I cry. 'Faster! Quicker! More!'

A final rotation. The next will hit. He doesn't seem to care.
I shout to Magnificat and Citizen, 'Close your eyes!'

I can't see whether they do. I can only hope.

Before Richard's face flashes one last time, I stab a paw into the chilli and hurl it at him.
Eyes closed against the fire spice, I hear screams.

'Cat!'

'Korma that, Dickie Dickster!'

I open my eyes. They sting red. Richard staggers back, clasping his face.

I shout,
'Now. Swing the cat! Faster, faster. Smack him into the pit.'

I wedge myself against the cauldron, tucked against Bran's head. He groans and groans.
The stink is disgusting. I grip my claws into his scalp and duck as Magnificat and Citizen slam the cauldron into Richard's head. Again and again.
As he stumbles back, I look out. He shakes his head, lumbers, holding his sword.

Magnificat and Citizen smash again and again.
He hurls the sword at me. It crashes against the pot. Bran screams. We circle again, faster and faster, bashing Richard more and more.

'To the pit!' I cry.

With one last thump, helpless, blinded, stunned by blows, Richard tumbles into the hole. The cauldron thumps to the ground as Magnificat and Citizen collapse on the grass. Citizen throws up. Bran moans. I kick off his forehead and stagger out.

'We're not finished.' I say.

'You're right,' says Mags. 'What are we going to do about them?' She looks up, staggering to her paws.

Above us, ghouls hiss. They've watched the fight. Now they're ready for their own.

'Now,' I say. 'Fireworks time! Halloween meets Bonfire Night!'

'What?' says Citizen.

I get back in the cauldron and sink my claws into Bran's head.
This time, he barely even groans.

'Hurl me up into the ghouls!'

'We've no strength left, Teufel.'

'Well find some!'

'We'll help,' says a deep throaty voice.

It's Charles. The lions. They're up!

I pull at the chilli tub, claws and teeth trying to get the doggin' thing to open further. Mouth screaming from chilli, I shout,
'When you throw me, you run. Get everyone under the stairs. Just run!'

The lions hurl me, Bran, and the cauldron up into the ghouls and run. I arrive in the cloud, pull the lid and the red powder falls through the ghouls as I cling to Bran.
I tumble and tumble with the pot.
Around us ghouls rage,
faces screaming at the stinging dust.
The chilli hits the dragon.
It gets mad. Really mad.
Sparks fire from its mouth. Billows of smoke. And the flames come.
The sky ablaze with dragon fire! Cordite and carbon swirl as each flame dies.
More flames blaze. Ghouls cry as the flailing dragon torches their last existence. Screams terror my ears as the cauldron falls.
Bursting cries as flames toast ghoul after ghoul.
Bran moans beneath me.

Ghouls vaporise to smells of burned bone and leather.
Bodies burst into ash that crumbles to dust that falls into nothing.
The cauldron smacks the ground. I tumble and roll, slamming against the iron.

Daggers and swords fall.
The country is safe.
The Chaplain and Mrs C.
My friends.
And me.

The cauldron comes to a stop. I'm trapped inside, upside down. Bran's over me.
Crushing down.

Doggin' off-cheese smells clamber over my fur.
A silence. A weird, small silence. Just me.

Bran moans. The fire sting of chilli hangs. I can't move. The cauldron lifts at the side.
A new smell. Coal and death. The dragon's snout, grunts under the gap.
Smoke fills the cauldron. Thick, carbon, burned. Black. Bran coughs.

'Yo, scale-head.' I say.

The dragon snorts.

'Come on, scaly. Come to papa.'

The red snout lifts the cauldron. A yellow snake-eye faces me. I double-kick Bran.
'Dod!' I shout. 'Dod! Dod!'

'Dod,' screams Bran.

The noise is deafening. Bran's mouth opens like a black prison. A wind comes.
A strange, sweet wind, sucking.

A crumpling sound.
The dragon's snout crumples. It sucks into Bran's open mouth.

The body follows, melding, collapsing down.

A red dragon becomes a seething,
speeding, scaly, liquid stream of giant-head soup.
The remaining ghouls follow. A stream of swirling, screaming grey,
sucking up from the ground and down from the sky into the mouth of Bran.

Bran burps then shuts his mouth. I slump on his scalp. My world
goes to the greatest colour in the world, the colour from where all life and light comes,

black.

FORTY

A giant, black paw comes under the cauldron.
'Not such a titch,' says Edward the lion, lifting the pot.

Smoke mixes in my chillified bad-cheese lungs. I clamber out feeling like the bad end of a restaurant bin. Thousands of celebrating rats rush at me. Elvis arrives first.

He jumps on my back.
'Cat! The best fight of my life! Shall we do it again?'
He laughs and rolls off.

I cock my head.
'Are you mad?'

He looks to the cauldron.
'What's in there that toasts big fire-monster dragons?'

'Bran. A giant's head. He protects Britain, like you've just done.'

'I can look after it if you want?'

'No chance.' I say, spitting chilli dust. 'It's going where it belongs. In that pit. Keeping guard of whatever's left down there. Where are Mags and Citizen?'

Elvis looks beyond the cauldron. They're lying splayed on the grass. We go over.

'We did it!' I say.

Neither respond. They're out. Sparko.
Not even a head lift.
Swinging the cauldron has knocked them out.

Elvis gives them a sniff. 'They're okay.'

I sit on the grass.
We did this.
I did this.

'Perhaps the head instead of the aftershave?' asks Elvis.

'You're not having that head. Let's check on the lions.'

We head over. Elvis beams pride as the lions stretch.
'Giants! Giants of Africa.' He begins to dance as we step.

'You're the giant,' I say, 'and your mates. Without you...'

He hugs me, big brown arms grabbing my sides.
'You are lions, too!'

Over his shoulder, Henry plucks a lump of ghoul from a claw. 'What a night.'
'I'm sticking with pigeons,' says George. 'No more, Big Ben, cat. Ever.'

'I won't, don't worry!'

His nose twitches and he grunts. 'We'd better check on your birds.'

The seven ravens are flat-out by the scaffold, wings spread.
Are they alive? I can't see movement. Chests look still. We get closer.

Thor is the nearest. Wings out, head at an odd angle.
I sniff his beak. The tiniest of snores filters to my nose. A contented breath. He's okay.

Elvis and I go to the others. They seem okay, too.

Last is Baldrick. His beak slightly open. Almost like a smile. I look at my chilli-red paw.
Move it towards him, but then think, nah. There's something in letting go. Sometimes.

Up over the steps is home. The house asleep, dark in slumber, content.
I glance back to the cauldron.

'Let's get Bran sorted,' I say to the lions. 'Can you help?'

'More work?' says George. He crouches down and offers his back.

Elvis and I get up between his ears and we stride across the grass.

'Careful with Bran's eyes,' I say. 'Mags says he's like a Medusa. A soul-sucker.'

'Cat. I'm a lion of Trafalgar.'

The giant's leathery head is half out of the cauldron. George bats him back in and then lifts the handle with his mouth.

'Rydych chi'r Saeson môr anghwrtais,' Bran grunts.
'Dqim diolch hyd yn oed.'

'What was that?' I say.

'No idea,' says George. 'Probably, thank you.'

He places the pot at the pit's edge. Elvis and I jump down.

Richard's hand clambers up the side of the hole.

'Oh, dog off,' says George, swiping Bran and the cauldron into Richard's face.

They tumble into the abyss.
The other lions shove the rock back in place and the pit is sealed.

'Now, where were we?' George says. 'Home time and a cup of tea?'

The lawn is a war zone.

'Why didn't any humans wake up?' asks George.

'Richard drugged everyone with sleeping tablets,' I say. 'But when they do, the CCTV is going to be some kind of show.'

'Leave that to me,' says Elvis.

'You?'

He nods. 'Where's the security control room?
Everything needs cables. Rats love cables.'

'No idea. Mags will know. But what about things like that?'
There's a huge dent where the rock was.
'The Governor won't like it, or the ravens being out,
nor all these swords and daggers.'

'You need to see things the rat way,' says Elvis.
'Problems are opportunities.'
He rises up, whistles then shouts, 'Rank and file!'

Rats blaze the lawn until we face a perfect formation, whiskers at full attention.

He puffs his chest.
'Company One! Ravens to cages.
Company Two, cutlery back inside White Tower.'

A company of rats race off to the ravens, creating platforms with their backs by each bird. Other rats lift them on. Company Two collects the swords and daggers, rat-handling them up White Tower's stairs.

'Amazing, Elvis,' I say, 'your guys...'

That hearty, rat laugh booms at me.
'My girls, Teufel. Nothing fights better than a female rat.
The boys have other business.'

'You've got more than this?'

'Of course! Grow or die. I'm eyeing the West End.
Bond Street. Tasty restaurants. This has been good training.'

Across the grass, Citizen and Magnificat stir.

Elvis barrels over.
'Up! Up! No time for sleep!'

'Dog off,' says Mags, with a smile.

She gets to her paws. Citizen stands, too. I pad over.

'Mags, Elvis needs to know where the security room is, and can you hover the lawn up? There's a big divot where the rock was that needs fixing.'

Magnificat scowls.
'You seen what we've been through? Why's he want the control room?'

'Scrub the cameras. Get all this evidence wiped.'

'Good idea.'
She scurries to Elvis's ear and whispers instructions.

Citizen turns for the dent.
'Mags, come on.'

They lift the divot then slump on the grass.

'Happy?' he asks. 'I could sleep for a week.'

'Not really,' I say. 'Soil's poking out everywhere. The lawn's like a rugby field, it should be all tennis-y – you know, Wimbledon-like.'

'My girls will fix that,' says Elvis. 'At your service.'

'What about all the chilli ghoul dust?'

'You think my girls can't handle a bit of curry?
We are Bethnal Green, brother!
We know our Lau Chingri from our Machher Jhol!'
He turns and shouts, 'Companies! Lawn style! It's spicy!'

Rats speed across the lawn, prod and poke, pull and push, until the grass is back to lawn-tennis smooth. A spotty brown-and-white rat approaches.

'All fine, General.'

'Thank you, Matilda.
Brothers and sister we must bid you farewell.'
He comes whisper-close to my ear.
'Any more ghouls you wanna bust up, dogs, anything, you call.
That was fun. Holler down the drain.'

'Thank you, Elvis, for everything.'
I shout to the rest of the rats. 'You saved us. Thank you all! You are friends.'

'Matilda,' says Elvis. 'Operation Exit!'

'Yes, General.'

Matilda whistles and a thousand rodents race from the lawn.

'We better be off, too,' says George. The lions bow, shuffle manes, flex a stretch and then launch in the direction of the Governor's house, flying over the roof.

Magnificat watches them go.
'What a team!'

'I know.'

'Court won't believe this. I'm gonna wake them up.'

'Thought they pray all night?'

'Nah. Once Anne falls to sleep, we drift off, too.'

'They slept through that?'

'Walls are thick here, bro. See you in a bit.'
And with that, she mists away.

'What about you and the Governor?' asks Citizen.

'I don't know, and I don't care. Let's check the ravens.'

The birds are splayed across the cages. The rats didn't put them in the huts.

Citizen pads to Thor and gives him a ghostly bash.
'Oi, bird.'

Thor's eye flicks open. He tries to stand but wobbles and falls.
Wings spread for balance, he tries again.

Finally up, he ignores Citizen and glares at me with eyes borrowed from hell.

'What are you doing here?'

FORTY ONE

Thor flaps to his perch and checks his family across the cages. Satisfied, he sidles back down and stares at Citizen.

'Who the fox are you?'

'Citizen. We've just saved all your feathers, the Tower and the country!'

He shakes his beak.

'What nonsense are you talking?'

'Richard III drugged you with rotten meat. We've had a dragon, ghouls and swords – everything's been flying around here.'

'Cat crap.' He looks around. 'Everything is normal.'

'Evil everywhere, all over the night sky. We played whack-a-king with the head of Bran.'

Thor wobbles. He steps towards Citizen.

'What? Bran? You found Bran... the Raven King?'

I'm confused. I come back from rinsing my paws in Thor's water bowl.

'He's the king of ravens?'

Thor scowls. 'Bran was a Welsh king. Bran means raven. His head was buried here millennia ago to stop Britain being invaded. What happened, precisely?'

'I tricked the dragon into toasting the ghouls. Got Bran to say *dod*. And he sucked them into his mouth. I was pretty awesome.'

Thor nods. 'Bran's Welsh.'

'You know Welsh?' I ask.

'I am Welsh. Ravens from across Britain guard the Tower.'

The other ravens stagger up, looking about, stretching their wings.

'This isn't my cage,' says Thor.

'I'll sort that,' says Citizen.

He mists the door open. Thor hops onto the lawn.

'Everything seems normal. You sure this happened? Is this a trick?' Thor turns to me.

'We've had a rat army here, the Trafalgar lions...'

'Now I know you are telling me lies.'

'The army was mine,' says Elvis, coming across the grass, chewing a thin bouncy, silver thread.

'I see no army,' says Thor. 'No proof of anything.'

'Look at the scaffold. There's still meat on the ground. You must remember.'

'No. My head is a rage. But if what you say is true, thank you. Halloween is a dangerous night. You've done a great service.'

'So...' I say, 'an apology, fella. For the poo? The attacks?'

Thor swings his beak.
'Nothing from me.'

'Excuse me?'

'This is a job. Attacking us is attacking the country.
There are untold dangers you know
nothing about. We are not just a tourist attraction.
But I'm prepared to start over.
If you are?'

My tail beats. Peace with birds? Hmmm...

'Maybe,' I say. 'If there's less attitude from bozo over there.' I nod to Baldrick.

'It's simple,' says Thor. 'If our days are peaceful. Yours are, too.
It could have been that from the beginning.'

'I'm a cat.'

'And we are ravens. At the Tower of London. And speaking of which. The Governor won't be happy you're back. But if you've helped us, I can help you.'
He turns to Citizen.
'Can you open the bolts to these cages at 6am?'

'Aye, I can,' says Citizen.

'Then, Teufel, meet us on the lawn outside the Governor's house at 06.15 on the dot. Alone.'

I nod.
'06.15.'

'Now, if you don't mind. We'd like to be in our correct homes.'

Citizen stares across the cages, sliding each bolt and door. Thor gathers his ravens into a huddle on the grass.

There's movement at Wakefield Tower.
Court mist through the wall. The guards leading, halberds forward on full spike.

'Who goes there?' shouts One-Eye.

'You know who it is, you muppet.' I call.

'That orange cat. And the... err... rat.'

'Heroes,' I say.

Anne steps past One-Eye.
'Out of the way... *All hail the ravens.*'

She nods to Thor. The Bishop, Walter and Lady Jane do the same.

Heads pop up from the raven huddle, then return.
They spread their wings for more privacy.

Citizen whispers to me.
'What do I do? Can't imagine I'm popular with the Court.'

'I'll handle it.'

Magnificat mists in at my side.
'I've explained, ish...' she says. 'They're a bit shocked...'

Anne lifts the trail of her dress and turns to me. 'You did this, cat?'

'Stooled it up, Ma'am. Magnificat, the Trafalgar lions, a thousand rats under Elvis here, and if I might introduce, Citizen – who was a traitor, but, I've brought him over to the dark side.'

Her face greys to a scowl.
'He's a traitor?'

'Fully redeemed,' I say. 'Without him, we wouldn't be here. Any of us.'

'And who's this rat that eats before a queen?'

Elvis bounds forward, tucks an arm and bends into a bow.
'Elvis, Your Majesty. King of outside,' he says, gesturing
beyond the Tower. 'Well, at my level, you know.
This eating is fibre optic. Good for teeth. Nice dress...'

A flush of colour returns to Anne's face.
She smiles.
'Not shy, are you? So, Dicko Richard's been about has he? Such a poo-bag.'
She turns to Sir Walter. 'Thunderpaws did the trick after all, Waltz?'

Sir Walter bows. 'Thank you, Ma'am.'

She scowls at the Bishop. 'You, Bosher, need to step up.'
Anne bends down. A misty finger tickles my chin.
'Good work, Sir Magnificent. And what about this rat?'

'He saved the lions of Trafalgar. Sorted the CCTV too.'

'All that? A rat?'

'Me and a thousand or two of my finest, Ma'am,' says
Elvis. 'Data cables severed. Hard disks scratched.
Power inverted. Everything gone and broken.'

He gets closer and offers his head for a scratch.

Anne rubs his ear. 'So, you're good with technology?' she says.
'Tell me, have you heard of this thing called
the internet?'

6.13am, London in darkness.

I'm on Tower Green outside the Governor's house, dew under paw, surrounded by a circle of ravens that guard Britain, the Tower, and now me. Upstairs at the Governor's, a light flicks on.

'Here we go,' says Thor, from the front of the circle.

Lights come on downstairs. We wait in silence. A living-room curtain opens.
The Governor stands in red pyjamas, sipping at a mug. His eyes slowly find focus.
The mug drops. He dances against the hot liquid then disappears.

The front door flies open. He storms out, coffee-soaked, mobile in hand,
staring so hard you'd think he'd seen ghosts.

'What the –?'

He stabs the phone and puts it to his ear.

'RM, you better come. Your ravens are
on my lawn, guarding that damn cat of the Chaplain's.'

He ends the call and steps onto the grass. The ravens bow, wings spread, tails fanned.
The Governor is lost. I sit in the middle, cleaning. Whatever the ravens' plan, it might be working. Hands on hips, the Governor's stumped. The Ravenmaster appears from the steps, buttoning his top.

'You locked the cages, RM?'

'Always.'

'Something's up. I feel damn weird, truth be told. I just dropped my coffee.'

The Ravenmaster shakes his head.
'I'm not in full fettle myself. Let's see what they're up to.'
He approaches the birds with low, open hands.

The raven circle tightens.
A standoff.

'Teufel,' calls the Governor, his tone soft and light. 'The Chaplain says he's intelligent, RM. Let's see. Teufel, come.'

I get up.

Thor checks back. 'You know what you're doing?'

I nod.
'Humans are rubbish liars. I'm okay.'

Thor opens the circle and I pad through to the Governor, tail high.

He bends down and rubs my head. 'Come.'

We walk together at an easy pace towards home. The Governor mounts the step and knocks, three sharp raps. Chap's feet thud down the stairs. His face peers from behind the door.

'Your cat is back, Chaplain. Keep him in line, will you.'

The Chaplain pulls the door fully open – dumbfounded.
'Yes, Governor. Of course. Best behaviour.'

I scoot in to the kitchen.

'We'll talk later,' says the Governor.

Chap shuts the door and shouts,
'Love, you better come down!'

I sit by the fridge and wait for his summer-blue eyes.

*

Mrs C rushes into the kitchen. In seconds I'm twirling with her dressing gown. Chap grabs a can of Tuna à la Teuf. Result. Released to the floor, I tuck in.

'The Governor turned up,' says Chap. 'Goes, here you are...'
He rubs under his glasses.
'I'm at a loss.'

The house phone rings. Chap heads to the front room to answer. Mrs C hits the radio. On comes Radio 4, their favourite station, Big Ben bonging from the speaker.

'THERE YOU ARE,' SAYS A CRISP MALE VOICE. 'BIG BEN CHIMING A THIRTEENTH TIME. I COUNTED THEM ALL. OFFICIALS AT WESTMINSTER CAN'T EXPLAIN IT. ALL OTHER CHIMES WERE NORMAL. NO ONE'S SURE WHAT HAPPENED, JOHN. A RODENT DROPPING OR TWO, BUT IT'S NOT BEEN PUT DOWN TO MICE, YET.'

A chirpy voice breaks in.

'THANK YOU, BRIAN. MOST STRANGE. IN OTHER NEWS, A CERTAIN ROCK STAR'S AT IT AGAIN, ALLEGEDLY. HIS SPEEDBOAT WAS FOUND CRASHED BY THE TOWER OF LONDON. THE STAR, WHO CANNOT BE NAMED DUE TO LEGAL REASONS, MAINTAINS HE WAS PLAYING SCRABBLE. THE MARINE POLICING UNIT ARE TESTING FOR FINGERPRINTS. MORE LATER, I'M SURE.'

I jump to the table.

'Well, well,' says Mrs C, hand on my tail.
'Was that how you got back?' she laughs.

Chap comes in.
'You won't believe this.'

'And you won't believe what was just on the radio,' she says.

'Every aftershave in the Tower. Gone,' says Chap.

Mrs C straightens in her chair.
'Every bottle?'

'Yep. Not a trace. A few open doors, but no clues. The Tower's wild with speculation. Exorcism requests left, right and centre. Everyone's saying ghosts.'

*

While Chap goes house to house, casemate to casemate, Mrs C keeps me in for the day. Out of sight of the Governor.

Silly, but understandable. A gentle reintroduction to public life might be wise – wouldn't want to mess anything up.

With nothing to do but sleep, my mind races over last night and
Mushika. Where did she go?
It was up to me. And I did it. But never again.

I wonder what those ghouls did to get trapped down there? A prison under a prison. And no living soul except me and a few ravens know about it. I'm a cat of secrets.

On stretch-and-patrol missions, I search the house for Mushika, but not a flash. I'll give her some when she does turn up. I saved a country, the whole world. I should be meeting the Queen, the prime minister. Proper world-beating famous with more prawns than the sea.

Mags and Citizen come with news of a Royal Court party. We're to meet up the third staircase in the Casemates, tonight at ten. The afternoon and evening laze by with sleep, tuna, chicken, and no whale poo.

Tourists gone and the Governor home, I'm finally allowed out into a proper London November night – dark, crisp and cold.

The inner ward of the Tower is silent. I pad by White Tower with something on my mind. The right thing to do. Even if it's doggin' strange to feel it. I'll keep it quick.

I weave through the railings by the old wall and pass over the pit where Richard and Fawkes' now reside, and there in the first cage is Baldrick. Just the bird.

'Alright, Teufel,' he says.

'Yeah. You?'

He nods.

'This is weird.' I say. 'And you don't say nothing after, right?

'Maybe? What?'

'Sorry.'

'You what?' he looks about. 'Yeah, maybe I owe you one, too. But you know nothing of us. We ain't just birds. Not that there's nothing wrong with being just a bird. Life is life.'

'I was doing what cats do.'

'And I was doing what ravens do,' he says. 'Fun, though.'

'Yeah, kinda.'

'Teufel.' Munin calls from a further cage.

'She's got you a present,' says Baldrick.

Weird.

'Go over.'

'Catch you later.'

He flies up to his perch.
'You haven't yet.'

I pad over to Thor
and Munin's cage. 'Hey.'

'We had a talk this morning, Teufel,' says Munin.
'In recognition of last night, we'd like to offer you something.'

Thor scrapes the gravel.
'It's a little unusual,' he gruffs, 'but, we'd like you to
become an honorary Her Majesty's Raven.'

An honorary bird? Can things get any stranger?

'If you accept,' says Thor, 'you must guard this Tower as we do. And its secrets.'

'An oath, I suppose?'

'In the form of your word, yes.'

'Then I'd be delighted.' I say. 'Honoured.'

'Excellent,' says Munin.

'But! But! No spreading the news. No cat can know. Big or small. Or I'm leaving. No part of it. You got that?'

Thor laughs.

'You lot coming to the party?' I say.

He shakes his beak.
'On guard, always. Our presence is older than the Tower.
This century is proving a tricky one.'
He taps the ground.

'You gonna hit me up on loads of Tower secrets?'

'You know more than any non-corvid already. It's enough for now.'

'Well, better get going. Don't want to be late. See you all.'

The ravens flap their wings goodbye and I head for the party, an honorary flapper.

FORTY THREE

Past the Tower's exit, beneath the great wall, I pass the Casemates, each a cannon housing and now a Yeoman's home. One staircase, two and three. Through an arched walkway, past arrow slits cut into the stone, I come to a flat long roof. Dotted with skylights, satellite dishes, washing lines, plastic tables and chairs; floodlights illuminate the Tower wall above.

The whole Court is here, the lions and the polar bear, everyone except the sleeping King. They all look super happy, apart from the Bishop still in his sunglasses, and the bear, who seems nervous and uncomfortable. I spy the faceless women.
My fur sharpens, but then, very un-catlike, I let it go.

We're in the right place. The right thing happened. The ladies were doing what they believed, beliefs are strong.

The guards are preparing a table of food. Chicken and salmon waft on the breeze. One-Eye sees me, winks and glides a finger along his axe blade. He's alright – just. Other guards hold banners with the Royal standard – the three golden lions emblazoned against a deep red.

'Hey, Teuf,' says Lady Jane.
She's in a dark green brocade dress and her sneakers.

'Nice curtains.' I say, nodding at the dress. 'Banging party?'

'Thanks.' She raises her misty eyebrows. 'Royal business coming up, preparing for the light. If you will follow me.'

She leads me to the front.
Magnificat is stood before a low wide stool, gleaming like she's got six tons of cream.

'Take a seat,' says Jane. 'Tail still, eyes forward, no cleaning.'

I can feel a formality, so do as I'm told. She moves away.

Queen Anne comes and stands before us.
'Cat. Up,' says Anne, gesturing to the stool.

I lift my paws onto the step and sit bolt straight. Jane and Sir Walter arrive at her side.

'Teufel,' Anne says. 'You are promoted from stool boy to
the Duke of Magnificence!'

A duke! Every fur tingles. I look around. The Duke of Magnificence! What a title!
Everyone smiles. Can you believe it!

She looks to Magnificat.
'Trixie. Up.'

Magnificat gets up on the stool, too. I'm confused.
I go to speak, but Jane pulls a finger to her mouth.

Anne gazes down.
'Trixie, our kitchen cat from Hackney who calls herself Magnificat.
Weaselled her way into an earl's affections, and now a queen's. Well done.'
Anne leans forward. 'After four hundred years, do you still really want to be a
lady-in-waiting, the role I've always denied you, because you're a commoner?'

Magnificat nods so fast her head might fall off.

'Well, you can't,' says the Queen, straightening herself with a smile.

Magnificat *slumps*.

'You are to be *the Duchess of Hackney and the Tower of London*!'

Her whiskers explode! She glows more than me. Sir Walter beams above his ruffle.
He signals behind us.
'One-Eye, your sword please.'

One-Eye steps forward and presents his gleaming broadsword to the Queen. She taps
it to our shoulders to signify our ascent into nobility then chucks it back to One-Eye.

'Congratulations,' she says. 'You may now arise, Duke and Duchess.'

'Your Majesty,' we say in unison.

I rise, stunned. I want to test this dukeship. There's another right thing to do.
'Ma'am. As a duke, can I ask questions and not be imprisoned in pit-holes of doom?'

'Perhaps,' she smiles, 'what is it?'

'It's the polar bear, Gnut.'

The polar bear lifts his head, his eyes pure panic.

'What of it?' says Anne.

I give her my cutest look – cocked head and everything.
'Can we remove his chain?'

Her eyebrows tighten. 'Why?'

I look around.
'Because no one else is chained.'

She gazes at the assembled Court.
'I suppose. One-Eye, remove the bear's chain.'

'Yes, Your Majesty.' One-Eye clunks over and removes the chain.

The queen looks at me.
'Acceptable, Duke?'

'Yes, Ma'am. Very.'

'Girls,' she says. 'Hit the music!'

With that, everyone chitchats. The two faceless women get the party going with a lute and a dulcimer, and the guards uncover the fabulous feast. Gnut jumps on the lions and starts a play fight, which breaks into a giant, kitten chase. I need a word with Lady Jane. She's stood by a skylight, watching the Queen summon Walter and the Bishop with her long curling finger.

I jump onto the skylight.
'Jane. Will Citizen be duked too?'

'He refused an honour,' she says, still watching the Queen. 'Friendship and respect are enough. He'll be along soon. Didn't want a fuss.'

What crazy fool refuses a dukedom?

'We'll talk later, Teufel,' she says. The Queen's long finger is summoning her too. 'Anne wants to discuss the light. She's obsessed.'

She lifts the trail of her dress and heads over. I pad beside her, then break off to Margaret Pole who's sat watching the princes play stick and ball.
I jump to an adjacent chair.

'Mrs Pole, Prince Edward, Prince Richard.'

Margaret smiles. 'Hello, Your Grace.'

'And hello to you, Countess...'

'A delight to meet our saviour.'

'Thank you,' I say, curling my tail. 'It was nothing. Sorry about your uncle, King Richard, Your Highnesses.'

Edward's face is relaxed.
'We're used to him, never our favourite.'

He sticks the ball to his brother.

'Did he murder you two, then?' I say.

The two princes go still. Margaret glares.
'Teufel, that's a very inappropriate question.'

'Sorry. Not dukey, I suppose?'

'Correct.'

'My apologies. It's just it's the Tower's most famous mystery.'

'A mystery that shall remain!'

Better change the subject.
'Why are you always running?'

Her eyes twitch and flick, white hair lifting.

I'm poked in my side.
'Teuf. A word.'

It's Citizen.

'When did you mist in?'

'Ease up,' he says. 'Ghosts don't need reminders of their pain.'

The princes cuddle Margaret and stroke her cheeks.

'Sorry.'

'You've been here five seconds. We've been living this stuff for centuries'

'Okay. Okay.'

'Take it easy and listen. You will find it welcomed by everyone.'

'Gotcha.'

'Let's get some food.'

'Yeah.'

We make our way to the table and jump up to a royal spread of meats and fish. I eye the salmon.

'What's all this for, if you're ghosts?'

'For memories, boy!' Citizen hovers a chunk of guinea fowl into his mouth, parks his bum over the table edge. It trundles through his body and falls to the floor. 'Only a hint of flavour, but enough. Yum. Feeds the foxes later, too.'

'Another question. Jane's sneakers and M's hat. How are, they – you know, ghosty?'

'Stolen from modern ghosts,' he looks to the city. 'It's wild out there. I've got a question for you, actually.'

I lift my head up from the salmon.

'Yup?'

'I've listened and watched for a while as you know, and I'm curious.'

'Fire away.'

'Just how many birds have you killed?'

I drop the fish. 'Errrrmmmm... Well, erm... Like what? Since being here?'

'You know, ever since you came up from kittenhood.'

'Errrrmmmm... Well. Okay, let me count.' I stare into the night. 'Well, there was that one and that one and that one and that one, and those ones and that one, errrrmmmm, yep it's, oh... I don't know, let me count, errrrmmmm, it's, errrrmmmm, yep, okay, errrrmmmm... It's... One.'

'One?'

'Yes, one.'

'Really, Teufel?'

'Errrrmmmm... Oh, this is not fair. Okay... Okay... It was dead when I found it. I ain't too good at stalking. I get excited.'

'Oh, so that's why they call you Thunderpaws?'

I nod.

'Can we change the subject? This is a party, you know. Happy chit-chat?'

He laughs.
'Our plan relied on a mouse that roars like a lion.
I can give you a few pointers on birds if you want?'

'Not that kind of hungry anymore. And less of the mouse stuff. Speaking of which, that Mushika. I could throttle her, but I guess where she's led us to has been alright.'

We say nothing more and tuck in. A friendly harmony descends as the party continues. The faceless ladies strum and bash, managing quite a tune. Margaret's calm. The boys play. Lady Jane appears bored as the Bishop outlines something on the wall. He lifts his sunglasses, showing a thick black eye.

Queen Anne and Sir Walter are deep in conversation. He's frowning, arms crossed, while she scowls – lips flat, black eyes emotionless. Some people just can't enjoy parties. Anne summons Jane and the Bishop with her finger.

I wonder what juicy gossip I can pick up. Citizen said learn, after all.

4 November

A spark flashes by the clock, Mushika sniffs the air.

'Afternoon.'

I haul myself from the sofa.

'There you are! Where have you been?'

'I had to check on something. News from home.' She scoots along the mantelpiece then jumps for Chap's chair. 'I know more about Zeus now.'

I stomp over the cushions.

'Oooh, Teufel, how did it go... After I dropped you into the mother of all dog poo and left you to it? Fine, Mushika, thanks for asking!'

'I knew you'd be okay. You're Thunderpaws. I chose well – the whole thing. See how it panned out – beautiful. I'm good at this. You, me, Citizen and Mags, that's a team. You ready for tomorrow?'

'Tomorrow?'

'Bonfire Night? The light, Zeus? Big kahuna?'

'Yeah...' I look away for a moment, 'I'm not going.'

Her tail slumps. She sits, ears flat.

'That is your decision?'

'I'm a duke. I have friends, respect. No one calls me Thunderpaws. Tourist treats coming out of my ears... It's enough.'

'Enough?' Her eyes cast around the room. 'I'm out of jerky. Any biscuits? I'm starving.'

'No, I haven't got any biscuits! I did it. Saved the country and quite possibly the whole world, that's what you should be talking about!'

She scurries from the arm to the cushion.
'Enough? You've not even started. But you need to want this.
Let me show you something.'

'What?'

'It's in the secret garden. The kitchen window's open. We can leave through there.'

'Strange, it wasn't earlier?'

'Mrs C did it. Fresh air and all that.'

Mushika jumps to the table, drops to the floor and leaves. Doesn't check if I've followed or anything.

Out the kitchen window, Mushika tucks between my front paws and we cross the Tower, my collar tinkling and me feeling well stupid with a mouse between my legs.
Down in the garden, we stop at my poo bush of all places.

'See that?' she says, whiskering at the ground.

'The soil? What of it?'

'That's where you'll be buried.'

'What?'

My gut snaps tight. A dry wretch in my throat.

'By the Chaplain and Mrs C.
All tears and sob-sob.
The Ravenmaster and the Governor come, too.
The Oggle showed me.
That fact is still fixed.'

'Your Oggle does the future?'

'Time is a complex thing,' she says.
'Let's not go there.'

I'm buried in my own poo.
This is gross.
'Why are you telling me this?'

Her head bows.

'Life is choices. Moments. Opportunities. Choice after choice. Chance after chance. Chances for change. It's the universal gift. Life doesn't stand still, though you can if you're not careful. And suddenly it's gone. You, Mr Teufel, can be the hero who saved the world twice, or the cat too scared to try a second time. I know who I think you are.'

'You're right. See you...' I don't move. 'Do you?' I say.

'I do. It's best if you view what happened on Halloween as practice. You see, if you don't come, and Zeus appears in the beam, travels into history and does whatever he wants, this whole place could disappear. You might simply vanish, or the world could have invented space travel in 1876, I don't know. But everything will change. It's impossible for it not to. I know you want more from life than getting chunky off tourists.'

'Do I?' I gulp. 'But if I go, what happens to the Chaplain and Mrs C. They will miss me.'

'While you're in history, your time here won't move on.'

'We'll come.'

I turn. It's Magnificat and Citizen.

'What are you doing here?'

Magnificat flexes her cap.
'Mushika told us. The light, Zeus. It's time. Our time. Everyone's. We have to try. To not try– ' She shakes her head.

'It might be a laugh,' says Citizen, misty claws on a tree.

'You what?' I say.

He rakes the bark.
'Adventure. Always wanted to see the world. Plus we'll be inside you. That's got to be an experience.'

I glare at him. '*Justa*, 'scuse me a second, a...'

'Ah, yes,' says Mushika. 'The safest thing is that they travel inside you, while in the beam. We can't have their mists lost in history.'

I shake my fur. 'That is not happening!'

'No other way,' she says. 'Unless you want to do it alone?'

I'm being ganged up on here.

'Are we on?' she says.

I gulp, roll my eyes and nod, more annoyed than Chap in hell.
I can't believe this.

'Excellent,' says Mushika. 'Now, don't panic, but I've got to leave.'

I look at her gone out.

'I know, I know,' she says. 'Again...
The news from home wasn't the best,
and I need to help. I'll catch you all later.'

'Things okay?' says Mags.

'They will be.'

With a spark she is gone. I stare at Magnificat and Citizen.

Inside me... I mean... How the...?

We head for home in silence;
all that needs to be said loud and clear in our looming future.

*

Thor lands on the path before us.
'Teufel, a word.'

What now?

'Sure,' I say, being polite.

He turns to Citizen and Magnificat.

'Just, Teufel.' He swoops off towards the huts.

'I'll catch you up,' I say to Mags and Citizen. 'Obviously, secret important Tower business. Dukey things.'

I pad over the path, squeeze through the railings and out onto the grass. I find him tucked behind the last hut.
'What's up?' I say.

He looks me up and down.
'What happened to Bran?' he says.

'The head? Got rid. Why?'

He taps the lawn with his feet.
'There are things happening. You didn't, by any chance, put him in the pit, did you?'

'With the cauldron, yes.'

'The what?'

Has he gone deaf or something?
'The cauldron. *Cau...l...dron.*'

I've never seen a raven beyond panic.

'Er, what cauldron?' he says.

'His head was in a big pot. That's what we dragged him from Little Ease in. Avoiding Medusa eyes, vacuum mouth and all that!'

Thor turns and bangs his beak against the ancient stone wall.
After five strikes, he stops
and meets me with a hard, black-eyed stare.

'Teufel! You've put the lord of the underworld in an underworld that contains the monsters of men, with the cauldron that brings things to life –
otherwise known as the holy grail.
Could you possibly cat things up any more than that?'

'The holy grail? The monsters of men?' I say.

He nods.

'You're not going to mention happy endings next are you?'

'No.
Down there is every dream-wrenching, murderous, giant, vicious, evil thing humans have ever dreamt up. That's what we protect the world from.
The nightmares, the terrors and darkness that humans for some reason chose to imagine. Every wicked monster from every wicked story.
The ghouls and the dragon were only a taste.'

'But they were alive already. So nothing to do with me!'

'They're alive because human flesh got into the network in Siberia in 1908.
All those energies started to become physical. Now, the whole planet has a seething mass of evil just under the surface, trapped in the dimension we guard.
But for how long, we don't know.
There are so many, we can barely cope.
It's a relief to be able to talk about it with someone, to be honest.'

'A network?'

'Access points all over the world. We guard the London one.
Our legend here is the cover story.'

'You're winding me up.'

'I wish I was.'

'Who puts these bad energies in your network?'

'Birds,' he says.

'Birds?' I say, dumbfounded. Flappers do that?
'So, it's your fault anyway?'

'No. Other birds. And they do a great service for the whole world.
They carry negative energies away from the newly dead,
and drop them onto distribution lines that bring them into the network.
The souls are freed of their earthly troubles,
and the bad stuff is brought to us to kind of compost.
Some humans call the distribution network: ley lines.'

No way am I taking the blame for all this as well. I push up to him.
'This prison of yours. This networked dimension. It's locked right?'

He nods.

'They can't get out?' I say. 'Nothing can, unless it's midnight on Halloween and you're all dead?'

He nods again.

'And that's the same for every lock across the world with ravens and other corvids? That's what you are. The lock and the key? That's what you're saying?'

'Yes. That's true.'

'Then, there you are.' I get closer than his mother.
'There's no problem. Stop panicking. You've got this.'

'Stop panicking?' Thor repeats.

'You looked after it before. No one got in. Just carry on. Put another lock on it. Breed more ravens, whatever. Get a grip.'

'You're a raven,' Thor says.

'Oh, no. You can dog off, mate,' I say, taking a step back, my fur fluffing. 'Forget trying that. Honorary. That's what you said. Honorary ain't real. No feathers. No beak. You're fine. Your job. No one better. Anyway, I've got other stuff on.'

I turn to leave.

'I'll see you later. I want some time with the Chap and Mrs C. Might be away for a bit. Carry on! Excellent work. Don't mention this to anybody. That's my recommendation. This is all your fault, after all.'

Around the corner, behind the farthest cage,

I throw up.

FORTY FIVE

The clock above Waterloo Barracks shows fifteen minutes to midnight.

Bonfire Night, the 5th of November. London's yearly riot of fireworks is over. The odd rocket whizzes, but otherwise the city is quiet.

Court are ready. They've met Mushika. They have their beliefs. She has hers. I have mine.

One-Eye leads Court up the steps, the royal standard before him, Mushika on his shoulder. Magnificat, Citizen and I follow, then the polar bear and the lions, and then finally, Court, with the Bishop following at the rear. I've got my head around the plan, and now I'm so excited I could pee.

I turn to Citizen.

'This is going to be awesome.'

'You're certain on your plan?'

'Yep. Find him. Mash him. Done. Home by tomorrow, I reckon.'

'Aren't you worried, that it might be – you know – a bit more complex? About where we're going? The *past?*'

'You haven't got it, have you? We're from the future. We got Mags' history knowledge. We'll know more than those idiots could ever dream. A bunch of thickos. And him, this Zoom fella, he's never been here. He'll stand out like a pink banana. We'll mash him up. I fancy setting dogs on him.'

The procession halts by the chapel. I study home, the dark bricks and summer-blue door. Upstairs, the bedroom light switches off, Mr and Mrs Chap ready for dreams.

Back soon, guys. Breakfast time, you can tuna this kahuna.

Sir Walter turns and addresses Court.
'Ma'am, if we could all stand back please... We know nothing yet.'

Anne smiles up at the moonlit sky.
'We climb this light and we get to Heaven, Walter? That's what you said.
You better be right...'

Court shuffles back. The guards create a perimeter around Magnificat, Citizen and I.
The clock shows two minutes to midnight.

We step forward, assume position and ready ourselves. The Bishop stands to the side,
a thin smile across his face.

'I'm checking first, Ma'am,' says Sir Walter. 'At your service. Climbing for you.
That song you love. A stairway to... A king's dream cannot be mere mice-meddling.'

I look to Magnificat.
'What have you been saying, Mags?'

She gives me stern tail.
'You want me to lie? To my Queen?'

Mushika slides down One-Eye's armour. She arrives at my feet, tugging my paw.
'Why don't they believe me?'

Citizen nudges my opposite shoulder.
'The collar. I want it back.'

'Why?' I say, turning. 'Hang on, Mush.'

'We don't know what's down there,' he says. 'It gives me confidence.'

'The beam lands in minutes and you come up with this? No way. You inside me
is bad enough. I'm not having a bell and a buckle there too. I ain't coughing that up, and
I'm certainly not... How do I work it if anything goes wrong?
Ask questions and that. What is it, a password?'

Mushika's nails stabs at my paw.
'Oi, ease it,' I say.

'You just said password,' she says.

'Yeah, he won't tell me, tight git. I want to try this information thing. I can't get it to
work. I'm not even sure it's real.'

Mushika glares at Citizen.
'What information? Where's that collar from?'

'Appeared when I was in the wall. Told me things. I've got a lot of attachment to that collar, and he won't give it back.'

Mushika darts up my leg, claws digging fur. Next second, she's hanging off my neck.

'Oi, what you doing?'

'It's an Oggle,' she says. 'Oh, gods.'

I feel a tug. She drops to the flagstones with the collar. Her eyes fix on me.
'How long have you had this, Teufel?'

'I don't know. A while, why?'

'The bottom of that bell is a camera. Zeus has seen and heard everything!
This is why everything is so wild at home. It makes sense now.'

'What makes sense?' says Magnificat.

'I didn't mention, because I didn't think you'd believe me,
but Zeus is coming to take over Earth.'

'Yeah, right.' I say. 'How's a cat going to do that?'

'He can enter minds. In the past, he'll know the future. Knowledge is power.
With a lot of power, you can appear a god. Trust me, he's very talented,
I didn't say Death Star for nothing.'

I stare at her.
'And you didn't think this would be good for us to know, earlier than
one minute to midnight?'

'You wouldn't have come. You wouldn't have believed me.
You can save your loved ones. I need to save mine. He's got my parents.
We're in this together. Same risk, same reward.'

'Excuse me?' I look at Magnificat and Citizen. 'What are we going to do?'

Only blankness replies.
The clock booms midnight.
Light flashes in the black, black sky.

A thick beam of light arrows down and strikes the lawn with a fizzing hum. It stays there, shimmering – a line from another universe passing deep into ours. The guards and Court pull back. We peer into the beam, not getting too close.

'Get on with it!' shouts Anne. 'Jump in.'

'Not yet,' says Mushika.

'What are we waiting for?' Citizen asks.

Mushika looks up.

'There.
He's coming.'

Mushika clambers up my shoulder. A huge spinning blob blasts down the beam. It flies past and disappears into the Earth.

'Erm...' I say. 'I'm not so sure about this–'

The air shudders and cracks. Copper clouds explode across the sky, then anvil to black.

All around us, reality fractures.

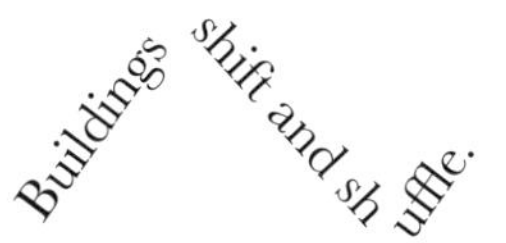

Skyscrapers burst up around the Tower, each plastered in huge screens.

My house and the adjoining one disappear. My house and the adjoining one disappear.

Castles rumble, giant banners unfurl down their sides.

A symbol on each. Ears and fangs in a circle.

'What's happening?' shouts Magnificat.

'I don't know,' I say.

We all cower.

'It's Zeus,' says Mushika.

'What do you mean? We've not even started.'

'Exactly. He's already in the past. Everything he's done has been done. He's won.'

Screeches blast around the Tower. From above the skyscrapers, dragons appear, wings beating the night. Around the Tower, zombies and ghouls smash through windows.

The monsters of men are on us!

The giant screens kick into life, showing a glowing, round hole set against a red lightening storm. Through the hole are spring fields, mountains and sunshine. The circular symbol emerges from the hole, the word *Come* beneath it.

A dragon swoops down, breath shooting blasts of hot, yellow fire.

On top, is Richard!
'Here's Dickie!'

Mushika shouts to Mags and Citizen.
'Inside Teufel, quick!'

Magnificat and Citizen disappear in mist.
I feel nothing.
Are they inside me or not?

'Jump, Teufel, jump!' Mushika shouts. 'Jump!'

And we
f
a
l
l

i
n
t
o

t
h
e

l
i
g
h
t

Be first to hear about the sequel, provisionally titled, *The Cat and the King*

If you'd like to be first to hear about the sequel to *Thunderpaws and The Tower of London*, sign up at the link below. If you are under thirteen please seek the permission of a parent or guardian. No spam, just glorious nosh.

www.thunderpaws.com/treats

If you've enjoyed Thunderpaws – please leave a review at your favourite book-buying location and tell your friends.

If you enjoyed it so much you wished there was an audiobook, there is! Search your favourite store and the delightful Mr Adam Gillen will be there waiting to tickle your ears with his fantastic audio version acted with over forty voices.

The Tower of London
If you would like to find out more about the Tower of London visit:
www.hrp.org.uk/tower-of-london

Battersea Cats and Dogs Home
(Battersea Dogs Home at the time of this story) is a famous charity dedicated to the care of cats and dogs. More information can be found at:
www.battersea.org.uk

Visit London:
www.visitlondon.com

Battersea Park
www.wandsworth.gov.uk/batterseapark

UK Parliament (Big Ben)
www.parliament.uk/bigben

Acknowledgements

Books involve a lot of people… Jane Leggett has almost read more versions than me and certainly done the most to help deliver a promising idea into reality. Kathryn Clark has read drafts with patience and provided timely, thoughtful input.

This book would not have been possible without the kindness of Jane & Sheg, the Knotts of Tobago, the Robinsons of London and the foresight of the Chaplain and Jennifer Jessup.

Help with reads on various drafts: Sarah House, Fran Lebowitz, Kathryn Jane Robinson Price, MJ Hyland, Trevor Byrne, Kaitlyn Johnson, Mary Kole, Gary Smailes, Brooke Vitale. Proofing, Johnny Sharp, Emily Thomas.

Friends, family and work colleagues as willing beta readers (apologies to any accidentally omitted) and helpers in other ways: Lucy Leverett, Thomas Walker, Emi Morimoto, Matt East, Pedro Caldeira, Chieko Aoki, Leigh Howden, Lynne Stelling, Joanne Parrish, Friederike Bubenzer, Clare Gyde, Lucrecia Kampenga, Stefanie Teichmann, Sarah Sharp, Uma Jocelyn, Clara Jocelyn, Ellie Maw, Sarah Treadway, Kim Siler, Daniel Miles, Charlie Dunster, Andreea Dumitrascu, Joan O'Connor, John Luck, Jackie Duff, Nick Clark, Krista Webb Carney, Richard Jocelyn, Yavini Chetty, James Simpson, Christopher Ross, Dafydd Balston, John Sparrow.

Others who have helped in different ways, Kate Housden, Peter Housden, Paul Skelton, Alice Skelton, my families, the Hoffies, Julie Coke, Roben Penny and Armien Abrahams, Alex Cautaerts, Lukas Lee, Zoe Dale, Michael Pender, Rebecca Beer. With thanks to Lana Del Rey, Jack Antonoff, Lin-Manuel Miranda, Greg Gonzalez, Johan Söderqvist and Patrik Andrén for the musical company over the last drafts.

Lastly, but *so not last* – MonoKubo, Robyn Lawrence and Adam Gillen for helping bring it all to life in beautiful, beautiful ways.

About the author

Ben Housden was born to teenage parents in the throws of revolution in the white-hot electric-cool of rural Shropshire, England. Turning one, he was the youngest resident of the University of Essex and part-time watchman of a café in a caravan. Aged three was hippie communes, marauding north London. He moved to Yorkshire at four – to bring on the revolution. Great adventures followed as an agitprop theatre roadie, budding entrepreneur and bus-fare dodger. Aged eight, he moved to a stately home, unfortunately to an asbestos hut around the back and a job glass-collecting in the student bar. A village of humungous pies came and went. A city next. Sheffield Steel. A failing education was ignored (Jackie Collins' for your English Literature book project anyone?), university failed. Record company, nightclub, investment banking (not as a banker), broken, light, copywriting, a good friend Jennifer Jessup said: 'I've got this story… a cat at the Tower of London.'

2021, Thunderpaws…
Books 2 and 3 are in process…